"I was thinking I could sail with you to Butterfly Harbor..." Sienna still had an ounce of hope.

Monty didn't choke. Not exactly. But he did clear his throat and his eyes were dazed. He practically gasped when he blurted, "You want to what?"

"Just hear me out!" She held up both hands. "I've been on boats my whole life. My grandmother taught me so I'd have something in common with my father. Not that that went any... Never mind."

She always babbled when she panicked. "I cook pretty well, so we wouldn't starve and you could eat more than peanut-butter sandwiches. I've always felt at home on the water, as if it's where I belong, and maybe that's what I need now. Just some time away from...everything. While I figure out what to do. I promise, once we get to Butterfly Harbor, you'll never see me again."

She'd get everything figured out by then.

She'd have to.

Dear Reader,

Monty Bettencourt was a character I knew I would have fun with. From the time we met him in his twin sister Frankie's story, I was imagining his HEA and who it was going to be with. Even better? I was looking forward to taking Butterfly Harbor on the road! And nothing says the road more than a runaway bride.

So what did I know about Sienna Fairchild when the story began? Not much other than the fact she most definitely does not want to get married. But what does she want? Even she doesn't know. Thanks to a man who doesn't judge but gently guides, and a cranky, determined parrot with a penchant for singing, she may find out.

With every one of these books, I've tried to do something different, especially with my characters. And as readers of this series know, people always find their hearts in Butterfly Harbor.

I hope you enjoy this visit to my small West Coast town. You'll see familiar faces and meet new ones, and if you're like me, by the end you're going to be wondering if maybe owning a parrot wouldn't be such a bad idea!

Anna

HEARTWARMING

Bride on the Run

—

Anna J. Stewart

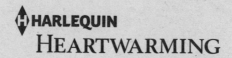

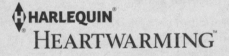

HARLEQUIN®
HEARTWARMING™

Recycling programs
for this product may
not exist in your area.

ISBN-13: 978-1-335-17970-8

Bride on the Run

Copyright © 2021 by Anna J. Stewart

All rights reserved. No part of this book may be used or reproduced in any manner whatsoever without written permission except in the case of brief quotations embodied in critical articles and reviews.

This is a work of fiction. Names, characters, places and incidents are either the product of the author's imagination or are used fictitiously. Any resemblance to actual persons, living or dead, businesses, companies, events or locales is entirely coincidental.

This edition published by arrangement with Harlequin Books S.A.

For questions and comments about the quality of this book, please contact us at CustomerService@Harlequin.com.

Harlequin Enterprises ULC
22 Adelaide St. West, 40th Floor
Toronto, Ontario M5H 4E3, Canada
www.Harlequin.com

Printed in U.S.A.

Bestselling author **Anna J. Stewart** is living her dream writing romances for Harlequin's Romantic Suspense and Heartwarming lines. In between bouts of binge-watching her favorite TV shows and movies, she puts fingers to keyboard and loses herself in endless stories of happily-ever-after. Anna lives in Northern California, where she tries to wrangle two rapscallion cats named Rosie and Sherlock, possibly the most fiendish felines known to humankind.

Books by Anna J. Stewart

Harlequin Romantic Suspense

Honor Bound

Reunited with the P.I.
More Than a Lawman
Gone in the Night
Guarding His Midnight Witness

Harlequin Heartwarming

Return of the Blackwell Brothers

The Rancher's Homecoming

Butterfly Harbor Stories

Recipe for Redemption
A Dad for Charlie
Always the Hero
Holiday Kisses
Safe in His Arms
The Firefighter's Thanksgiving Wish
A Match Made Perfect

Visit the Author Profile page
at Harlequin.com for more titles.

For Marie McLetchie Sarnell

Cousin, little sister and friend

CHAPTER ONE

"WHAT AM I doing getting married?"

Sienna Fairchild stared at herself in the full-length mirror and wondered if she was real. She pressed damp palms against her colorless cheeks. The neatly arranged cascading raven curls perfectly framed her expertly made-up face. The diamond choker sparkled against her pale throat. The weighty emerald engagement ring that dragged her down like an anchor sparkled against the late afternoon sun. The rays streaming through the bay window of the bridal suite at the San Diego Empire Yacht Club. She'd grown up here, spent countless hours exploring the boats and dock where first her grandmother and then Vincent Fairchild, Sienna's father, had served as president.

"Nana, where are you when I need you?" Tears of grief stung the back of her throat. It had been two months since her grandmother had died; two months that had passed excruciatingly slow and yet flashed by in the blink of an eye ever since Richard Somersby had proposed.

Richard Somersby, her father's latest business partner, and someone who could ensure the Fairchild fortune for generations to come, should have been a dream come true. Handsome, wealthy, charming. Oh, so charming. Too charming? Sienna frowned.

Richard had turned his attention on Sienna the instant he'd seen her at her father's birthday party, which had happened not long after her grandmother's funeral. Richard had been exciting and different and…her head had spun, given his interest, and her normally distant father had been thrilled.

She had most definitely been charmed. She'd also been neck-deep in sleepless grief over having lost the only parental figure she'd really had growing up.

Winnifred Fairchild, teenage bride, WWII factory worker, former CEO of Fairchild International, mother of four sons, only two of whom had lived past childhood, would have moved heaven and earth for Sienna; *had* moved it, in some respects. Before Winnie's death, Sienna's father never would have considered pushing Sienna into marriage, let alone into one that would solidify his business connections.

Nana never would have allowed it unless she was convinced it was what Sienna wanted.

It had been what she'd wanted, Sienna thought now. At least it had been until fifteen minutes ago, when she'd looked at herself in the mirror.

And didn't see a trace of herself.

"I need help, Nana." The whispered plea echoed in the empty room, against the brocade curtains, the striped gold wallpaper and the silver tray that housed a champagne bucket and glasses. The one-of-a-kind designer gown felt like a straitjacket despite the strapless corset top. The sweeping, elegant tulle skirt with satin lining brushed against the floor. Embroidery, beads, rhinestones and appliqué added intricate patterns of perfection any bride would be thrilled with. Yet all Sienna could hear, even above the lapping waves of the marina and the cries of seagulls, was her panicked breathing and the voice screaming in her head that something wasn't right.

She gripped her skirt in her fists and moved to the French doors overlooking the marina.

The ocean. Peace instantly settled over her; the water always had provided solace. It had been her grandmother's coping mechanism, as well, one Winnie had embraced fully a few years before when she'd purchased a cozy home on the beach less than ten miles from where Sienna currently stood—a house Sienna was poised to inherit now that Winnie had died.

"What are you doing?" Tabitha, her cousin and maid of honor, rushed into the room. Her expression was frantic, her long blond locks solidified with enough hair product to supply a salon. "Let go of your dress! It's getting wrinkled. You have pictures in less than fifteen minutes." She slapped at Sienna's hands, kneeled down and smoothed the expensive material. "There. It's okay." Tabitha let out a long, relieved breath. "I don't think we need to steam it again."

"I can't do this." The words were barely a whisper. Sienna cleared her throat. "I can't marry Richard."

"Don't be silly—of course you can." Tabitha stood and flipped a curl behind Sienna's shoulder. "Richard's a woman's dream come true. It's last-minute jitters." But Tabitha didn't meet her gaze. If anything, she seemed to be purposely avoiding it.

"I don't know him." Not the real him, Sienna thought. Oh, he was a pretty enough picture and well established in the financial world, but what were his dreams? His ambitions? And he'd never asked about her dreams, her plans. Her...

"What's to know?" Tabitha asked. "He's crazy about you and he can pay for anything you ever want or need." Tabitha turned critical, almost accusing eyes on her.

Sienna swallowed hard. She saw it, a moment before Tabitha covered it, but it was there. A momentary flash of envy. "Now." Tabitha nodded. "Let's head downstairs. Richard and his groomsmen are finishing up with the photographer. We're up next."

The roar in Sienna's ears intensified as Tabitha pushed the bouquet of red and white roses into her hands. She followed her cousin out of the room to the winding staircase and thought this had to be what an out-of-body experience felt like.

"I'm going to go get the others," Tabitha told her, referring to Sienna's bridesmaids. Tabitha took Sienna's arms and planted her in an alcove at the bottom of the stairs. She fluffed up the veil a bit, tsked a few times, then smiled. "Don't move. We'll all be right back."

Tabitha disappeared in a flash of bloodred, a fitting color for the attendants' A-line gowns, Sienna thought against the giggle of hysteria that bubbled up. This was it. The first day of the rest of her life. Married to a successful man, a man whose parties and appearances and professional successes would soon be hers, while her own dreams...

Every ounce of warmth drained out of Sienna's body. Her own dreams, whatever they were, would wither and die, forever unrealized and unachieved, because she'd been so determined to fulfill the only request her father had ever made of her.

She shouldn't have waited so long to listen to the doubts. She should have confided in one or more of her friends, asked for their advice, but they were all so busy with their own lives, their own relationships and jobs. She didn't want to bother them with something she should be able to work out for herself.

A cool breeze drifted in through the side door. The early spring rainstorm that had crossed through the area last night had long since moved on, leaving in its wake the promise of blue skies and crisp, refreshing days. The sunshine beckoned her, like a beacon of escape she only now realized was within reach.

She walked to the door, set the bouquet on the nearby table and pulled off her veil.

It drifted to the floor as she stepped outside.

She took a deep breath. Held it. Released it. The belt of panic that had been tightening around her loosened. It continued to ease with each step she took away from the club. Her spiked heels clicked on the cement stairs she descended. Bending down, she caught huge wads of fabric in her hands and hiked up her dress, walking quickly along the stone path to the marina entrance. She welcomed the warmth of the sun beating down on her.

Sienna surrendered to instinct. She'd practically grown up at the club, where her father had been president for most of her childhood. The boats were all different, of course, but they were also the same. She had no idea where she was going or what she was going to do when she got there. But she most definitely was not going to get married. Not now. Maybe not ever.

There was commotion behind her and it

caused her to pick up her pace. She couldn't be certain it had anything to do with her, of course. But the sooner she got out of sight and took some time to decide what came next, the better.

Except no boat felt right. Every schooner, yacht or cruiser she eyed had her scrambling onward. Her heel caught between two planks. Foot stuck, she pitched forward and cried out, landing awkwardly. Probably looking like a marshmallow factory that had exploded, she pushed herself up and shoved her hair out of her face. She twisted around to pull her foot free from her shoe, but froze, blinking at the fiberglass boat right in front of her.

Nana's Dream.

Her stomach clenched. More cries and calls and shouts came from the direction of the club. Her pulse kicked into top speed. She finally yanked out the shoe from between the planks and practically dived onto the boat. She scrambled across the deck toward the open hatch, her dress billowing around her.

Once inside, she stopped. A time warp to the eighties? Dark painted wood paneling, hideous pastel floral-print cushions on the bench seats and nautical-themed drapes over the lone grimy window.

Boy, did this boat need some TLC ASAP.

She bunched up her dress and squeezed past the galley kitchen, then began pulling open doors. She heard distinct and all-too-familiar voices shouting from the dock, including her father's loud baritone.

Expecting a bathroom behind the next door, she ended up wedging herself into a narrow closet where old fishing rods and gear were stored. It also had one shelf. With a fast sweep of her arm, she cleared it. After tucking the dress up and around her, she hoisted herself up, reached out and pulled the door closed.

Only then did she realize she'd lost her shoe.

DUFFEL SLUNG OVER his shoulder, grocery bag in the other hand, Monty Bettencourt whistled his way down the path toward the marina that housed *Nana's Dream*.

It had taken him three months of negotiating the price to something he could afford—barely—but the extra hassle had been worth it. This latest acquisition to his expanding fleet for Wind Walkers Tours would be the perfect honeymoon rental once he knocked some shape into it. He could also book it out for a college-buddies' reunion or moms' get-away. It would take time, and a boatload of cash he no longer had, but eventually she'd shine.

His cell phone buzzed in his pocket. Even before he pulled it free, he knew who was calling. He stopped, setting down the bag. "What now, Frankie?"

"Foregoing the pleasantries, are we?" His twin sister's borderline-uptight voice didn't even register on his freaking-out meter.

"I'm saving time." He looked over his shoulder as a group of men about his age stampeded out of the yacht club and split off like struck tuxedoed pool balls. Now *they* were uptight. "What did Ezzie do this time?"

"Nothing horrible. To me, anyway." Frankie's voice softened when talking about her soon-to-be mother-in-law. "I know she means well, I really do, but you need to get back here. She's trying to plan Roman's bachelor party!"

Monty dodged to one side to avoid a racing groomsman. "No fair. As best man, that's my territory." After discussing said event with his future brother-in-law, he'd planned an early morning, catered fishing-trip excursion.

"That's what I told her. When are you getting back?"

"Not for a few days at least." *Nana's Dream* couldn't cope with a fast dash up the coast; he was cautiously optimistic the engine would hold out long enough to get him back to Butterfly Harbor in central California. He'd figured four, maybe five days tops if he could give the engine a significant nightly break. Parts for a boat this age weren't easy to come by, so he needed to preserve this engine long enough to replace it. "You want me to call Ezzie?"

"Just to remind her this is your thing. Roman's horrified at the idea of his mother planning his party. It could scar him for the honeymoon."

"We wouldn't want that." Monty had to bite his cheek to stop from laughing. It was two weeks until Fire Chief Frankie Bettencourt married her co-chief, Roman Salazar, in what was sure to be one of Butterfly Harbor's biggest social events of the year. He couldn't think of anyone in town they hadn't invited—or who hadn't invited themselves. One could only hope Skipper Park was large enough to accommodate everyone. "I'll give her a ring before I cast off." Cell reception was notoriously horrible out on the water. All this wedding talk was making him strangely sentimental. Watching Frankie and Roman together had made him think about his own future and whether he was going to continue as he was, alone but not lonely, or jump deeper into the dating pool. "And I'll keep your name out of the conversation, don't worry." No use getting Frankie into trouble this close to her wedding day.

"Thank you. All finally good with *Dream*?"

"Paperwork and licensing finalized this morning. She's officially ours."

Since she was one of his business partners, he kept Frankie abreast of his acquisitions, but when it had come to *Nana's Dream*, she'd been adamant he buy her. Too bad he couldn't get the boat in running shape before his sister's honeymoon. Then again… Monty shuddered. He really didn't want to think about that aspect of his sister's life.

Back at the club he saw four women emerge, each wearing various styles of a red gown and flailing about with bouquets as they looked in every direction for something they clearly weren't finding.

"I gotta go, Frankie." More people, presumably wedding guests, began flooding outside, all of them looking equally surprised and put out. "I think there's a scandal erupting at the yacht club."

"Safe trip home. Don't rush." She hesitated. "But don't take too long."

"Noted. Talk later." He hung up, picked up his bag and pushed through the waist-high metal gate to the docks. "What's going on?" he called to one of the men speeding toward him.

The man, a good three inches taller than Monty's six feet, but about thirty pounds slimmer, skidded to a halt. A white-rose boutonniere hung limply against the lapel of his tux, and the spinning dismay in the man's eyes told Monty everything he needed to know. "Have you seen a young woman? Dark hair. Wedding dress. Anywhere around here?"

"You have a runaway bride?" Monty thought that only happened in movies. "Ah, sorry, no." He would not laugh. He would not. The poor guy looked seriously stressed out.

"Her name's Sienna. I don't know where she went or why. I need her to come back."

"I'm sure if she loves you, she will." Monty had the strange urge to pat the guy on the shoulder.

"If she what?" For an instant, the man looked confused. "Oh, love, right, yeah. Of course."

Uh-huh. Monty refrained from rolling his eyes, much in the way his teenage goddaughter, Mandy, often did. "Good luck, buddy." Yeah. Sienna the runaway bride was gone for good.

He started whistling again, not an easy task when he couldn't quit grinning. He was a lucky, lucky man. The only thing he had to worry about was living his dream; Wind Walkers Tours was operating in the black and he was already booked halfway through summer, and it was only early April. His sister was about to settle down—first time that had happened ever—and he was gaining a brother-in-law he considered a good friend. Add to that the happy nuptials of his best friend Sebastian with his first love, along with the girders going in at the butterfly sanctuary back home, and Monty didn't have a care in the world. He certainly didn't have a runaway bride to worry about.

Whoever that poor guy was, his fiancée sounded like a mess of trouble.

Monty paused on the dock, taking a moment to appreciate the worn fiberglass hull, faded padded seats and fraying lashings. She'd had a good life prior to his purchase, the last ten years of which had been spent moored right here in this berth, but he was going to give her an even better life now. One where she was appreciated, cared for and, most of all, used.

Fifty-footers like *Nana's Dream* weren't meant to be stabled. They were meant to be out there on the water, riding the waves, steering into sunsets and dreams.

Monty tossed his bag onto the deck, but was more careful with the groceries, then he walked the width of the dock to give *Dream* one last check. Tomorrow morning was the perfect time to head out, right when the sun was peeking over the horizon. A cup of hot coffee, the last of the homemade bagels Ezzie Salazar had packed in his bag yesterday when he'd flown down to San Diego and the wheel in his hand. There truly was no better way to start the day.

Nor was there a better way to end a day than with a good eight to ten hours of shuteye. He stretched his arms over his head, pulled off his jacket and threw it on top of his bag.

The runaway bride   or rather, her absence—

was causing a major ruckus on the dock. He kept his ears open as he stepped onto the boat, then slowed to get a good feel for her while making mental notes as to what needed to be repaired or replaced. When he caught sight of a group of the tuxedoed men heading in his direction, he rested a foot on the railing and leaned his elbows on his knee.

"Something I can help you with?" It was obvious they wanted him for something. The question was, what?

"Someone said they saw Sienna get on your boat," the man he'd spoken to earlier accused, any grudging politeness having evaporated. "I want to search it."

"Do you?" Normally Monty would have told him to have at it, but the man's snotty attitude had him thinking otherwise. "It's a shame you didn't ask nicely."

"Richard." An older man stepped forward as Richard scowled at Monty. Monty simply arched an eyebrow. He'd dealt with dozens of guys like this Richard dude. They didn't faze him. They barely entertained him. Rich, privileged and happy to run over anyone they thought was an obstacle. Monty much preferred to be the immovable boulder. "I'm sorry," the older man said, offering his hand.

"Vincent Fairchild. It's my daughter, Sienna, we're looking for. She's…fragile. We just want to make sure she's all right."

"Monty Bettencourt." Monty shook the man's hand. "How about I take a look myself? You'll understand if I'd rather not have you all traipsing around my boat."

"Of course, thank you."

Monty silently sighed. Good manners didn't hide Vincent's irritation. Clearly the older man didn't appreciate Monty's suggestion. He also was probably used to getting what he wanted. All the more reason for Monty to needle him. He didn't have anything else to do at the moment. "Be back in a sec." He gave Richard a quick grin before he turned toward the stairs that led below to the cabin. Instantly, his blood pressure spiked.

From his vantage point above, he could see, in the middle of the floor, a solitary sparkling white shoe with rhinestones. A seriously sexy shoe. But that wasn't his only surprise.

The closet door opened, inch by inch, hinges creaking. A long, tanned arm reached out, and pink-tipped fingers grasped the shoe's strap.

"Something wrong?" Vincent stepped onto the boat and Monty spun around.

"No. I have this inner ear condition." He pretended to sway. "I move too fast and I get all... Be right back." He hurried down the ladder just as the closet door closed, arm and shoe out of sight.

His mind raced as he feigned searching for his stowaway. He opened doors, slammed them shut, all the while asking himself what he was going to do about the woman in his closet. Clearly she didn't want to go with Vincent and Richard. She knew they were here yet remained hidden. Having met the guys, Monty could understand her reticence. He could at least play along with her for a while. Maybe long enough for her to make a real getaway.

He rapped his knuckles on the closet door as he passed and thought he heard a yelp, then he returned up the stairs.

"Sorry. I didn't see her." Not a lie. He hadn't seen—well, at least not all of her. "You sure they said my boat?"

"They did." Richard bolted forward again, but Vincent stopped him with a hand on his chest.

"She's not here, Richard," Monty said, erasing all humor from his voice. "Unless you plan on calling me a liar and having the police conduct a legal search, I suggest you get off my property."

"It's fine. It's fine," Vincent repeated when Richard started to argue. "She can't have gotten out of the club without someone seeing her. She's here somewhere. We'll just have to look elsewhere." He faced Monty. "Thank you for checking. If you do see her—"

"I'll send up a flare." Monty shoved his hands in his back pockets and smirked at Richard. Depriving him of even a bit of triumph felt like an accomplishment.

Monty waited calmly, watching as the men retreated and disappeared into the yacht club. Only when he was sure no one was watching did he let out the breath he'd been holding and head to the cabin below.

This time he didn't spare a knock, but yanked open the closet door, only to stare into the most stunning brown eyes he'd ever seen in his life. She stared back at him, unblinking, defiance shining as she struggled to keep hold of her monstrous dress and one sparkly shoe.

"Sienna Fairchild, I assume? Monty Bettencourt." He bowed slightly and held out his hand. "Welcome aboard."

CHAPTER TWO

Sienna was rarely at a loss for words. Nana had often told her she'd been born talking; it had just taken a few years for people to be able to understand her. It was, perhaps, the one quality she'd gotten from her father that she actually appreciated. She could talk to anyone. About anything. Except for now.

She felt her mouth move, a bit like a goldfish struggling for air—open, close…open, close—as if the words couldn't quite settle on her tongue. Maybe it was delayed shock from her escape. Maybe it was the fact she was crammed into a linen closet to the point that she may very well have suffocated. Or it could be that the man looking down at her had one of the most disarming, carefree, friendly smiles she'd seen in a very long time. A smile that set his stunning green eyes twinkling brighter than her emerald engagement ring.

Careful, she warned herself. The last time she'd let herself be charmed by a smile like that she'd ended up trussed into a wedding gown that attempted to smother her.

Finally, she managed to respond with a slightly strangled sound that had the color rushing to her cheeks.

His smile faded. "Are you all right?"

"Mmm." She nodded, noticed his open palm. Never in her life had she wanted to accept an offering more. Her right hand flexed around the bundle of fabric and the strap of her shoe. Her left tingled at the fingertips.

"I won't hurt you," he said in a serious tone.

She frowned. Funny. That thought hadn't even crossed her mind. It probably should have. He was a stranger. They were in a confined space together. And she was in a rather vulnerable and ridiculous situation. Yep. Sienna took a deep breath. Just a typical day in the life of Sienna Fairchild.

She gripped his hand, ignoring the tiny jolts of excitement that danced across her palm when his skin touched hers. He gave a gentle tug. Sienna shifted too quickly, tried to get her feet under her before she dropped from the shelf.

"Careful!" His warning came too late. She felt her dress catch, heard a distinctive rip and before she knew it, she'd landed face-first on the floor of his boat.

She raised her head and coughed. The worn carpet, which was the color of rusted metal, smelled like it had been laid at the turn of the century. Before she could even think of righting herself, he'd scooped both hands under her arms and hoisted her up.

"Whew." That almost sounded like a word. She stepped to one side and shoved down her skirt, only to have her ankle give way and send her toppling over. "Ooooow!" She tried to break her second fall in as many minutes, but missed the closet door handle by inches.

He caught her again, this time locking his hands around her arms and pushing her back against the bulkhead. "Better now?" He hadn't released her; seemed a bit reluctant to, given his furrowed brow.

"Better." She nodded, then winced when she tried to put weight on her foot. "Ah, except for that. Ouch!" She would have hopped if she hadn't thought she'd give herself a concussion on the overhead. "I must have twisted it when I got my shoe caught in the planks."

"Best get your weight off it until we're sure it isn't broken."

He swept her off her feet and deposited

her on one of the padded benches surrounding a scarred Formica table. "It's fine," she protested when he bent down on one knee. Given her billowing skirts and his gallantry, Sienna felt as if she'd been caught up in a nautical version of "Cinderella." Except, instead of obnoxious stepsisters, she had an overbearing father and fiancé. Although…she didn't have them. Not since her escape. What on earth was she going to do now?

She shivered against the skim of Monty Bettencourt's fingers as they pressed and prodded her ankle. His hair was the color of tamed fire, with hints of sun-kissed red and yellow intermingling beneath darker hues of brown. Such an odd combination. Her fingers itched to touch it, to see if it was as soft as it appeared. He had the look of a man who spent time outdoors with tanned skin and biceps that appeared to be challenging his navy T-shirt. His hands were firm, yet rough and calloused. Honed by physical labor. He had lifted her as effortlessly as if she'd been a feather.

Sienna flinched when he flexed her foot. It no longer hurt, just throbbed in protest. "I don't think it's broken." The rumble of his deep voice had her quivering inside.

"No." She shook her head and almost

laughed as he extricated himself from beneath the white fabric of her dress. "I, um, thank you. For not telling them where I was."

"Wasn't that difficult," he said with a flash of that heart-tugging smile. He pushed to his feet, took two steps away and pulled open the door to a small refrigerator under the counter. "Fortunately, ol' Richard made it an easy decision." He produced an old-fashioned metal ice-cube tray and dropped it upside down into the sink.

"Scoot back." He motioned for her to sit back in the booth and once her foot was up on the bench, he tied the towel-encased ice cubes with a rubber band and plopped the makeshift ice pack onto her injured ankle. "Better?"

"It will be, thanks." He was acting as if strange women stashed themselves in his linen closet every day. "You're being awfully nice about this."

"About what?" He hurried off, then returned with a duffel bag, jacket and stuffed recyclable grocery tote. He tossed his duffel through the opening under the ladder into what she assumed was one of the berth compartments.

"About finding a stowaway on your boat."

He shrugged. "It beats finding a leak. Are you hungry?" After setting the groceries on the chipped counter, he began unloading the items.

"Starved." Tabitha had put her on such a strict diet this past week, Sienna couldn't remember the last time she'd chewed.

"I don't have a huge selection I'm afraid. I can get by on peanut butter most days." Her stomach growled and he smiled again, chuckling. "Peanut butter it is. Strawberry jam okay?"

"Sounds great." Tears burned the back of her eyes and she tried to distract herself by looking around the cabin. It was…homey, she supposed. Clearly, he had interesting interior-design ideas, no doubt inspired by classic 80s television. "Are you a renter?"

"The *Dream*?" Monty turned slightly and she could watch him slathering the bread. "Nope. This beauty is all mine now. Just finalized the purchase. Heading home come sunrise."

"Oh." So much for offering to buy him out of his lease so she could stay. Not that the thought had been a serious one. It was more than slightly pathetic, hiding on a stranger's boat because she couldn't stand up to her father. Still. She caught her lip in her teeth. This did seem like the perfect hiding place while she tried to figure out what she did now that she most definitely was not going to marry Richard.

"That's a disappointed *oh*." Monty slapped another piece of white bread on top of his swirled masterpiece and slid the sandwich onto a napkin. He set it, along with a butter knife, on the table for her.

She blinked and a solitary tear slipped down her cheek.

"Is it your ankle? Are you in pain?" He shifted toward the ice pack, but she shook her head.

She tried to smile and swiped a hand under her eye. "My nana used to fix me peanut-butter-and-jam sandwiches when I was having a rough day. She died a few months ago." She touched a finger to the pillow-like bread. "I really miss her." Her voice hitched. "Sorry. I'm such a mess. If you don't mind me hanging around until the club closes, I'll sneak out of the marina after dark."

He finished making his own sandwich, grabbed a couple of bottles of water from the bag and joined her at the table. "I'm no expert, but I don't think you'll be sneaking anywhere in that dress."

She pulled her sandwich closer, looked down at the embroidered top of her gown and sighed. "I guess I will kind of glow in the dark." Still, what choice did she have? She couldn't go home. Her father would find her there immediately. She couldn't think of one friend or acquaintance she had who would understand what she'd done.

After all, Richard Somersby was considered one of the best catches in singledom. She was probably going to be labeled a pariah the second that word got around she'd ditched Richard at the altar.

She needed a plan. And fast. But for now, she'd do the one thing that was completely in her control and enjoy her sandwich and pretend as if she hadn't just pitched her entire life into the ocean.

As expected, the second she bit into the bread she felt better.

"I'll tell you what," Monty said, breaking the silence. "Let's give your bridal party some time to clear out, then I'll hit the gift shop. I'm sure I saw some sweatshirts and stuff in the window."

Suddenly it became very difficult to swallow. Sienna nearly choked in her rush to answer. "You don't have to do that. Why would you…? I mean…" What did she mean?

"I'm a sucker for a damsel in distress." He grinned over his water, then cringed. "Wait! Scratch that. My sister would strangle me for even thinking of using that phrase. Let's just say I like to help where I can. If it makes you feel better, I'll give you my info and you can send me the money when you're able to."

It did make her feel better. Now if she only knew how to retrieve her purse and cell phone, which, if she was lucky, were still up in the bridal suite at the club. She was literally up a creek without a paddle. "Are you and your sister close?"

"As close as siblings can get. Frankie's my twin. Older by a few minutes, which she never lets me forget."

Sienna had envied her friends who'd had siblings growing up. Tabitha had been a close cousin, but despite the time they'd spent together, Sienna had never really considered her a real friend.

So much of Sienna's life had been put on hold during her grandmother's illness, including her friendships. She wanted to explore that life now, figure out exactly what she could do. What she wanted to do. Despite the chaos she'd caused, for the first time, she truly felt free. No guilt, she ordered herself. She rejected even the notion of it.

"Shoot." He snapped his fingers and brought Sienna out of her reverie. "I need to make a phone call. Be right back."

Sienna nodded, pretending not to listen in on his phone call, but she welcomed the distraction of someone else's life. She should, she supposed, be grateful that Richard had been so adamant about finding her. That must mean he actually cared about her, right? Or did he just care about appearances and not disappointing her father? Given their business connections, and her luck, she could guess the answer.

In between bites of her sandwich, she removed bobby pins from her hair. With each one she set on the table, she felt remarkably lighter as her hair fell in waves around her shoulders. The tightness in her skull eased. The tension in her shoulders melted away and soon she was looking at a stack of pins amid the scattered crumbs of her PB and J.

Monty's voice was raised and she distinctly heard the mention of a bachelor party. Sienna shifted to watch him pace from port to starboard, dragging a hand through his hair before he dropped his head back and stared up at the sky. When he quit the call and ducked inside again, she couldn't help herself and asked, "When are you getting married?"

"Married?" He looked as if she'd just thrown an anchor into his arms. "Oh, no. It's not *my* bachelor party. I'm just in charge of it for my future brother-in-law. My sister, Frankie, is taking the plunge in a couple of weeks."

Unexpected relief slid through her. "Oh."

"Roman's the groom, and his mother, Ezzie, has some ideas as to what I should be planning. I had to tell her I didn't think Roman would appreciate having his stag arranged by his mother."

Sienna's lips twitched. "No." She shook her head. "I wouldn't think so." She knew Richard had had a bachelor party last week sometime. Thursday? she thought. She hadn't really paid much attention. She hadn't really cared.

"Still, she wasn't wrong about me needing to get back to Butterfly Harbor. Guess I'm going to put this girl through her paces." Monty tapped his hand against the bulkhead.

"Engine might need some work on the way, but we'll get there, won't we, *Dream*?"

"If she has so many issues, why did you buy her?" The question came out so quickly she didn't have time to really consider how she'd said it.

If he took offense to her tone, however, he didn't let on. "Because she's got an old soul. Boats like this, they've got a history, a feel about them. It feels like home. A really dated home," he added with a laugh. "But she'll fit perfectly into my fleet. Wind Walkers," he added at her perplexed expression. "I run a tour-and-diving company out of Butterfly Harbor."

She'd heard the name before. Where had she…? Sienna frowned, thinking. "Butterfly Harbor. That's near Monterey, isn't it? Jason Corwin opened a new restaurant there around the time he got married." She'd watched the behind-the-scenes TV show featuring Jason's Christmas wedding almost two years ago.

"That's my town. Do you know Jason?"

"I met him once. My father flew him and his brother out for one of the firm's big holiday events, just after they'd hit it big on television." Her father was always one to try to latch on to the latest celebrity or trend to show his clients how on-top-of-things he was. "It was horrible, what happened to Jason's brother." Jason and his brother, David, had been twins like Monty and his sister. But unlike Monty, Jason lost his sibling in a plane crash. "I'm glad to hear Jason's doing all right."

"He's more than all right. He and his wife, Abby, are expecting a baby in about a month. It's a boy. They're naming him David, after Jason's brother."

"That's lovely." She smothered a yawn, probably the result of a massive adrenaline crash.

"You look wiped out," Monty said. "Why don't you get some rest? There's a separate berth right down there." He pointed at the narrow hall ahead of him. "I've already grabbed the one at the back."

"You wouldn't mind?" He was racking up serious Sir Galahad points. She hadn't had a decent night's sleep in weeks. The idea of even a few hours sounded like heaven.

"Not at all. I've got stuff to do on the boat before I can leave the marina, and then I'll hit that gift shop. Oh, and I'll see if I can get the gossip about your nonwedding wedding."

Tears burned her eyes again, but she

blinked them back. "I'll never be able to thank you for all this."

"Nothing to thank me for. That look on your fiancé's face was enough."

Richard. Her father. The reality of what waited for her beyond the marina rushed over her like a tidal wave. But her anxiety and fear about what to do next disappeared for the moment, thanks to a stranger's kindness. "You haven't asked me."

"Asked you what?"

"Why I ran away," she stated.

Monty's half smile didn't reach his eyes. "It's none of my business. If you want to talk about it, I'm happy to listen. Otherwise, consider this sanctuary until you decide what you want to do."

"Just be gone before the morning tide, right?" Sienna forced a laugh as she struggled out of the booth. The pinching and tightening of her dress reminded her of the uncomfortable situation she was currently in. "There is one thing I need your help with. If you don't mind?"

"Name it."

Her face went hot. "I'd really love to get this dress off." She turned around so she wouldn't have to look at him. She pulled her hair into one hand, then drew it over her shoulder. "There's no way to get these buttons myself. Could you just—"

"Yeah." His strangled response had her biting back a smile. "Sure. I can do that."

MONTY FLEXED HIS suddenly sore fingers and watched Sienna Fairchild shove her way down the narrow passageway toward the forward berth. Never in his life had he seen such teeny, tiny buttons. Or so many of them. But he'd managed, finally, to pop the last one free and send her on her way. She'd stumbled, limped and fumbled, trying to keep her dress in place.

She was going to be lucky not to fall and sprain something else.

While he'd be lucky not to be haunted by images of what she wore under the dress.

For him, his planned nap was clearly out of the question. He picked up her shoes and stashed them in a cubby under the bench. While he'd bought the boat as is, and that included most everything left behind by the now elderly owner, it wasn't anywhere close to well stocked or outfitted. The bare necessities indeed, which was exactly the tune Monty hummed as he cleaned up the remnants of the sandwiches and put away the remainder of the groceries.

The six previous boats he'd purchased for his fleet had all been in better condition than *Nana's Dream*. There was a reason his brain chimed like a cash register whenever he stepped onto her. Normally he didn't worry about money; in his experience it tended to arrive when it was needed or his patience won out over impulse. Truth was he wanted to take his time with her; she could very well end up being the best investment he'd made yet.

He'd meant it when he'd told Sienna about the boat's soul; he'd felt the life in *Dream* as soon as he'd seen her online. Even before Frankie had pushed for the purchase, he'd known he'd buy her. Now that he'd done so, he had to deal with the consequences.

He pulled out his phone, tapped open the notepad app and began dictating the list of things he'd need to do, from refitting the cabinetry to ripping up the carpeting and replacing it with durable vinyl flooring. Tasks like that he could hire Kendall Davidson and her construction crew to handle. The army vet knew her way around restoration projects and he'd bet she wouldn't mind adding boat work to what her company offered. The smaller stuff he could pass on to Kyle Knight, who was looking for opportunities to build up his construction experience for the contractor's license he planned to test for.

Monty took pictures of the rest of the interior, avoiding the bow berth until it was unoccupied. The head would need a complete overhaul, as would the appliances in the galley. Cosmetics would come later, including a new coat of paint and maybe—*maybe* a new name.

He'd have to spend some time with *Dream* to decide. Whatever her name, he'd make certain it would fit.

He glanced toward the closed door at the end of the passageway. Sienna Fairchild definitely had a way about her. She hadn't seemed fazed by the close quarters on the vessel and had clearly been comfortable enough with boats in general that she'd escaped onto his. Regardless, she was way out of his league. That necklace around her neck, the ring on her finger… Obviously she lived in a world he couldn't begin to fathom. He was perfectly content living his small-town life. Nothing about Sienna Fairchild said "small town." She'd probably been places he'd only pinned up pictures of on a bulletin board. At least he'd have an entertaining story to tell once he got home. He'd leave out how his heart beat double time when he'd touched her or how he'd inhaled the scent of jasmine threading through her hair. Or how soft her skin had felt beneath his touch.

"I need to get out of here," he muttered. Making sure he had his wallet and phone, he headed above deck into the fresh afternoon air. The crowd he'd seen hours before had dissipated, apart from the caterers reloading white vans in the service entrance and the group of men who had been scurrying around the dock. Out in plain sight were a furious-looking Richard and Sienna's father.

Monty ducked back inside and scribbled a note for Sienna, on the off chance she woke up while he was gone. Best she keep out of sight for the rest of the day. Then, whistling, as was his habit, he left *Dream* and headed down the dock toward the club.

He knew right when Richard had spotted him. It was like a red-hot laser beam hitting him between his shoulder blades. Monty ignored the sensation, figuring it was better to have them focusing on him rather than the boat and who might be inside.

Monty had only been inside the Empire

Yacht Club a few times before, mostly on the invitation of a member when he had been on a buying trip. The blinding whiteness of the building reminded him of Liberty Lighthouse back in Butterfly Harbor, standing tall and resolute against the sky and ocean beyond. Clapboard siding gave the club building a bit of historic character, as did the hand-carved wooden signs with gold lettering. Bypassing the bar-and-grill restaurant, he turned into the expansive gift shop and set his sights on the clothes.

He heard voices in the distance. Richard again. And it didn't sound as if he'd gotten his temper under control.

"Don't try to stop me!" Richard's voice exploded in the store. "I know what I'm doing. You!"

Rolling his eyes, Monty held up the gray sweatshirt with the club's logo as if he was judging the size. "Still looking for your bride, Richard?"

The man's cheeks went bright red. "Where is she?"

Monty shook his head. "Nothing's changed since we last spoke," he lied. "Haven't seen her."

"Oh, yeah?" Richard strode over, snatched

the sweatshirt out of Monty's grasp and waved it in front of his face. "Then what's this?"

"That's a sweatshirt, Richard." Monty kept his voice calm. Rising to the bait wasn't going to help anyone, least of all Sienna. "And I'm sorry, but I think that's too small for you." But it was perfect for Sienna. He plucked it free and draped it over his arm. Just for kicks, he turned his attention to the sweats-and-shorts section.

"They're too small for you, too," Richard seethed. "You know where she is. I know you do."

"Richard, you're being rude." Vincent Fairchild's voice intimated he'd clearly had enough of his almost son-in-law's behavior. He, unlike Richard, appeared to have surrendered to the fact that there would be no wedding. He'd changed out of his tuxedo and now looked like a senior cover model for *Seven Sails* magazine. "Mr. Bettencourt, my apologies once again. We're only trying to find Sienna before she does something drastic."

He made Sienna sound like a wilting flower when she seemed anything but. "From where I'm standing, I'd say leaving him at the altar was smart, not drastic," Monty said slowly. "I'm sorry, Mr. Fairchild, but I can't help you."

"Can't or won't?" Richard snapped. "Those clothes fit her. I'm sure of it."

Monty's temper caught, a dull flame of anger taking form in his belly. "They will also fit my sister."

"Yeah, right," Richard snorted.

Monty pulled out his phone and flashed a picture, one of the few of Frankie where she wasn't in her firefighter's uniform. "She collects sweatshirts. And shoes." He added a pair of deck shoes to his growing pile. Sienna was going to need some getting-around clothes if she was breaking out of the marina. "Do you know if they have sunglasses?" He ignored the prices, even as he heard that darn cash register ringing in his head again.

Richard and Vincent trailed behind him to the checkout, where he found an excellent selection of shades with the club logo in the corner of the lens.

The young woman behind the counter cast nervous looks over Monty's shoulder, and it wasn't until he saw the current newsletter displaying Vincent Fairchild's photo as yacht-club president that he realized why. Monty merely smiled and engaged her in small talk, easing her nerves as she packaged up his purchases.

"If you'd just let us search your boat it would solve everything," Vincent said as they followed him back to the marina.

"Step foot on my boat and I'll have you arrested for trespassing," Monty said.

"I can call the police myself." Vincent's arrogant tone let Monty know exactly the type of person he was dealing with. "The local sheriff is a good friend of the family. He understands how these things work."

"Well, if you do, tell Chris that Monty says hello." Monty did a slow turn and relished the shock on Vincent and Richard's faces. "I had breakfast with him just this morning. He and my dad worked together years ago fighting wildfires. We've kept in touch. So, yeah. Go ahead and call." Monty's lips twitched. "I'd be happy to fill him in on the harassment I've received from you both this afternoon."

"Why you—"

"Richard!" Vincent caught the younger man's arm to stop him from lunging. The temper on his face eased and the older man laughed. It was a sound that carried no humor, but the promise of something more. "I think

Mr. Bettencourt and I understand each other, don't we?"

"We sure do." Without waiting for a response, Monty sauntered back to the boat, resisting the temptation to look over his shoulder to see if the men were still watching. The less suspicious he acted, the better.

He ducked into the cabin, headed down the hall and quietly opened the door wide enough to check on Sienna. She was wrapped up in the blankets on one of the twin beds, her wedding dress lying in a heap on the floor. She was sound asleep.

Monty set the paper bag by the bed and quietly backed out of the room.

CHAPTER THREE

DESPITE HER HOPES, clarity with respect to her situation did not present itself when Sienna woke up.

It did, however, take her a few moments to remember where she was. The small, dank cabin-type room. The tarnished brass lampshade near the door. The high narrow windows on either side of the pair of beds told her she'd slept the day away.

Her stomach pitched as if she'd been thrown into a storm-tossed sea. She sat up, dislodging the blankets, and stared in blank horror at the pile of wedding dress pooled on the floor at her feet. "I've really made a mess of things, haven't I?"

Despite her earlier vow, she waited for the guilt and regret to surface, but as she sat there, the boat swaying gently in its moored state, the faint sound of water lapping against the hull, neither emotion made an appearance. The more she thought about what she'd done, the more she realized her unsettled state had more to do with ambiguity about her future rather than the choice she'd made to abandon her wedding. Somehow she'd launched herself from a safe, predictable life into a typhoon of uncertainty, and yet…

And yet.

She chewed on her manicured thumbnail, thoughts racing at peak speed. For the past two months she'd let her father and Richard run everything, from insisting they could take care of all of Nana's funeral arrangements to pushing for a fast marriage for herself and Richard. But what was worse, she'd let them because her father had asked her to, because it was easier than making a scene, easier than being a problem.

Easier than living her own life.

"Well, you're certainly about to start living it now." She carefully planted her feet on the floor, then breathed a sigh of relief when there was barely a twinge of pain. She twisted and shimmied, running her fingers under the elastic band of the underwire bra she'd tucked herself into this morning. The undergarments were nearly as uncomfortable as the gown itself. Even as she struggled to ease the band of the bra, she caught sight of the paper bag sitting beside the bed.

All the jagged edges of her day smoothed out as she found the sweatshirt and other items of clothing Monty had left for her. Affection swelled inside of her. With silent thanks, she ditched what was left of her wedding attire. Once she'd slipped into the gray sweatshirt and matching pants, she arranged her wedding gown, along with the ostentatious necklace, on the matching twin bed. The deck shoes were a little too big, so she ditched them before sitting on the edge of the bed and staring down at her engagement ring.

"You never really fit, did you?" She twisted the ring, wincing as it clung to her finger like a leech. She was meant to have it resized after the wedding. She tugged and pulled until her finger hurt and she'd left red welts on her skin. "Great. You'll just have to stay put for now."

She tried to tick off a mental list of things she had going for her, but said list began and ended with "being on her own." At least until she got her inheritance from her grandmother. She'd never had a career. She and Nana had traveled so much, especially after Sienna graduated from college, that Sienna had found it easier to work part-time jobs. She knew it made her seem flighty and frivolous, especially in her father's eyes, bouncing from employer to employer, but that flexibility had made it easier when her grandmother's health had taken a turn for the worse.

In the months since then, Sienna had been too busy dealing with a fast-tracked wedding and moving plans to even think about finding another job, let alone deciding on a career.

Besides, Richard had often said he'd like her to continue with her and her grandmother's past volunteer efforts and committee works; it would build up his social status and allow him to expand his contacts list—in essence, make him look good by extension.

She actually shuddered. By breaking up with Richard she'd probably dodged the biggest bore in the world.

She definitely was not getting married. Nor would she be moving out of the house she'd lived in with Nana for the past ten-plus years. In two weeks, she'd have more options. In two weeks, she'd turn twenty-five and the inheritance her grandmother had left her would officially become hers. But until then...

Until then, her life was as empty as the nightstand between the two twin beds. She needed a break, needed some time to think things through, and maybe, finally, figure out who she was and what she really wanted.

Her nose twitched and she sniffed the air. Her stomach rumbled and her blood began to pound. Oh, thank heavens. Actual food. After weeks of starving herself into her wedding dress, her nautical host was cooking something that smelled deliciously caloric. Sienna angled her head, a smile spreading across her lips at the sound of Monty humming on the other side of the door. Just being around him made her feel more at ease. Happier. The nerves he caused were entirely different from the ones she'd struggled with in front of the mirror this morning in the bridal suite.

That Monty hadn't balked at finding her on his boat was only part of it. That he wasn't inclined to reveal her whereabouts to her father and fiancé was another point in his favor. He hadn't pushed or prodded her for answers; he'd even offered her a bed to ease her exhaustion. Sienna's smile brightened. He was entirely too good to be true.

Still…she bit the inside of her cheek, an idea forming out of desperation. She had no life to get back to, at least not one she wanted to get back to. But she wasn't ready to face her father and Richard. Not yet. Not until she had the security of her inheritance behind her and a plan of action in front of her.

How ironic she felt most solid on a gently swaying boat that belonged to a stranger.

She pushed to her feet and walked to the door, getting used to the dull throbbing in her ankle. After the drama of what she'd done this morning, this should be easy.

Sienna found Monty where she expected to, puttering around the galley, keeping one eye on the juicy hamburgers cooking on the stove. The lights were on in the cabin now; they had to be, considering it was pitch-black outside. She could see the tiniest sliver of moonlight shining through the window over the table.

"I had a feeling these might wake you up." Once again, Monty took her appearance in stride. "How's your ankle?"

"Better, thanks." She tucked a disobedient curl behind her ear. "The burgers smell great."

"One of my prelaunch traditions. You eat meat, don't you?"

"I will tonight." Heck, she was hungry enough to eat a full cow.

"Great."

She leaned against the table and watched as he stacked lettuce, tomato and other fixings onto a paper plate. He really was handsome, Sienna thought. Even more than she'd realized at first. Maybe it was his kindness affecting her judgment. Or maybe it was the stunning combination of green eyes and fiery hair overwhelming her. Now, in the dim light of the cabin, watching him move so gracefully in the small space, she was definitely appreciating more than his generosity. Gentle hands, a caring touch, an easy smile… Was there anything more appealing in a man?

She cleared her throat, shifting uncomfortably. Definitely not the track she needed to be on considering what she was about to ask.

"I take it you slept okay?"

"Better than I have in ages." She hugged her arms around her torso, then thought better of it and let her arms drop. "Thank you for the clothes. They're perfect."

"You look the same size as Frankie so it wasn't hard." His grin dipped a little. "I ran into Richard and your father while I was buying them."

Her stomach clenched again, the way it always did when she wasn't sure what would happen next. The worst he could say was no.

"Speaking of them… I have been doing some thinking."

"Second thoughts about canceling the wedding?"

"Any second thoughts I might have are more to do with how I let myself get talked into the engagement in the first place. Not that I'm ready to discuss that with him. Or my father."

Monty flipped the burgers, then after she nodded, poured them each a mug of fresh-brewed coffee. He motioned for her to sit. "You probably don't want to hear this, but I don't think either of them is convinced you've left the marina."

"No?" She swallowed the wonderfully hot coffee and nearly swooned. It was perfection, with the slightest hint of… She sipped again, frowned, and sent him a quizzical look.

"Cardamom. Just a little." He drank. "Tones down the bitterness."

"It's lovely. Reminds me of a drink I liked in India." Despite the scalding temperature, she eagerly sipped again. "You got the sense they're going to wait me out?"

"If they don't do it themselves, I'd bet they get someone to. Your father even threatened to call the sheriff to search my boat."

Sienna winced. "He did not..." She could understand her father's frustration with her, but this was taking things too far. "I'm so sorry. There's no call for that. I'm a grown woman, after all, and in charge of my life." All evidence to the contrary. She nearly snorted into her coffee.

"Yes," Monty said with a twinkle in his eye. "Yes, you are. It's no big deal. I told him to go ahead. But don't worry." He held up a hand. "The sheriff's an old family friend. Even if Chris did come on board and search, he wouldn't give you away if you didn't want him to."

"I feel like a teenager who's run away from home," she grumbled. Not that she ever had. By the time she was old enough to think about it, she knew very well her father didn't care enough to come after her. Which was why this situation with Richard was so perplexing. Why bother with her now after ignoring her for so many years?

"Yeah, well, since it seems neither of them is going to stop looking for you anytime soon," Monty said as he got up to pull the burgers off the heat, "maybe you should go ahead and face them now rather than draw it out any longer?"

"I suppose that's one option." She swallowed, gathering her courage. "Or there's another one."

"What's that?" He opened a bag of chips, popped one in his mouth and sat down. She waited until his mouth was full before she answered.

"I was thinking I could come with you to Butterfly Harbor."

He didn't choke. Not exactly. But he did push a fisted hand against his mouth as his eyes widened and watered. When he finally swallowed, he practically gasped, "You want to what?"

"Just hear me out!" She held up both hands and dived into her rehearsed plea. "I know how to sail. I've been on boats my whole life. My grandmother taught me so I'd have something in common with my father. Not that that went any… Never mind." She was babbling. She always babbled when she was panicked. "I cook pretty well, so we wouldn't starve and you could eat more than peanut butter and hamburgers. I've always felt at home on the water, as if it's where I belong, and maybe that's what I need now. Just some time away from…everything. While I figure out what to do. I promise, once we get to Butterfly

Harbor in a few days, you never have to see me again." Monty stared at her, and for the first time she couldn't decipher the expression on his face.

"On the other hand," she added, "if you were hoping for solitude, I can keep out of your way. I'll even lock myself in the forward berth—"

"I wouldn't ask you to do that," Monty said, cutting her off.

Hope welled and surfaced like an inflatable dinghy. "Is that a yes?"

"It's a… I don't know." Monty cringed. "This trip's going to be unpredictable. The boat isn't in great shape. The engine's temperamental. I can't guarantee we're going to get anywhere at a specific time. Could be up to a week before we get there."

"Lucky for me I have no pending appointments." A week. Not a lot of time, but it was more than she'd have if he said no.

It seemed like an eternity before he spoke again, and when he did, her stomach turned over. "I don't think it's a good idea, Sienna. As much as I'd like to help you, you'd just be delaying the situation you're in. Take it from me. It'll just make things worse."

"Frankly, they couldn't get much worse,"

she countered. "And no offense, but dealing with my father and my fiancé is my problem. I need time to clear my head. Really clear it. I've been in this haze since my grandmother died. It didn't begin to clear until I looked at myself in the mirror, standing there in that dress, minutes away from marrying a man I barely know because it was what other people wanted." Because she'd finally done something that had made her father happy. How ironic that pleasing him had made her absolutely miserable. "Running away might seem rash and irresponsible to you, but for me, it feels like I'm breaking free. A little extra time to sort everything out. If it helps," she added when Monty still didn't look convinced, "I can pay you."

His eyes sparked with irritation an instant before they narrowed. "Not everything comes with a dollar sign. I don't want your money."

"Maybe not want, but I bet you need it." She motioned to the cabin's interior, reminded once again that time had a way of standing still in the oddest of places. "I imagine this boat cost you quite a bit. And it'll take even more to fix it up to become the star of your fleet." She could see he was surprised that she'd been listening to him earlier. "Seems to me the only thing standing in your path to make an instant profit with *Dream* is a lack of money."

All her life she'd been Winnifred Fairchild's granddaughter, Vincent Fairchild's daughter, solitary heiress to a fortune that could set her feet on any path she chose. It never occurred to her not to pay people's way; to host the parties, arrange the trips. She'd been two years into college before she realized most of those friendships weren't real. For some, she'd been a walking ATM. The rich girl so desperate for friends and emotional connections she'd literally bought and paid for them.

Now here she was, doing it again. "Well?"

"Well what?" His eyes went cold.

"How much will it cost for you to take me to Butterfly Harbor."

"You don't listen very well, do you?" He stood up, began gathering up his trash. "If you want to come with me, all right. I still believe you're making the wrong choice by running away, but it's your mistake to make. I do not, however—and I want you to hear me on this—I do not want your money."

She snapped her mouth shut. This didn't make any sense. Who turned down money for doing something he was going to do anyway?

Still, when she thought about continuing the argument, she realized he was standing stone-like, daring her to challenge him.

"All right." She nodded. "We won't talk about payment again." Until he wanted to. He'd change his mind. Of course, he would. In a few days or a few weeks, he'd see how much he could get done with a large check.

"I'd still like to get access to my bank account. Enough to help cover my travel expenses. Is that acceptable?"

"I suppose." He narrowed his eyes. "Just how expensive are you?"

"Not very. Just…particular." She smiled. "Is there somewhere we can stop to get cash? And maybe a new cell phone." And with a longer stay on his boat she was going to need clothes.

"There's a small town only a couple of hours north." Monty nodded. "We can stop there tomorrow and get supplies."

"Great! So we have a deal?" She held out her hand. He seemed to wait an extra beat, then shook it.

"Yeah." He curled his fingers around hers. "We have a deal."

HE'D SEEN IT, Monty thought a few hours later as he tried to sleep. He'd seen surprise and shock on Sienna's face when he'd passed on her offer. It had been as clear as the Pacific on a summer day. It was as if no one had ever told her no before. Or turned down her financial favors. What kind of life had she led where she thought everyone had a price?

His business sense was screaming at him. Of course, he could have used the money. The sooner he could get *Dream* operating, the faster he'd recoup his investment. Practically speaking, he was an idiot for saying no.

But taking money for helping her out of a tricky situation just felt…skeezy. Not to mention the fact that he could hear his father's disappointment with him from the afterlife. Bettencourts didn't help people for profit— they helped because it was the right thing to do. And it seemed that transporting Sienna Fairchild to his hometown was the right thing. It was certainly going to be a complicated thing.

His suggestion that she talk everything out with her father and fiancé had been an honest, well-intentioned one. Getting everything out in the open when you had issues with people was much less messy than running away or ignoring them. Communication was the way to move forward and start afresh. He hadn't really expected her to take the advice; it had only been a few hours since she'd introduced herself to him. And the only price he'd have to pay would be sharing this very small boat with one very beautiful and distracting socialite.

He groaned, rubbed both hands down his face. What had he been thinking saying yes?

And why did he have the sneaking suspicion he would be the one who ended up regretting it by the time they reached Butterfly Harbor?

He'd just have to make sure they got there in as short a time as possible. Five days max. Maybe six. He could manage that, right? Although being in close quarters with a raven-haired knockout with a penchant for teasing smiles and heart-lightening laughter was going to be…well, a new kind of challenge, that was for sure. The uncertain "good night" he'd received a short time after their handshake should make keeping his distance easier.

"That's probably for the best," Monty muttered as he shifted in bed. A woman like Sienna Fairchild, who was probably into a million things, and traveled here, there and everywhere, wasn't for someone like him. He liked his calm, routine life just how it was. Sure, he thought about getting married, settling down and having a couple of kids, especially now that his twin sister was about to. Not to mention most of his friends had done the same. He was fast becoming the spare wheel.

Sienna Fairchild, however appealing, however entertaining, was not the solution to anything.

He had absolutely no doubt once she saw Butterfly Harbor and the reality of the very mundane life he and his friends and family lived, she'd quickly realize exactly what she'd given up by leaving Richard at the altar. She'd probably call her ex the second they docked and beg him to take her back.

Yeah. Monty squeezed his eyes shut and forced himself to believe that. That's exactly what would happen. Just as well to not get involved with her more than he already had.

He grabbed his phone and looked at the clock. One o'clock. He planned to be out of the marina by six with a clear head, but a lack of sleep was not going to make that happen.

Monty closed his eyes, willing his mind to slow, for the peaceful sound of the water lapping against the boat to lull him into the darkness.

A soft thunk overhead had his eyes shooting open. He waited, listening, and wondered if maybe Sienna had left her berth and was clomping around the boat. Except she didn't clomp. With her injured foot, she barely walked.

Another clunk, a hiss of pain and a muttered curse that was definitely a male voice had Monty throwing his legs over the side of the bed and pulling on his jeans.

He shoved his phone into his back pocket, quietly headed to the door and pulled it open. He nearly jumped out of his skin when he found Sienna on the other side, hand raised to knock.

"What are you doing?" he whispered.

"I heard a noise." She was still wearing the sweatshirt, only she'd changed into the shorts that proved what he'd already discovered. Sienna Fairchild had fabulous legs. "I thought it was you."

"Well, it wasn't." He quickly shifted places with her and pushed her inside. "Stay in here and lock the door."

"But—"

"My boat. My rules." Chances were it was

a group of drunk teenagers looking to break some marina rules—at least, he hoped it was that harmless. Regardless, he wasn't about to let anyone damage *Dream*. He waited until he heard the click of the lock on his door before he climbed the ladder and pushed open the hatch.

The cool night air rushed over him as he stepped onto the deck. He stood still, listening, waiting for an indication of where the intruder might be. Sure enough, he heard the stumbling footsteps again. Beneath the glow of the marina's lamps, he followed the shifting shadow along the aft and approached the dark figure, who was attempting to peer into one of the long narrow windows of the galley.

It was the blond hair that gave Richard away. That and the pale, almost glow-in-the-dark skin. The idiot hadn't even bothered to wear a cap. Monty might have laughed if he wasn't so annoyed. He leaned down and picked up the docking poll, and held the metal staff securely in his hand as he moved in behind a crouching Richard. He tapped him once on the back of the shoulder. "I told you to stay off my boat."

Richard let out a sound that reminded Monty of a wounded seal. He stumbled, tripped and, after trying to find his balance, pitched straight over the side of the boat and dropped into the water.

The splashing and swearing that ensued made Monty wonder if the guy even knew how to swim.

"Grab hold of the dock, Richard," Monty called. It had been pure luck Richard hadn't landed straight on the planks and broken his back. Shaking his head, Monty pulled out his phone and dialed. "Hey, Chris. It's Monty," he said when the sheriff answered.

"Monty? What the—? Do you know what time it is?"

"I do indeed." Monty watched as Richard tried, and failed, to haul himself onto the dock. The man looked like an inept octopus. "I've got a trespasser on my boat. Can you come get him and lock him up?"

CHAPTER FOUR

THERE WASN'T MUCH room to pace. Even though this cabin was larger than hers, she only managed five steps before she was spinning and moving in the opposite direction. The minutes seemed to stretch into an eternity. Of all nights for a burglar to appear on Monty's boat, it had to be tonight?

She sat on the edge of Monty's bed. Crossed her legs. Crossed them the other way. Folded her arms. Slid to her feet when she heard Monty's voice, and then another, all-too-familiar one let out a shriek seconds before a huge splash.

Sienna fumbled with the lock on the door, yanked it open and darted up the ladder. She found Monty standing by the railing, his back to her, a phone to his ear as he looked over the side.

"Is it…? Was it…?" Sienna let out a groan when she saw a sopping-wet Richard dragging himself onto the deck, water cascading off him. "You have got to be kidding me."

Still on the phone, Monty gently guided her back to the hatch. After he hung up, he spoke to her. "Looks like your fiancé is a man who doesn't take no for an answer."

Horrified, Sienna could only blink into the darkness. "I am so sorry."

"Not as sorry as he is. Sheriff's en route. Now stay off that ankle."

"The sheriff?" That got her attention. She gaped at him, mouth open. "Is that really necessary?"

"I told Richard to stay off my boat. He didn't." Monty rose to his full height. "I mean what I say, Sienna. Bullies only back down when you stand up to them."

"Yes, of course." She nodded, torn between laughing and screaming. She had to admit, she'd witnessed a side of Richard today she hadn't known existed. She really had been fortunate to escape marriage to him. "It's just…he's had a really rough day, Monty."

"He's not the only one."

Sienna's lips twitched. Monty, still shirtless and barefoot—and, boy, was that an image that would keep her up the rest of the night—

stepped off the boat and walked to where Richard was lying on the dock, groaning.

It might have crossed her mind to do a bit of soul-searching had the bright, spinning police lights not interrupted the darkness a few minutes later. Two patrol cars had pulled into the marina parking lot and soon three uniformed officers were heading toward *Nana's Dream*.

She perched on the padded bench and huddled next to the bulkhead for cover. The older officer took the lead, his silver hair shimmering in the lamppost light. He stepped aboard and gave her a quick nod of acknowledgment, then disappeared around the corner with his officers,

Unable to hear anything being said, Sienna shifted closer to the voices on the other side of the boat. She heard her name a few times, heard the distinctive irritable growling of Richard, who claimed his right to find his fiancée was more important than Monty's ownership of the boat.

Had she any doubts left about her decision to ditch Richard at the altar, they vanished with her ex-fiancé's declaration of "You'll be hearing from my lawyers." Honestly. She'd only ever heard people on TV shows use such a line. But she'd heard it now—and at full volume as Richard was hauled away by the deputies.

"Thanks, Chris." Monty was coming, so Sienna quickly summoned her courage and claimed the seat she'd abandoned. She sat there, legs bouncing against the cold, as Monty rounded the corner with an older-looking man.

"Gotta say, it's never boring with a Bettencourt around," the older man said with a chuckle. "Ma'am. I'm Sheriff Sutherland. You'd be Miss Fairchild?"

"Yes. Is Richard okay?"

"Better than he deserves to be," Monty muttered.

Sheriff Sutherland gave him a look. "I'd say he's suffering from busted pride at the moment, but otherwise he's uninjured."

"How long can you keep him?" Monty asked.

"Depends. How long do you need me to?" He laughed. "Don't answer that. I can keep him until you come in and sign your complaint. He's already asking for a lawyer, so the window will close fast on that one."

"Understood. Appreciate you coming out yourself, Chris. I owe you one."

"Son, I think this is one I'll owe you. Never in my life did I think I'd be arresting a waterlogged Somersby. Now that's something we'll celebrate at this year's Christmas party. What about you, ma'am. Do you want to file a complaint?" He glanced at Sienna, who turned pleading eyes on Monty.

"He's been through enough already," she said. "This would only add insult to injury."

Monty sighed, ran both hands through his hair and shook his head. "I'll probably regret this...but tell him to leave Sienna alone, then let him go."

"Thank you," Sienna whispered. She could only hope that once they finally hit open water her luck would begin to change.

"All right then." Sheriff Sutherland looked at each of them in turn. "Safe journey."

"Thanks," Monty said. "I'll see you in a few weeks."

"Adele and I are looking forward to Frankie's wedding. You tell your sister if she needs anything to let me know."

"Will do." Monty watched the sheriff return to his car and drive away. "Well. That's an interesting start to our journey."

"I suppose it is." Shivering, Sienna shoved herself to her feet. "If you've changed your mind about taking me, I understand."

"Have you changed yours?" he asked when he faced her again.

"No." If anything she was even more determined. "The offer to pay you is still open, though."

"That isn't what I meant." There was no smile now, only irritation. "I meant do you still want to go with me?"

"Yes."

"Then I'll knock on your door in a few hours. Try to get some sleep."

"All right." She went down first, because he insisted, but when she turned to say "good night" again, he'd already closed his door.

SOMEHOW, DESPITE THE midnight excitement, Monty managed to grab a couple hours' sleep before his alarm went off.

Strange how being awakened by an obnoxious ringtone made for a more difficult start to the morning than waking up on his own, which he usually did. Just about everything felt off to him. "I wonder why that is?"

His frustration only grew. The third time he hit his elbow against the water-stained shower wall made him curse. The solitary bathroom, located in the narrow hallway between Sienna's bedroom and the galley, had not been designed for anyone close to his height and breadth. By the time he got to port in Butterfly Harbor he was going to be one big bruise. Towel slung around his waist, he shoved open the accordion-style door and nearly stumbled back into the shower stall.

"Sorry." Sienna beamed at him and seeing the laughter in her dark eyes set his teeth on edge. They hadn't even left the marina and he was already wondering how he would deal with her in such close proximity. "Maybe I should start wearing a bell around my neck?"

"I'll add it to our shopping list." The top of her head brushed his chin as they exchanged places. He could smell gardenias dancing off her hair and the scent brought to mind a lazy cruise around the Hawaiian islands against the setting sun. Oh, yeah. This trip was going to be worse than he thought. "There's a little town about three hours north where we can get supplies, and there's a dealer there who specializes in old boat engines. We should also be able to get you a phone and online to connect to your bank."

"It's your boat. I'm just along for the ride." There was that smile again, a smile that told him she'd shaken off whatever trepidation she might have been feeling and was ready for a new adventure.

"Great. I'll get dressed and do a final check on the engine."

"Sounds like a plan."

He glanced out the narrow window over the galley table. "It's a plan all right—at least, it is for now." With that, he headed back to his cabin. He heard the scream before he shut his door. Still grasping his towel, he raced back to the bathroom. Monty had his hand on the door handle, then hesitated. "Sienna? You okay?"

"No, I'm not okay." She yanked open the door and countered his own towel with one of her own. Her face was drenched, her hair sopping. Her eyes flashed danger when she pinned him with a look. "You used all the hot water!"

He couldn't help it. He grinned. "Sorry about that."

"You know what? I don't think you are."

His grin widened. "You can go first tomorrow, princess. Quirks of the *Dream*. Better get used to it." This time he whistled on his way back to his cabin.

CHAPTER FIVE

IF SHE'D KNOWN all it would take to improve Monty's mood after encountering Richard was to get pummeled by ice-cold water, she'd have showered as soon as the sheriff had driven away. She managed to get clean in record time despite getting distracted by the citrus-scented shampoo that smelled distinctly like Monty Bettencourt's hair. Practicality dictated she braid her hair, which she did, before pulling her sweatshirt and pants back on. Her ankle gave her barely a twinge as she finished getting dressed and headed out to start the day.

Finding coffee already steaming and ready to pour, she grabbed the two mugs from last night, washed them and refilled them and carried them up the ladder toward the wheelhouse, where she found Monty checking gauges and testing the radio.

"I'm not naturally sneaky," she said after making a show of climbing the short staircase. He glanced over his shoulder as she joined him. "I'll try not to scare you again."

"You can scare me all you want if you bring coffee." He accepted the offered mug with a quick smile. "Thanks."

"Everything okay?" The view from the window was nothing more than a collection of boats and cruisers—a view she'd seen hundreds of times over the years. The view behind her—the view waiting for them—now that was another story.

"Electricity seems to be working. I'm going to try not to push the engine too hard our first trip out. The ride to Plover Bay should be a good test."

"Like I said, I'm just along for the ride."

"Oh, you're more than that." He took a long drink of coffee. "You're crew now."

"In that case, Captain, your wish is my command. If I don't know how to do something, I'll let you know or figure it out myself."

"Fair enough. You know how to unmoor us?"

"Yep." She set down her mug in a cup receptacle. "Quick start out, huh?"

He nodded and she unfastened the lashings, looping each thick rope the way her grandmother had taught her back before Sienna had hit double digits. When she heard the roar of the engine catching, she picked up speed, wanting to watch the horizon come closer as they pulled out of dock.

The morning was cool, as most mornings were this time in early April, and the wind chill increased as the boat began to move. She tilted her head, listened to the odd sounds of the engine. It definitely wasn't as smooth as she was used to, but then, this boat had been made well before she'd been born.

She stood at the bow, feet braced apart, hands gently clasping the brass railing as *Nana's Dream* pull-putted its restrictive four miles per hour out of the marina water space.

She'd never found anything better than the ocean wind blowing across her face as open water lay ahead. The wind made her eyes blur, and she shivered, but she stood fast, the anxiety that had been plaguing her for the past couple months fading the farther from the marina they went.

They passed early-morning fishermen and late-night cruises on their return to the harbor. Horns blared occasionally in greeting, and soon, as Sienna closed her eyes and dropped her head back, the Empire Marina was out of sight.

Monty steered *Dream* north, kicking up their speed enough to have them bouncing lightly along the current. How she loved that *slap, slap, slap* against the boat—it was like music to her ears, the vibration of the sea beneath the soles of her shoes reassuring. She felt the last of the emotional shackles she'd been wearing drop away and, head tilted back, she raised her arms and made like a bird soaring across the waves.

Seagulls cawed overhead, along with a flash of bright green interspersed among the feathered creatures. A distinctive squawk had her lips curving into a smile and she returned to the wheelhouse and joined Monty.

"Get your fill already?" Monty called over the noise of the wind and engine, his brow arched in challenge.

"Never!" She stood beside him, feet braced apart again, and balanced herself as she drank her coffee and sighed. "This might be the best morning of my life."

"It's about to get better." He rustled up a paper bag from nearby and pulled out an over-sized bagel. He tore it apart and offered her half. "My last one for the trip. Homemade by Roman's mother, Ezzie."

"Thank you." Too hungry to refuse, she accepted and bit in, her taste buds exploding with crunchy, soft, herbed goodness. "It's delicious."

"Better than New York if you ask me. Not that I'd know. Chrysalis Bakery in town does pretty good ones, but I'm partial to Ezzie's. Plus they're free 'cause she likes me." There was that charming smile again, the one that made her stomach do odd things.

The sun arched higher into the sky, warming the air around them. "If you're still hungry, you can check the fridge," Monty called.

She wasn't, mainly because she wasn't normally a breakfast person, but she suspected that wasn't the reason he'd mentioned it. "I take it that's code for you want something to eat?"

"See? You're learning to speak my language already."

"Or I could take the wheel?" She'd meant it to tease him, but the skeptical expression on his face clearly meant she'd failed. "Kidding! Believe me, even I'm smart enough to know not to get between a man and his... wheel this soon out. I'll just..." She gathered up the now-empty mugs and paper bag and headed downstairs.

She found a scribbled list of supplies on the table, most of which she couldn't read. The man's writing was atrocious. She'd need a code-breaker to decipher it. What she did do was take a quick inventory of all he had brought on the boat with him yesterday, noting his particular penchant for all things carbohydrate. Beyond the giant jars of peanut butter and strawberry jam, he'd brought two different kinds of bread, cookies, breakfast toaster pastries and… She pulled out a family-size bag of chocolate-coated-peanut candy.

"A man after my own heart." Her blood sugar was spiking just holding it. Well, she might not be much of a cook, but she could throw together some mean salads, so she added to his list, making sure each and every item was legible.

More than once she'd caught herself reaching for her cell phone, which, of course, she didn't have. She practically itched without it. Withdrawal, she told herself. So she set aside the impulse and made him a peanut-butter sandwich. She picked it up, along with another cup of coffee, this one in a new travel cylinder she found on the shelf next to the sink.

It hadn't taken her long to get her sea legs back, other than learning to try to keep as much weight off her ankle as she could. She added painkillers to the grocery list, then took his second breakfast upstairs.

This was something she could easily get used to. Waking up in the morning with nothing around her but open water and clear sky. It was a dream, she knew. Not every morning was like this and the ocean certainly wasn't always friendly, but this was a day she'd remember for a very long time. No matter what else might come down the line, she could cling to that. And smile.

"I added to the grocery list," Sienna said as she handed him his sandwich and set his metal tumbler where he'd had his mug previously. "Hope that's okay."

"Of course." He had taken a seat in the padded chair, had one hand casually on the wheel, not steering necessarily, but guiding and making sure the boat stayed on course. "So, Plover Bay, here we come. Not sure what cell company you use—"

She told him.

"Okay, same as mine. There's a satellite store there, so we should be able to solve at least one of your problems."

"I'm already itching not having mine," she admitted.

"They also have a pretty good farmer's market on the weekends."

"How often have you been there?"

"Too often to count. I've run charter fishing groups down the coast of California. They like to find out-of-the-way spots and so do I. It doesn't have all the tourist trappings of say…well, San Diego." His lips twitched.

"Yes, California is known for its lack of tourist traps." Sienna laughed in agreement. "Where does your Butterfly Harbor fall in? Seems to me it's a tourist spot, isn't it?"

"Touché," he said. "Butterfly Harbor's special. It nearly went under a few years ago. Tons of foreclosures due to financial malfeasance on the part of the main bank in town. Took all of us coming together and fighting to save it. The current mayor's better than the last. Mostly. We're on the other side now and flourishing."

"Sounds like an interesting place." Not that much different than most cities and towns she supposed. "It looked lovely when I saw it on a TV special. The one they aired about celebrity chef Jason Corwin and his wedding." She could remember the images clearly; the coastal town with expansive beaches, high cliffsides and cypress trees outlining the rocky shores. There was a historic inn painted a bright summer yellow with white shutters and trim, perched at the highest point overlooking the town. The Flutterby Inn. From the moment she'd seen it on screen, she'd wanted to go there. Somehow, she'd forgotten about that.

"The town got its name from the butterfly migratory patterns. Monarchs especially," Monty said. "Every year from October through December, the eucalyptus trees are filled with them. Thousands upon thousands. There are other towns in the area that get their share, as well, but we're hoping to bring tourists in year-round with the new sanctuary that's being built. Especially in November, when we have a month-long butterfly festival."

"Sounds promising."

Monty nodded. "It is. It'll include a nature education center, as well. Its location is perfect, right near Duskywing Farm, an organic outfit run by one of our locals, Calliope Costas. If you don't go anywhere else before you leave, you have to make a stop there. Calliope's…well,

Calliope's got a special manner with flora and fauna."

"Flora and fauna?" Sienna laughed.

"Hang around Calliope long enough and you start speaking her language. It's a good place, Butterfly Harbor. A happy place. It's not perfect, of course. But it comes pretty darn close as far as I'm concerned."

"You've lived there all your life?"

"That's right. My father was a firefighter there when Frankie and I were born. Became chief a few years later. Never knew a man more proud of his town, more proud of his fellow residents."

Sienna could name at least one who was equally, if not more proud. "Is he still chief? Your father?"

The cloud that passed over Monty's face was one Sienna had seen many times before in her own mirror.

"He died fighting a wildfire when Frankie and I were sixteen. One of those freak wind changes that steals a life away in the blink of an eye. Two lives in this case. My dad and another fighter out of the Bay Area."

"I'm sorry," she whispered, but even against the wind he heard her.

"Thanks. He was a good man, but he was

an even better father. Anything that's good about me is because of him."

"What about your mother?"

Monty shook his head. "Suffice it to say, Roxie was always more interested in Roxie than being a parent."

Odd to call a mother by her first name, wasn't it? Not that Sienna would know. She'd never known her mother and she'd learned early on that asking about her would only shut down her father faster.

An odd clunking sound emanated from somewhere below and behind them. An instant knot of unease tightened in her belly. Monty eased up on their speed until they came to a stop. With barely a flicker of concern, he turned off the engine. "Let's see what's going on."

It was one thing, Sienna thought as she watched him descend to the lower deck, to be told they could have engine issues. It was another thing to actually experience it in the middle of the ocean. A part of her knew she should stay out of the way, but another part of her was curious. She was, after all, along for the ride, and while she knew the basics about sailing—admittedly with a sailboat—there wasn't any reason she couldn't learn more.

She followed him below and found him wedged into a closet that was jam-packed with electrical wires, gauges and boxes. Everything was covered in a lot of dust, which he was blowing off with every wire he lifted to check.

"I just want to make sure it's not electrical before I dive in to look at the engine." He kept testing wires as he spoke.

"What's worse? Engine or electrical?"

"Neither is great." His brow furrowed in concentration. "I took a good look before I made my final offer. Really thought she'd make it at least a couple of days before I ended up with issues. Hand me a rag, would you?"

He held out his hand, so she hurried to the kitchen, found a ratty towel under the sink and passed it to him. As he started to use it, she knew it wasn't going to do him much good. She returned to the spot under the sink to grab a paintbrush she'd seen in the back corner.

"Here. Let's try this." She reached across him and began brushing away the dust and debris . It was quicker than the towel, and did a better job.

"Great. Thanks." He flipped open a fuse

box and ran his fingers down each outlet. "Nothing feels unusually hot." He bent down, then quietly asked for the brush, which she handed over. "Ah, okay. This could be the culprit." He motioned to an exposed wire barely hanging on to its connection.

"I saw some electrical tape in one of the drawers. It looked ancient," he continued, as she was already retrieving it, "but it should work or at least for a little bit." She bent down next to him, handed him the role of shiny black tape.

"A woman of hidden talents."

"I told you." The memories came fast, like a spinning film reel. "My grandmother was a very self-sufficient woman. She told me there's nothing a man can fix that a woman can't. You need me to tear that for you?"

"Yeah, if you can." He winced as she accepted the tape, deftly tore off a piece and handed it to him. Soon he was pinching the sticky stuff around the wires.

She shifted closer, her arms tight between his chest and the electrical panel. "You see any other exposed wires?"

"No." He inclined his head so that it hit the back of the cabinet. "I'm going to take a quick look at the engine, though, just to be sure." He braced his hands on his knees and shoved himself up. "Not exactly the pleasure cruise you were expecting, I'm sure."

"I'm not expecting anything." She backed away to let him out. "But whatever happens, you aren't alone."

ONE THING HE'D neglected to understand upon his agreeing to be Sienna's ride was that he would, in essence, be taking responsibility for her. For her safety. For her intact arrival in Butterfly Harbor.

It was one thing to take off in the run-down *Dream* on his own; he had no issues dealing with whatever consequences that followed. He'd purposely kept close to land, though, so as not to be considered offshore; some risks, even alone, he wasn't about to take. He did a quick evaluation of the intake valves, the bilge pump and, specifically, the head gaskets. If they blew one of those they'd be dead in the water. Literally.

Despite the years *Dream* had spent unoccupied and moored, she was in pretty good shape. Until he got her into dry dock and really dug into the engine, however, he couldn't risk burning her out completely.

"Well?" Sienna asked when he slammed the engine hatch shut. "What's the verdict?"

"All the things I really worry about seem okay. Let's start her back up." He walked around Sienna and climbed back into the pilot cabin.

"We've only been out on the water a short time. How far have we gone?" She took a tentative seat on the bench beside him.

"About thirty miles." He might have to reduce speed even more. "Hopefully we'll catch some fast water, otherwise we're looking at over a week to get home." He smiled. "Though I bet you'd be good with longer."

"I would be, yes." She didn't look anxious to get anywhere. "But I know you need to get back for your sister."

"Only because Ezzie's driving her nuts. I'm a good buffer. Let's see how we do at a slower pace this time."

They were no sooner on their way again than the radio crackled.

"Monty, you out there? Over."

Sienna's eyebrows went up as Monty picked up the radio receiver. "Here. Over. What's up, Luke?" He mouthed "the sheriff" at Sienna, who wore a confused expression.

"I've got a couple of mischief makers here who want to ask you a favor. Over."

"Mischief makers?" Sienna moved closer so she could hear better. She rested her hand on the back of his chair.

"That's code for Luke's son, Simon, and his friend Charlie. Charlie's a girl, by the way," Monty added with a grin. "They have a talent for getting into trouble. Remind me to tell you about Charlie's adventure in the caves sometime." He clicked the receiver. "Put them on, Luke. Over."

"Monty, we had the best idea ever but we need your help." Charlie Bradley's excited voice could have lightened anyone's mood. "We have a science report due next week and we have to display information about different animals in our environment. We want to do the ocean. Oh, yeah, sorry. Over."

"Can't exactly come get you right now, Charlie. Over."

"Give me that." A young boy's voice came over the speaker. "Our teacher said as long as we do the report and find the information, it can be anything. So we were thinking maybe you could take some pictures for us? Over."

Monty glanced at Sienna, who shrugged. "I can keep lookout for sea life," she offered.

"Okay, Simon," Monty told him. "We'll do what we can. Just don't be disappointed if it's not an orca or great white shark. Over."

"There aren't any great white sharks around here," Charlie said with what sounded like exaggerated patience. "But there are sea turtles and dolphins. Over."

"What is it with her and dolphins?" Monty asked Sienna.

"For me it was always seals."

"Okay, kiddo," Monty responded. "I'll email any pictures we take to you when I make a stop on dry land. Over."

"Cool. Thanks, Monty!" Scrambling and shuffling ensued before Charlie's voice exploded once more. "Right. Over! Bye! See, I told you he'd do it, Dad!"

"Appreciate this, Monty," Luke said. "Simon was talking about swimming out to find what he could for himself. Thankfully cooler heads prevailed. See you when you're back. Over."

Monty chuckled. "Charlie is most definitely the cooler head," he told Sienna. "Here." He handed her his cell phone. "Since you volunteered, you're officially life-form patrol. We're about ninety minutes from Plover Bay."

"Aye, aye, Captain." She descended the ladder with new purpose.

He turned the engine back to full, half-expecting that clanging noise to start again, but it was sounding smooth. Relatively confident, he accelerated and resumed course.

Sure enough, by the time he radioed ahead to the marina for an open slip, the boat was still running fine.

"What a cute little town." Sienna popped back into the wheelhouse and, standing beside him, shielded her eyes as he pulled into a small marina. "I've never even heard of it." The stretch of local businesses took up most of the street on the opposite side of the marina. The fish stall was doing a brisk trade, as was the fresh-lemonade-and-organic-fruit-bowl stand that was new since he'd last been here.

The telltale hint of treetops a few blocks away belied the park beneath the barely blooming blossoms and branches. The few blocks of downtown wound in and around each other, but it was one of those places that appealed to him. Just like home.

"It's definitely a blink-and-miss-it kind of town, but it has a lot of charm," Monty said as he waved at a group of sport fishermen heading out in a trawler for the day. "They're getting a late start."

"How early do they normally go?"

"I've got my groups out and their lines in the water by six thirty at the latest." Monty craned his neck to see where he was going. "Besides, earlier I'm out, earlier I'm back."

"And you make a good living with your business?"

"Wind Walkers. And, yes. Don't sound so skeptical. I just need enough to get by, not break the bank."

"I didn't mean to sound judgmental. I was just curious how the son of a firefighter ends up as a tour guide."

"Water-excursion specialist," Monty corrected with what he hoped was a smile. "And the answer's easy. Firefighting wasn't my thing. Frankie, on the other hand—"

"Your sister's a firefighter?"

There was no misinterpreting the shock in her voice. "Not just a firefighter, she's cochief. From the time we were kids, it's all she ever wanted to be. She's good at it, too." But as good as she was, it hadn't stopped Frankie from getting seriously injured last Christmas Eve.

He could still remember what it felt like, standing out there in the darkness lit by the very fire ripping through the town's onetime pub that had been serving as a temporary mayor's office. He'd watched it burn…with his sister inside. And he hadn't been able to do anything about it.

He hadn't felt so helpless, so useless, so scared, since their father had been killed. "Frankie is a multifaceted woman," he said before he dwelled too much on the fear he'd managed to bank. He couldn't worry about her; he shouldn't. Not when she was so capable at her job. Nor could he silence that little voice in the back of his head that asked if one day the flames were going to be too much and he'd lose the only family he had left. "There's nothing she hasn't been good at, but firefighting? That's where she excels."

"Whereas your place is on the water. Opposite elements," Sienna said as he pulled back on the throttle and turned off the boat. "You balance each other."

He chuckled. "Oh, yeah. You and Calliope Costas would get along great. She has a lot of insight and shares it frequently, too. Come on. Let's see if we can reconnect you and a little cell phone technology."

CHAPTER SIX

SIENNA HAD DONE her share of traveling. Nana had always thought it important to expose Sienna to as much of the world as possible. It was also, Sienna learned at an early age, the best strategy to make sure she appreciated her own home, her own neighborhood. Her own life.

Stepping off *Dream* and onto the dock in Plover Bay reminded her instantly of some of the smaller Greek or Italian islands she'd visited. The smattering of colorful boats, street stalls and quaint hole-in-the-wall businesses were familiar to her and made her smile. "My grandmother would have loved this spot."

"You think?" Monty sounded surprised. "All that jet-setting you two did?"

"We'd always travel off the beaten path. Go out on our own, just see where roads took us. She loved visiting new places, especially if they were ones that hadn't been touched by a lot of tourism and commercialism."

"Sounds like a woman after my own heart," Monty said.

"Yeah." Sienna looked up at the sky, and pretended that the morning sun rays came straight from Winnie.

They wandered past various businesses including a tiny tourist shop with starfish holiday ornaments and ships in bottles displayed in the windows, and a store filled with handmade candles. He wasn't kidding, Sienna thought. Plover Bay was absolutely charming.

At the hardware store, Monty bought a few emergency tools and spare bits and bobs for the engine. Next they hit up Aft to Stern Parts and Supplies, proving to Sienna her grandmother hadn't come close to teaching her all there was to know about boating. But something told her she'd be much more informed about engines by the time they reached their destination.

To save time, they visited the grocery store and left loaded down with kitchen supplies and healthier food alternatives before taking it back to the boat.

Trip two consisted of a couple of bags of fruits and vegetables from the farmer's market, along with bottles of red wine made just a few miles away. She was still chuckling at the horrified expression on his face when she'd grabbed a handful—or two—of kale. He was most definitely not a fan, but she'd take it as a challenge to convert him.

A last-minute detour into a bookstore had Sienna realizing just how long it had been since she'd read anything for pleasure and, making up for lost time and with Monty's encouragement and contributions, she ended up with a selection of mysteries, romances and the latest Stephen King thriller.

"You're adding these to my expense sheet, right?" Her teasing smile faded at his guarded expression. "What? What's wrong?"

"You might want to rethink getting another cell phone." He moved to block her view of the periodicals stand.

"What?" She pushed him to the side. "What don't you want me to…see?" Her jaw dropped. On the front page of a major San Diego newspaper was her picture with the headline "Runaway Bride Sienna Fairchild Goes Missing at Empire Marina." "Oh, no."

"Afraid so." Monty gently pulled her away and, after offering the cashier a distracting smile, flipped over the paper. "If it's made the papers you can only imagine what social media's like about now."

"My Instagram page runneth over, I'm sure," she grumbled. "And it was turning into such a nice day."

"Still is."

Monty paid while she asked the cashier for the local branch of her bank.

"It closed a few months back," the young woman said with a snap of her gum. She didn't even look up as she ran Monty's card. "Closest one now is about twenty miles inland. But they're closed today."

Even if she found a way there, her ATM card was back in her purse in San Diego. "Right." Sienna wasn't enjoying this part of the journey. At least she'd get a replacement cell phone at the nearby store. That hope was quickly dashed by her lack of ID.

"I'm sorry, but it's company policy." The friendly middle-aged man behind the counter at the cell-phone store blinked at her. He reminded her a little of a frog with over-round eyes and an equally round face. The fact that his shirt was the color of algae probably didn't help. His name badge read Herb. She didn't like Herb at the moment.

"But I told you, I've lost my ID." Not exactly true, but close enough.

"There must be an exception to the rule,"

Monty said, resting a hand on her arm. "People lose their wallets and phones all the time. You don't refuse to replace them all, so what's the catch?"

"No catch." Herb pointed to the sign over the back counter. "It's our policy."

"Hold on," Sienna said. "If I requested a new phone online they wouldn't need my ID to mail it to me, would they?"

Herb blinked again as if the thought hadn't occurred to him. "I suppose they wouldn't."

"So we can just approach it that way," Monty clarified.

"Can't do it." Herb pointed behind him again. "Policy."

Sienna's temper caught. "Now look—"

"Excuse us a moment." Monty strode toward the door and gestured for her to follow him. "Don't alienate the only person who can get you what you want."

"Apparently he can't because of 'company policy.'" She made air quotes with her fingers. She looked out the window, saw the bookstore they'd just left. "Unless...wait here. Oh, do you have a dollar?"

"Yeah, sure. What's...?"

She didn't wait for him to finish his question. Sienna bolted from the phone store and returned with a copy of the San Diego newspaper, hurrying directly back to Herb.

"It's not an ID, but it's me." She slapped the paper down on the counter and pointed to her engagement photo staring up at them. The picture, she now realized, didn't really look a thing like her. But the ring on her finger was definitely distinctive. "See?" She pointed to the ring in the photo, then her own, then stuck her face in Herb's. "It's me."

He didn't look completely convinced. "That really you?"

"It really is."

"Says you're missing. You don't look missing to me. How come you ran away like that?"

"Long story," Sienna summed up. "Look, I can give you all the information that's on that computer," she persisted. "Name, address, PIN number to my online account. Please. I really need that replacement phone."

"Well, I suppose it's worth a try. What's the phone number again?"

Sienna recited it again, this time through gritted teeth.

"See, honey?" Monty draped an arm around her shoulders and squeezed. "I told you he'd take care of it for you."

Sienna glared up at him, then felt her

cheeks warm at the smile he aimed at her. *Oh...my.* That look in his eye... She took a deep breath and instantly wished she hadn't. He smelled like the fresh air when they had been on the open ocean, with a hint of citrus. The mixture was intoxicating; her reaction so...distracting. And one hundred percent inconvenient. She bit her lip, tried to remember what she was supposed to be focused on. "Thanks, *honey.* What would I do without you?" She fluttered her lashes and earned a quiet snort of amusement.

"How's it going, Herb?" Monty asked.

"It's going." Herb leaned closer to the screen. "The system's not stopping me from issuing you a new phone under the same plan, but..."

"But what?" Getting national security clearance would probably be easier at this point.

"I'm afraid we don't have that same model in this store. As you can see, we're pretty limited with our stock."

Sienna did see. The store wasn't that much bigger than Monty's boat and the display of phones lining the walls made her feel as if she'd entered another time warp to the pre-cell phone era. "Are there any I can sync with my backup in the cloud?"

"Uh, sure. I think so. Let me check in the back."

"You get the feeling he doesn't get many customers?" Monty asked when Herb disappeared through a door.

"I'm beginning to think the universe is telling me to stay unplugged."

Monty shrugged. "Chances are whatever's waiting for you isn't going to be anything you want to hear."

"Maybe. But I'd still like to get in touch with my bank." She didn't like the idea of spending even more of Monty's money.

"Found one!" Herb emerged from a back room, a faded yellow box in his hands. He blew off a layer of dust before rubbing the box on his shirt. "No bells and whistles, but it's got Wi-Fi and Bluetooth and cloud access."

"Perfect. Can you add that to my account?"

"Can, but there's a replacement fee. Two hundred." He set the box on the counter but inched it away when she reached for it.

"Two hundred dollars for an out-of-date phone?"

"Yep." Herb didn't look the least distressed.

In fact, he almost looked as if he was enjoying himself. "Sorry. Company—"

"Policy, right. You know what?" She took a deep breath. "I'm going to take the hint. Let's hit that internet café we passed on our walk here." If she could log into her bank account she could see what her options were for ordering a new card so it would be waiting for her in Butterfly Harbor. She left the cell phone store and Herb behind, with Monty leading her to the café.

The row of old computers inside the garishly painted building did not inspire confidence. "If it says 'you've got mail' in that creepy computer voice, I'm done," she muttered and slid into one of the many free chairs. Behind the register, a pair of teenagers played video games on the large screens.

Monty grabbed them two coffees, paid for an hour of time, then sat next to her and opened one of the romantic-suspense paperbacks she'd chosen. Sienna's fingers froze over the keyboard as that rush of warmth she'd felt back in the cell store washed over once more. He really was unflappable.

She found herself speculating how Richard might have reacted had he gone through the same past couple of hours with her. Before the wedding she'd have assumed everything would have rolled off his back; after yesterday and his creep-tastic appearance on Monty's boat? That didn't seem feasible.

It was more confirmation that she'd made the right choice leaving him at the altar and in San Diego.

She accessed her email quickly enough and sent the first one to the Realtor she and her father had been working with to put Nana's house on the market. She included Monty's cell number in case he needed to get in touch with her.

Next up, she went to her bank's website and attempted to log into her account. Denied.

She tried again, more carefully this time. Denied.

"What the…?" She typed slowly, repeating the letters to herself as she… Denied.

"What's wrong?" Monty leaned over.

"It's not letting me in. And now I've tried too many times from an unrecognized computer." She sagged back in her chair. "I'm locked out." Which meant trying to get on from an app on Monty's phone wasn't going to work, either.

"Okay. So you can finally stop worrying about this paying-me issue and we can move on?"

"Back to square one." *Darn it!* Roadblocks

everywhere she turned. "I guess I'll just have to wait until we get to Butterfly Harbor."

He reached over and pulled her hand off the keyboard. "I'm not worried, so you can stop."

This whole thing—walking out on her wedding, hiding from her father and Richard, stowing away on Monty's boat—had all been an effort to get a little distance and figure out where she went from here. She couldn't do that as long as she was still anchored to her old life. It might seem silly to him, but Sienna didn't like taking advantage of anyone's generosity, and having Monty cover her expenses, as well as transporting her, was more than she could accept.

Maybe this was a mistake. Maybe she should just let Monty go on and she'd find the means to head back to San Diego. "None of this feels right." She didn't realize she'd said that out loud until she felt his fingers brush the side of her cheek.

She glanced up, found his face close to hers, felt the warmth of his breath against her skin. Sienna blinked, licked her lips and watched his pupils contract as he lowered his gaze to her mouth. Was he going to kiss her? Anticipation coiled hot and tight in her belly. Oh, she hoped so. She wanted him to. She had wanted him to ever since she'd first seen him in the closet doorway.

"You're worried about things you can't control at the moment, Sienna. Reminds me of when I was a kid and I stole my dad's boat when he wouldn't take me. I got caught in a storm and I panicked. I wasn't paying attention to the moment. That I had everything I needed to make it through." He inclined his head, his mouth curving into a gentle smile. "You have all you need right now to make it through this storm."

"You're right." Emotion clogged her throat. "I have you."

He blinked, then pulled away from her. "We'll grab something to eat, then head back to the boat. With any luck, we can get another few hours out of her today. The sooner we're in Butterfly Harbor, the easier everything will be for both of us. You'll get your account issues sorted and you can get on with your life. Sound good?"

She nodded even as her throat tightened. "Yeah," she croaked. "You're right, of course." Apparently she was the only one thinking about what a kiss between them would be like.

"How do you feel about Mexican food?

There's a great little place on our way back to the boat. Want to give it a shot?"

"Sure." She managed a quick smile, then turned back to the computer, clearing the history and making sure to log out of her email. When she stood up, her fake smile was back in place. "Let's go. I'm starved."

MARTA'S COCINA WAS located at the end of the main thoroughfare of Plover Bay, nestled into a bungalow-style building under the thick foliage of palm trees and whimsical drooping peppertrees. They were seated in the shaded side patio in iron chairs painted in hues of pink, blue and green. Traditional Mexican artwork lined the exterior walls, from murals to tile work to metal sculptures and a rock-formed waterfall that made it feel as if they were in the middle of the rainforest.

"Senor Monty." The young woman seating them handed him a menu. "Nice to see you again."

"Thanks, Flora." Monty gave their server a wide smile. He'd only been here a handful of times, but after the first they knew him by name. One of the many reasons he came back. "This is my friend Sienna."

"Welcome, Senorita Sienna." Flora's dark

eyes crinkled when she offered her a menu. "Would you like to hear today's specials?"

"Please," Sienna said.

Monty only half listened as he took in the serene setting and half-filled restaurant. They were early for lunch; it was barely noon. In the distance, church bells chimed, announcing either the beginning or ending of services. He gave Marta's another half hour before every table was filled with both customers and complimentary oil-hot salty tortilla chips.

"The roasted-chicken-and-poblano tamales sound wonderful," Sienna said. "I won't even look at the menu."

"*Si*. My father is a wonder with tamales. Senor?" Flora turned her attention to Monty. "Your usual?"

"*Si*, Flora, gracias. What would you like to drink?" he asked Sienna.

She shrugged. "I'm open to anything, remember?" Her cheeks went pink almost instantly. "I mean—"

"Cervezas—*dos*. And an order of your blue cheese guacamole."

"Squawk! Duchess pretty girl."

"Oh!" Sienna twisted in her chair and looked up into the trees. A green-as-grass parrot with huge black eyes blinked down at her. "Well, hello there."

"Shoo, Duchess," Flora snapped and waved one of the menus at the bright green bird perched on a branch just beyond the gate of the restaurant. "I'm sorry. Poor thing belonged to the owner of the fitness center in town, but when it closed, Duchess got left behind."

"That's horrible!" Sienna gaped. "Who could leave such a pretty creature behind? Oh, wait!" She held out her hand for Monty's cell phone. "For Simon and Charlie."

"Is it my imagination," Monty said slowly, "or is that bird posing?"

"Guac," Duchess sang. "Guaca-mooleeeee!"

"She's a fan, too?" Monty teased.

"Unfortunately." Flora frowned. "I'm afraid she's a bit on the stubborn side. If you ignore her, she should go away. And no matter how much she asks, do not give her any guacamole. Avocados can be toxic to birds."

"Good to know," Sienna said. "We're probably encroaching on her space."

"If Duchess had her way, the entire town would be her space," Flora said. "I'll get your drinks. Please, relax and enjoy. Duchess! *Silencio ahora!*"

"Guaca-mooleeeee! Drop and give me fifty!"

Sienna laughed. She pushed back her chair, walked to the fence and lifted her hand. "I bet you miss your owner, don't you, girl?"

"Be careful," Monty warned. "They're known to bite."

"She just wants attention," Sienna said quietly. "My goodness, you are beautiful. Look at those feathers. You're like a flying rainbow."

"Senor Monty's regular! Squawk."

Sienna giggled and now Monty felt his cheeks heat. "That's just obnoxious. Go away, bird."

"Stop it," Sienna ordered, stretching up higher and managing to stroke a finger down Duchess's chest. "You aren't a duchess, are you? You're a queen."

"Queen Duchess! Pretty bird Queen. Four, three, two, one, pulse, pulse, pulse."

"Great. A workout with our lunch." Monty offered Flora a mouthed apology when she returned with their drinks and the guacamole.

Flora merely shook her head and laughed, her knee-length blue skirt bustling around her legs as she disappeared back into the cantina.

"You going to wash your hands after that?" Monty asked when Sienna took her seat again.

"I guess I should." Sienna winced. "Be back in a second." She darted off to the bathroom.

"Duchess Queen! Squawk!"

A flap of wings and a burst of air later and the parrot landed on the back of Sienna's vacant chair.

"Don't even think about it, bird." Sienna was absolutely right. Duchess was stunning. The majority of her body was covered in bright green feathers, but around her head, smatterings of yellow and red and blue accented her enormous eyes and beautifully curved beak. And those eyes were as dark as the deepest ocean.

"Guaca-mooleeeee!"

Monty sighed. Clearly Duchess had an agenda, if not a self-destructive one.

"Sorry, Duchess. No can do." Yesterday a stowaway bride and today a guacamole-obsessed parrot named Duchess. Life really was full of surprises. He tapped open his phone and scanned through the photos Sienna had taken the last few hours. A few seagulls, water shots that indicated fish near the surface. Lots of seaweed and a few dolphins keeping pace with *Dream*. He sent them, along with a few shots of Duchess, to

Luke's and Deputy Fletcher's emails. "Well, I guess I've been replaced." Sienna stopped beside the table and planted her hands on her hips. "Duchess, you're in my seat."

"Squawk! Don't be a slacker. Pedal to the metal. Spin, spin, spin." Duchess tilted her head from side to side, blinked widely at the two of them, then launched off the chair and disappeared into the trees.

"Typical," Monty said. "Runs when she doesn't get what she wants. You're making friends everywhere we go, aren't you?"

"Ha, ha. Herb at the phone store would disagree." Sienna retook her seat. She reached for a chip and dunked it nearly all the way into the guacamole. He waited, watching as she bit, for the explosion of happiness he knew was coming.

"Oh, wow." The chip broke and she caught the part that dropped in her palm as she licked the side of her hand. "Oh, wow, this is amazing!" She finished the first and went in for a second. "Who knew that combination would work. And no cilantro. Be still my heart."

"Not a fan?" He wasn't sure what he was enjoying more, his own portion or watching Sienna thoroughly like hers.

"Of cilantro? Yuck. Nuh-uh." She ate,

swallowed. "Tastes like soap to me. Do you like it?"

"I can take it or leave it." He resumed eating. "It's a genetic thing, did you know that?"

"I did." Sienna held up a chip. "Learned about it in my college biology class. We did testing to see who had a specific marker and how cilantro tasted to them. That's just weird, isn't it?" She squeezed and popped a wedge of lime into her beer bottle, then drank.

"One of those things. Frankie's like you with cilantro. Can't stand it. Must be one of those mutations I got hit with that she didn't."

When Flora brought their plates, once again Monty entertained himself by watching Sienna's eyes go wider than the platters. "There's enough here for three people," she gasped once Flora had gone. "You should have warned me."

"You were too busy flirting with the bird," he teased.

"What did you order?" She leaned over to examine his plate.

"*Carnitas.* Best I've ever had."

"Hmm." Sienna didn't look convinced. "San Diego's got some pretty amazing Mexican food."

"I totally agree. This is better."

"Small town versus big city, I suppose?" Sienna challenged.

He shrugged. "Just like us. Not everything is better because it's popular. Sometimes what's hidden away is the best treasure to be found."

Sienna grinned. "I will say the tamales are amazing, but it takes a special touch to get *carnitas* just right."

"Fine." He pushed his plate over a bit. "Help yourself. Just don't touch that corn. It's mine." He used his fork like a barrier, then refrained from saying "I told you so" when she sighed in culinary ecstasy. "Good thing I'm not one to say I told you so."

"No," she said, and laughed. "Good thing."

Silence fell as they ate, which gave Monty time to think. Normally he preferred to make trips on his own; he liked the long stretches out on his boats. It gave him time to get to know the vessels, understand their quirks and foibles. One of the things he'd learned early on, during excursions he'd taken with his father, was that every boat was different and he had to pay attention if he was going to get what he needed out of it. Talking about his dad with Sienna earlier had brought up a whole lot of memories, memories that put a smile on his face. They might have missed out on having a mother in their lives, but he and Frankie had hit the father jackpot. For as long as they'd had him.

"Do you mind if I ask you a question?"

Sienna's fork paused on its way to her mouth. She looked surprised at his inquiry. "Sure."

"It's about your father."

Her gaze went from curious to guarded and she suddenly seemed very interested in the pattern on her ceramic plate. "What do you want to know?"

"From what you said you aren't close."

"Not for lack of trying on my part. No," she added with a tight smile. "We aren't. He's always been very focused on his business, on finding the next big deal, the next money-making merger. That doesn't leave a lot of time for offspring."

"You mentioned your grandmother, but not your mom."

"She died when I was born. From what my grandmother said, it was very quick." Sienna had gone from shoveling food into her mouth to moving it almost absently around her plate. She sat back, lifted her bottle and drank. "I had nannies until I was

around twelve, then Nana took over. Dad…
well, from what I learned growing up, my
father was never an affectionate man. She'd
hoped losing my mother would make him
realize just how fleeting life could be, but
he went pretty much the other way. It broke
her heart, I think. Knowing he couldn't be
bothered with the only child he had. She'd
lost two of her own early on and my Uncle
Frank just a few years ago." Sienna examined how her beer glistened in the sun. "On
the bright side, she was amazing with me. A
real Auntie Mame, you know? Took me on
fabulous adventures. Vacations and excursions every summer. She didn't want me to
miss out on anything. When she got sick, she
was so angry. Angry that she was running out
of time. One night…" Sienna cough-laughed,
but Monty had witnessed enough grief that
he recognized a broken heart. "A few months
before she died, she woke me up at two in the
morning and told me she'd booked two tickets
to Paris. Just like that. We left the next afternoon. It was one of the best weeks of my life.
Of hers, too, I hope."

"I can understand why you miss her so
much." How many times had he done something similar; not that he could afford a trip

to Paris, but he often climbed on board one of his boats and set sail for parts unknown. There was something freeing about impulse, something life-affirming.

"She'd have liked you," Sienna confirmed. "You're very roll-with-the punches, much like she was. And your taste in boats?" She gave him a thumbs-up. "Since she's been gone I've become a bigger believer in signs. Seeing *Nana's Dream* right where I seemed to need her yesterday couldn't have been a bigger one."

"Glad to have been of assistance." His own life had certainly shifted off course because of it. "So what was the plan for after the wedding?"

"To live happily-ever-after." She toasted him with her bottle, but he didn't miss the sarcastic smirk. "Move to North Carolina. Take over his late mother's role on various charity boards. Throw parties for his clients and business associates."

"Sounds…fun?"

"It might have been, although I doubt it. But as my father reminded me, it wasn't like I had a career or anything to worry about. Richard was a safe bet. Or at least I thought he was."

"You definitely had him showing his true colors yesterday." Not that it was any of his business, but he was grateful for whatever clicked in her head. No one deserved to be tethered to a life that wasn't of their choosing, and it was clear, especially given where they sat at this moment, that the life her father had planned for her was not her choice.

"The ironic thing is," she mused, "Nana would have loathed Richard. It took me until yesterday morning to see that. I guess I saw a lot more in that mirror than just myself. Standing there, laced into a dress that didn't feel like me at all, I couldn't see myself. Or maybe I was seeing myself too clearly. But, yeah, she would definitely not have approved of me marrying Richard."

Monty chuckled. "There must have been something about him that got you that far."

"Daddy's approval. That's what Richard got me. For the first time in my life. Of course, Richard's firm means a whole new influx of cash to my father's company. I'm betting that deal's been blown to smithereens."

Monty didn't respond. He didn't want to be reminded of how different they were; what different life experiences they'd had. What vastly opposite worlds they inhabited. He liked her. More than he should. More than was rational and practical. Like Sienna, he decided to believe, at least for a little while longer, in the fairy-tale aspect of their current circumstance rather than the reality that would come crashing down on them once they reached Butterfly Harbor.

Sienna Fairchild wasn't one to have her wings clipped; her father and Richard had tried. Perhaps she still had some work to do on closing doors behind her when it came to life changes. But a woman with every advantage at her fingertips would never be happy or satisfied in the only place he could ever call home. He'd seen what happened when his mother had been forced into a place that couldn't contain her. He wouldn't wish that misery on anyone—not himself and certainly not Sienna. It sounded as if she'd had enough of that already. "What do you plan to do once the dust settles and you're back to your everyday life?"

"I have absolutely no idea." She leaned her head against the back of the chair and let out a heavy sigh.

"What did you want to do? Wait, scratch that." He pushed away his empty plate and rested his arms on the table. "What did you want to do before you started doing what you had to?"

Sienna narrowed her gaze. "That's a rather astute observation from a nonpsychiatrist."

"I tend to listen more than most people." Not just to the words, he thought. But to the thoughts beneath them. One reason Frankie never could lie to him—other than straight up being a terrible liar—was that he could read her far too well. "What was the first thing you wanted to be?"

"Oh, that's easy. A waitress." She laughed at his expression. One of those deep-from-her-belly, joyous laughs that made his own lips tug. "I'm serious. Nana and I used to go to this great little diner every once in a while. Usually on our way back from a weekend road trip. They had the most amazing old-fashioned cash register. The kind with the buttons for each amount. Every time you hit Total, a bell would ding. I loved watching the waitresses ring up the bills, so, of course, I thought that would be the coolest job ever. I was six, by the way." She held up a finger to clarify. "I bet when you were six you already knew what you wanted to be."

"Sure did." He could get used to this, just sitting in the early spring breeze, talking endlessly with her about…anything. Just being around her made him feel lighter. Happier. "I planned to be a pirate."

"Well, you came close, Captain Bettencourt." She saluted him. "Do you spend your free days searching for lost treasure and wrecked ships?"

"I do not. What happened after you were six? What else did you want to be?"

"I went through a lot of phases. For a while my career goals coincided with whatever book I was reading at the time. I even considered being a medical examiner for a while because of a series of crime fiction I was addicted to. Then I realized that would mean medical school, so I gave up that idea." Her eyes dimmed a bit. "I ended up majoring in business and marketing because I thought maybe I'd make an impression with my father. I was wrong." She drank the last of her beer. "He canceled coming to my graduation about an hour before the ceremony. And for the record, I have yet to have a job in either business or marketing. For the past few years I helped my grandmother catalog and organize her estate and took over a lot of her responsibilities for the different organizations she helped to run. You know, charity events, fundraisers. I even planned a few weddings for friends of the family. The kind of stuff Richard would have expected me to do." She took a deep breath and tilted her head to stare up at the cloudless sky. "How much we give up of ourselves trying to impress or please someone whose opinion, it turns out, doesn't really matter."

Monty didn't think he'd ever heard a sadder statement in his life.

"Go back to when you started college. If you'd had a choice, any choice. What would you have done?"

"I'd probably still do the business angle, but with a side of something more creative like event planning or maybe interior design. Not that high-end, don't-touch-it-or-even-breathe-on-it decor, but real-life design that works with people's lives. Our home, mine and Nana's, was always that. A home. I never worried about spilling something or getting the floors dirty. Sounds pretty silly, huh?"

"No." He shook his head, mildly impressed. "It doesn't sound silly at all."

Flora reappeared with their bill and took away their plates. A few minutes later they were off to find Sienna some new clothes at the only discount store in the area. She surprised him again by being selective about what she needed and how much she spent. Into the cart went another couple of pairs of shorts, a good selection of T-shirts in brilliant pinks and yellows, underwear, socks, a serviceable pair of sneakers and, of course, a bathing suit—a rather modest-looking turquoise one-piece that had him breathing in relief. He did not need images of Sienna in a bikini wreaking havoc on his concentration and ability to steer his boat.

He added a few towels while she visited the toiletries section. Once they reached the boat, the afternoon sun had been overtaken by storm clouds that seemed determined to dump rain all over them.

"I'm thinking we might be better-off staying here for the night after all." He climbed on board, then stepped back so she could head into the cabin first. "I'd rather save the engine for a good distance tomorrow rather than get caught in a storm out there tonight."

"Sounds like a plan to me. I'm going to go put all this stuff away."

After checking the weather report and his own barometer up in the wheelhouse, Monty was satisfied with the decision he'd made. If he'd been on his own it would have been one thing, but until he was more secure in understanding *Dream*'s idiosyncrasies, he wasn't about to try to traverse unpredictable weather with Sienna on board.

He went through the bag of supplies and equipment he'd bought at the hardware store—spark plugs, extra fuses, wire caps and electrical tape. He'd also purchased a basic tool kit he'd simply leave on the boat for emergencies and added a couple of different-sized wrenches for good measure.

Monty found his attention pulled toward the front of the boat, to the closed door of Sienna's cabin. With Frankie getting married in a few weeks, he had to admit the idea of settling down and starting a family had been in the back of his mind. So much so that he'd been dating here and there, but so far nothing had sparked. He'd been hopeful about Leah Ellis, a recent Butterfly Harbor transplant who had set up shop as the town's family lawyer, but it was clear there wasn't anything beyond friendly affection between them.

Nothing happening between himself and Leah had probably saved him serious drama given she was challenging Mayor Gil Hamilton in the upcoming special recall election. He'd help her out if he was asked to; he'd be thrilled—as would a lot of people in Butterfly Harbor—to have Gil replaced, but getting in the thick of politics really was not his thing.

Monty climbed up on deck just as the rain began to fall. He took a deep breath, then released it. No, he preferred his life as predictable as possible, moving like these smooth, calm waters. Which meant his mooning over Sienna Fairchild was completely ridiculous. Because he already knew the truth.

Women like Sienna didn't settle down.

They just kept running.

CHAPTER SEVEN

"YOU GOT AN early start." Sienna pulled herself up the ladder to the wheelhouse as the sun was peeking over the horizon.

"Couldn't sleep." Monty didn't even glance over his shoulder, but kept his eyes shifting between his cell and the boats moving in and around the marina. "I'm waiting for a follow-up call from Frankie." He glanced at his watch. "I'll give it another few minutes before we head out."

"What's going on with Frankie?" She braced her hip against the console and looked at him. He seemed pale, sitting in the padded chair, one knee bouncing up and down. "Bad news?"

"That's what I'm waiting to hear." He shook his head. "There was an accident at the sanctuary construction site in Butterfly Harbor yesterday."

"Was anyone hurt?"

"Yeah." The strain in his eyes, that he

hadn't shaved and that his hair was rumpled from nervous, anxious fingers, would have been enough of an answer. "A couple of the crew—the construction foreman and my goddaughter's boyfriend."

"You have a goddaughter old enough to have a boyfriend?" She moved a bit closer, wanting him to know she was here for him, whatever he might need.

"Mandy, yeah. She's fifteen going on thirty-five." His lips curved for a brief moment. "Frankie didn't have much information last night and Luke and the other deputies have been working nonstop." He gestured to the radio. "No one's available for me to call for an update and I don't want to bother them. Frankie said she'd call back when she could."

"Then I'm sure she will." She hesitated, wondering why he hadn't mentioned Mandy before. "Are you and your goddaughter close?"

"Mmm." He gave an absent nod, his eyes flickering between the phone and the view beyond. "Yeah. Very. Her dad, Sebastian, and I go way back."

Recognizing a potential positive distraction, she sat down, tucked in her legs and settled in. "How way back?"

"Kindergarten, I think. Frankie would know for sure. The three of us made peas in a pod seem like distant cousins."

She smiled even as the pang of envy struck stomach-deep. "He's your family."

"Absolutely. He's also a partner in Wind Walkers. Mandy works for me on school breaks and during the summer. On weekends, too. She's part fish. Can't keep her out of the water. She's planning on becoming a marine biologist. Or something along those lines." His lips twitched. "She's still deciding."

Monty sounded like a proud father. A familiar longing tugged at her heart. What she wouldn't have given to hear that kind of affection in her own father's voice for her. "Mandy wasn't with her boyfriend when he was hurt, was she?"

"No." That seemed to bring him a measure of relief. "No, she wasn't with Kyle, she was out on one of my boats with a group of snorkelers when it happened. I know how useless I'm feeling about now, so I can imagine how she must be dealing with this." He picked up his cell. "I should just call Frankie."

"No, you shouldn't." Sienna reached out and pressed his hand down to the console until he released the cell. "Your sister said she'd call you. She's working and if she hasn't contacted you, that probably means she doesn't have anything to tell you yet. Worrying about you worrying about them isn't going to do anyone any good."

Irritation flashed across his face. "Maybe Kendall can tell me something. Kyle's worked for her on his days off from the construction site. Maybe she knows——"

"Monty." She stood and moved closer to take hold of both hands, shifting in front of him so she was all he could see. "Stop running through the town's entire population. You're going to do what Frankie needs you to do right now and focus on getting home. Let's fix some breakfast and head out. There's an auxiliary radio down in the cabin, isn't there?"

He nodded. "Yeah, I didn't want to turn it on until you were up."

"I'm up." She smiled. "Sitting here willing the phone to ring won't help. Come on. I'm in the mood for bacon."

"Bacon?" He sounded rather dazed when he said it.

"Bacon makes everything better. And it's something I cook very well. I have a secret. The oven works, doesn't it?"

When he wasn't looking, she pocketed his cell phone and led him downstairs.

IF THERE WAS one thing Sienna did very well, it was distraction. She'd distracted her Nana for months, trying to get her grandmother's mind off the chemo treatments, off the pain and nausea when she was home. Board games she could play with her eyes shut; she was a master at cards and jigsaw puzzles. Easy peasy. What she'd found helped the most, however, was good conversation.

"Pop the toast," she urged and elbowed him gently. He'd been gazing blankly out the window again, which is why she'd taken over the scrambled eggs while the bacon finished cooking in the minuscule oven. "Unless you like it burnt."

"Sorry. Yeah." He clicked the lever and shook his head. "I don't know why this is hitting me this hard. I mean, I've known Kyle his whole life, but only by sight really. Until recently. This feels personal. Mandy's crazy about him, even if she is a little young to be dating him."

"How much older is he?" Sienna moved effortlessly around him, letting him say whatever he needed to.

"He's eighteen."

"Well." Sienna's eyes went wide. "Well. That's a surprise."

"I know. Believe me, we all know. Sebastian and I have gone through a number of long nights in the backyard with six-packs discussing it. Getting that serious that young feels a bit like history repeating itself."

"Whose history?" Out came the bacon, which she plopped onto paper towel, then she finished stirring the eggs and removed the pan from the burner.

"Sebastian and Brooke were nineteen when they had Mandy. They got pregnant when they were still in high school, but Brooke left Sebastian with the baby."

"Oh." Sienna blinked, her eyebrows knitting. "That must have been difficult for him. Nineteen and a single father?"

"He made it work. We all did. Me and Frankie, we helped as much as we could. And he had his parents until they moved away. The town really came together to lend a hand. She's a community kid and one of the best people I know."

"All the same, I couldn't imagine having a baby at nineteen." Who was she kidding? She couldn't imagine having a baby *now*.

Monty shrugged. "Sebastian was a natural with her from the moment she was born. He made her the center of his world. The kind of dad every kid deserves to have, you know?" He winced. "Sorry. I guess maybe you don't."

No. She didn't. But she was getting better at accepting that. "What happened with Mandy's mother?"

"Brooke? She came back to town unexpectedly earlier this year to, well, make amends really. She and Sebastian got married on Mandy's birthday last month."

What was it about this Butterfly Harbor place that they had so many weddings? "Happily-ever-after after all, huh?"

"It's been great, so, yeah, I don't want Mandy's heart broken, Sienna." He gripped the edge of the counter and bowed his head. "And, Kyle, he's had a really rough life until recently. But the last few years, he's turned things around. He doesn't deserve this. And then there are his parents, Lori and Matt." He scrubbed his hands down his face. "I can't even imagine what they must be going through."

"Then don't try." She turned him toward her, caught his face in her hands. "If you need to get back, we can get you on a plane. You can leave the boat here, with me. I'll watch over *Dream* while you get home to your family."

"I couldn't ask you to do that." But she could feel the tension leaving his body as she kept her confident gaze pinned to his.

"You aren't asking," she said softly. "What do you want to do?" *Don't go. Please don't go.* But she'd understand if he did.

"I—"

His cell phone buzzed in Sienna's pocket. She released him and handed the cell to him. "It's Frankie." His voice was barely a whisper when he answered. "Yeah. How's Kyle? How's Mandy doing?"

Sienna held her breath, praying for good news, but bracing herself for bad. She was about to serve their breakfast, but stopped when Monty caught hold of her shoulder, slid his hand down and threaded his fingers through hers.

Cold food didn't bother her; staying where she was needed, if only for a few minutes, mattered. She could hear the female voice on the other end of the call, but couldn't really make out anything she was saying. Judging by Monty's expression, good news had won out.

"How long will he be—?" Monty nodded.

"Of course. Tell Mandy not to worry about work. I can get someone to cover for whatever time she needs." His smile returned, not quite as bright as she would have liked, but it was there, and her own heart started beating again. "What about Matt and Lori? They need anything…yes, I know I'm not in a position to…Frankie…" Monty rolled his eyes and mouthed "sisters" at Sienna. "I can get on a plane if you need me to."

"You will not!"

Now that screech Sienna heard. She bit her lip to stop the laugh from emerging. Monty held the phone out a good six inches from his ear. "Okay," he said finally, when Frankie stopped yelling at him. "Okay, Frankie. I got it. Just one more…" He paused to listen some more. "Uh-huh. Wait…what? Frankie, stop for a sec. What happened at the site?"

Sienna watched his relief give way to anger, frustration and, finally, resignation. "Definitely not great news. Who's going to—? Oh. Okay. No. Don't worry. I'm not stepping into that hornet's nest. I'll just keep going as I am, but call me if there's anything you need me to do. Okay. I'll check in with you later… Uh-huh. Yeah. Give Mandy a hug for me. Lori, too. She's probably frantic about Kyle… Love you, too. Bye."

"Kyle's okay?" Sienna asked when he hung up and let out a long, controlled breath.

"By some miracle." He set down his phone.

"What happened?"

"From what Frankie found out, the cement holding the main pylons didn't set properly. Can cement set improperly? Anyway, the whole structure started to crumble. Jed Bishop, the construction foreman, and two other workers were inside when it started to go. Kyle ran in to try to get them out and got caught in the collapse himself."

"How bad were they hurt?"

"Jed's got a broken arm, scrapes and bruises. The other two workers are in about the same shape. Kyle got the brunt of it. Concussion, broken ribs and a busted leg. That's why surgery took so long. They had to put in a steel rod. Poor guy's looking at a good few months of recovery and rehab."

"I'm so sorry. But at least he's going to be all right." Sienna rubbed her hand down his back.

"That's definitely the good news. Not so sure about the future of the sanctuary. They've had to call in state investigators.

Construction's been halted. Frankie suspects the project will have to be started over again, which is going to put it off schedule. Then there's the question of who's to blame. If it's a substandard-material situation or faulty construction or…" He shook his head. "That project's been the mayor's claim to fame for the past couple of years. Gil's going to have one heck of a time climbing out of the rubble of this if he's involved somehow, especially with the election looming in November. It's going to be such a mess."

"A mess you can't do anything about right now. Kyle's okay. So's Mandy." He wasn't leaving the boat. Sienna breathed her own sigh of relief, then wondered when she'd become so used to him, so attached. It was something she'd have to think about later. For now, she'd make things easier for him here. "You can't ask for more than that right now. So maybe stop fretting. Have some breakfast. You'll feel better."

SIENNA WAS RIGHT. Monty did feel better. Hearing from Frankie had definitely helped, as had the bacon, along with half a pot of coffee. The engine was running smooth, last night's storm had passed, leaving only a pristine sky in its wake, and there was a beautiful woman flitting around his boat taking pictures of every creature, in the air or the sea, that made an appearance.

He could literally feel the worry lifting off his shoulders. *Dream* continued to pull them into the late afternoon with nary a hiccup. From his seat in the wheelhouse, he kept his attention divided between the open water and Sienna as she moved around the boat looking for new pictures to send to Charlie and Simon.

Occasionally she'd wave up to him and point at the water, and he'd ease back on the throttle, smiling as she gave him a thumbs-up that all but erased the uncertainty and doubt from his face. Had it really only been a couple days since he'd found her tucked into his closet? He rubbed a hand against his chest.

Funny. He was having a difficult time remembering what it was like being out on the water by himself. She was entertaining. And distracting. In all the right ways. He'd always thought of himself as an easygoing guy, but around Sienna, the real world really did seem to melt away.

Not a good mindset, he reminded himself, for the long term. The more time he spent around her, the harder it was to keep his distance. It had been a long time since he'd wanted to kiss a woman as badly as he wanted to kiss Sienna.

The idea wasn't only keeping him awake at night, but he was also having to fight off the desire during the day. Like now, for instance, as she darted to the other side of the boat, the sound of her laughter ringing in his ears as she played hide-and-seek with what he could only assume was one of their dolphin escorts.

He could try to believe that all he wanted was for the real world not to interfere, but it would.

Reality was exactly what was waiting for them once they docked.

He reached for his cold coffee, checked his gauges. It looked like it was clear sailing ahead, straight through to Butterfly Harbor.

And that, Monty tried to convince himself, was most definitely good news.

SIENNA LEFT THE bow of the ship and went to her favorite spot below the wheelhouse. Sitting down, she scanned through the photos she'd been taking, deleting and tweaking them so Monty could send a new batch to his proxy passengers. It was a small task, but big enough to keep her from focusing on what she'd be dealing with once they docked in Butterfly Harbor.

"Squawk! Guaca-mooleeee!"

Sienna yelped and shot up in her seat. The phone toppled out of her hand and clanged onto the deck.

She swung her legs down and, shielding her eyes, searched the boat. There, on the wheelhouse railing, was Duchess, perched in all her festooned, parroted glory.

"Duchess! What are you doing here?" Sienna stood up, wondering if she'd gone half-crazy by asking a bird a question.

"Squawk. Give us a kiss."

Sienna snort-laughed, covering her mouth as Monty emerged from below deck, wiping his hands on a rag.

"What's going on?"

Sienna couldn't do anything but point.

"Oh, for the love of Pete." Monty planted his hands on his waist and glared up at the bird. "I've only got room for one stowaway this trip, you silly bird. Shoo, Duchess."

"Shoes, glorious shoes!" Duchess sang in that high-pitched falsetto, then tilted her head almost upside down. "Work it. Work it. Squawk. Give us a kiss."

"I don't think so." Monty turned grumpy eyes on Sienna. "You're not helping at all, you know."

"I know." Sienna couldn't stop laughing. "Come on, Monty. This is too funny. You're beginning to attract stowaways now. Duchess, come here." Sienna put up her hand. "You need to come down."

Instead of complying, Duchess stretched out her wings, flapping them a good three times before settling where she was. "Kiss, kiss, kiss." She made smooching sounds, then turned her back to both of them.

"I'm not set up for birds," Monty grumbled.

"I don't think she cares. She came on her own. I wonder how she found us?"

"A trail of bread crumbs, perhaps?"

"Don't be such a grump. You've got a mascot now. Maybe she'll come with us all the way to Butterfly Harbor."

"If she does I'm giving her to Frankie as a wedding gift."

"I'll see if I can get her to leave," Sienna said, starting for the ladder. "You have to admit, she's pretty cute up there. Take a picture. At least one. It would make for great advertising. 'All creatures welcome at Wind Walkers Tours.' Go on. Go get your phone."

She kept her distance from Duchess while Monty did as she suggested. Personally, she was thrilled to have another living being around. Hanging out in close quarters with Monty Bettencourt was proving more difficult than she'd anticipated. Especially after that almost-kiss yesterday in the internet café. Not that he'd given any indication of wanting to repeat the scenario. If anything, he seemed a bit more standoffish. Was he not attracted to her or was he giving her space because he thought she was still hung up on Richard?

Richard. Ugh.

"Richard, ugh," Duchess repeated.

"Oh, no." Sienna flapped her hands wildly at the bird. She'd said that out loud? "No, no, don't repeat that, Duchess. I shouldn't have—"

"Richard, oh, no."

"No, Duchess. Richard bad. Very, very bad."

"Bad. Bad, bad, baaaaaaad!" It was like the parrot was writing her own opera.

"Do they make muzzles for birds?" Sienna muttered to herself. She peered down and saw Monty standing there with his cell phone, snapping pictures. She stayed out of view as Duchess turned in slow circles, preening and showing off as if she knew exactly what was going on.

"You want something to eat? I bet you're hungry, aren't you, Duchess?"

"Guaca-moleee!"

"Sorry, no can do. How about some strawberries?"

"Yum. Duchess Queen. Berries, berries." Duchess bent down and clanked her beak against the railing.

"Don't go pecking at his boat. It's got enough problems already," Sienna warned as she headed back down. "Or he really will kick you off."

Duchess let out what sounded oddly like a raspberry. All that was missing were crossed eyes and a tongue sticking out.

"Do you think she's normal for a bird?" Monty asked when Sienna had two feet on the deck.

"You are asking the wrong person. But maybe our best bet is to ignore her. If she gets bored, she'll leave."

"One can only hope. What are you doing?"

"Getting her something to eat."

"Isn't that counterproductive to us getting

her to leave? She's a wild animal. She can find food."

"What kind of hosts would we be if we let a guest starve?" She dug out one of the containers of strawberries from the back of the small fridge. "By the way, when you start working on this remodel, please install good appliances. This boat really could be amazing if it's outfitted right."

"Gee, if only I'd thought of that before I'd bought her," Monty said. "Don't worry. I've got plenty of ideas for what to do with her."

Why that statement made her blush, she didn't know. "Just an observation," she said. "I thought hearing the good news about Kyle would have made you less grumpy."

"I'm not grumpy," Monty countered as he shut the electrical closet door with more force than was necessary. "I'm frustrated."

"Obviously," she said, and rinsed off a couple of berries before she sliced them. "You're the one who's worried about burning out the engine."

"That's not what I'm frustrated about."

"Then what's the—oh!" She blinked up at him. All rational thought evaporated like steam when she caught the sweet, humble look in his eyes. "Monty?"

"Sienna?"

She searched for an answer. Her life had taken so many turns lately, so many unexpected detours, what was one more? Besides, it was an answer she wanted, wasn't it? She wanted to know—needed to know—if what she was feeling for Monty was real or if it was merely a reaction to his kindness for helping her to escape.

"I don't not want you to do this, or…yes." She slipped her fingers over his broad chest and felt her breath hitch in her own.

"Double negatives always fascinate me," he murmured and dipped his head.

She let out a sound—a gasp? A moan? She couldn't be sure until he stopped a breath away from the kiss he promised. His smile widened, those tiny crinkles in the corners of his eyes appearing as he slid one of his hands around her waist. He pulled her close.

His mouth brushed hers; a touch so light she wondered if she'd imagined it. In that moment, every cell in her body surged to life. The feel of his warm skin beneath her fingertips left her longing for more as his lips drank her in.

Until now, kisses like this had been relegated to the books she read, the movies she watched.

The kind of kiss that ignited a woman's blood and had her craving more from the man in her arms. His mouth was as perfect on hers as it was when he spoke to her; filled with humor and laughter and quiet intensity that demanded a response. There wasn't a part of her that wasn't filled with thoughts of Monty Bettencourt.

"Squawk! Nice flat back!"

Sienna pulled back before the laugh erupted. Her shoulders trembled as she struggled to hold it in, but it wasn't any use. She could sense the frustration in Monty, and even as she wanted to spring it loose, she wasn't sure the entertainment wasn't more satisfying.

"Go away, bird," Monty growled.

"Kiss, kiss, kiss." Duchess flapped into the cabin, her talons clicking on the table as she perched and twisted her head one way and then the other. "Berries for pretty girl." She clicked her beak.

Sienna swore she saw the bird grin.

CHAPTER EIGHT

"Squawk. Land ho. Reach for the sky!"

A flap of feathers and the now-familiar sound of sharp talons clacking onto the railing beside him announced Duchess's arrival in the wheelhouse. They'd spent most of the day on the water, making steady progress toward home.

"What's up, bird?"

Duchess belted a familiar tune about blue skies shining.

The perfectly pitched melody had Monty's lips twitching. It hadn't taken long for the bird to grow on him. Despite Monty's pleas to fly away, the parrot had yet to find other suitable accommodations and appeared to be sticking with them for the foreseeable future.

So there Monty sat in the captain's chair, arm draped over the steering wheel, with a fitness-obsessed bird as his copilot. Duchess pranced, searching for her spot. Monty counted his blessings she didn't perch on the steering wheel.

"Okay to come up?"

Monty glanced over his shoulder. Sienna was halfway up the ladder. She had her hair loose today, those long waves catching against the wind.

His resolve to keep his distance after that kiss they'd shared in the galley wavered. "Sure."

"I brought you coffee." She waggled the travel mug in one hand as she climbed up. "A peace offering."

"A what?" He accepted the metal container eagerly and shifted his empty mug out of the way.

"A peace offering. Things have been weird between us ever since…" Now she cringed as she stepped up behind Duchess and stroked the bird's back. "You know. Ever since we k-i-s-s-e-d."

Duchess squawked and did a little dance on the railing. "Ten more reps, baby!"

"Careful. I bet she can spell, too," Monty warned a pink-cheeked Sienna.

"Wouldn't surprise me. She's a clever bird."

"Clever bird. Very clever bird," Duchess agreed with a violent bob of her head.

"Are we really going to continue with the small bird talk rather than address the…rutabaga?" Sienna sighed.

"Ruta…oh." She was using a code word to prevent Duchess from trilling a new song about kissing. "No. We can talk about the… rutabaga." That sounded believable. "Sorry. You're right. Things have been weird and it's my fault." Feeling more secure about *Dream*'s engine performance, he kicked up their speed a bit. "I shouldn't have ki—er, rutabagaed you the other day."

"If I remember correctly, I didn't back away or tell you not to."

"Still, it wasn't right. You're dealing with a lot. The nonwedding wedding. Your father. And you're still grieving the loss of your grandmother. I shouldn't have—"

"Shouldn't have shown me what a real kiss feels like?" She sat on the padded bench and kicked up her feet. Leaning back on her hands, she lifted her face to the sun. "I'm sorry if you regret what happened, but I certainly don't. If anything, you made me realize exactly what was missing in my relationship with Richard. You're a very good kisser, Monty."

He felt the flush rising up his neck. "I'm not

entirely sure how to respond to that. What exactly was missing with Richard?" He shifted enough in his chair to look at her. Bad move. The instant his eyes landed on her, the more he realized he didn't want to *talk* about kissing anymore.

She shrugged slightly. "Passion. Interest. Emotion. I've had a lot of time to think the past few days and I've come to the conclusion that not marrying him was the smartest thing I have ever done. I mean, who wants to live without passion?"

"Who indeed," Monty choked out.

"Therefore, I probably owe you my thanks. For opening my eyes and showing me exactly what I want out of life."

"And what's that?"

She met his gaze. "Why don't you stop the boat and I'll show you?"

"Stop the boat?" He did a quick scan of their surroundings. Once again he'd been keeping land in sight, but the skies were as clear as the ocean was calm. One of the better days he'd seen in a while.

Sienna walked over to him, a sly smile on her full lips. She brushed her fingers over the back of his hand. "Stop the boat, Monty."

Entranced, he eased up on the throttle. By

the time the boat stopped, Sienna was stepping down the ladder. He looked at Duchess, who was looking at him as if he was a fool for taking too long. Making sure the boat was secure, he followed Sienna down to the deck and found her tugging her T-shirt over her head. The bright green-and-turquoise swimsuit she was wearing glimmered against the sun and all but transformed her into a sailor's dream.

"What are you—?" Clearly, she created brain fog for him because it took a beat to understand what she was doing. When her shorts hit the deck and she kicked off her shoes, he couldn't do anything but stand back and watch as she stepped up to the edge of the boat and, after a quick wave and grin at him, dived over the side.

She disappeared into the depths like a mermaid. He moved closer, heart in his throat, until he saw her surface a few feet away from *Dream*. She slicked back her hair and bobbed to the surface, a contented smile on her face. "It's glorious in here!" With the calm water and the clear sky, he could hear her without trouble. "I couldn't stand being cooped up on that boat for another second."

Monty grinned. He'd never been seduced into stopping his boat before.

She swam effortlessly until she twisted, tucked and dived back under. When she popped up again, she was reaching for the ladder at the side of the boat. "Are you coming in or not?"

"Not sure I can beat the view I have now."

She gave an approving nod and launched herself into the water once more.

She'd been beautiful, Monty thought, that first moment he'd seen her, tucked into his closet, surrounded by poofs of white fabric. The expertly applied makeup, the neatly arranged hair, her skin glowing around the jeweled necklace she'd worn above the fancy gown. But seeing her now, in the simple, pure image of nature that surrounded her, he could admit he'd never seen a more gorgeous sight in his life. He didn't want to move. Didn't want to breathe. He just wanted to stand here, for the rest of his life, and watch her in the water for the ethereal creature she might very well be.

A fantasy. That's what she'd created for him, making him see things, feel things he didn't think he ever could. Emotions he couldn't entirely trust. Falling for a woman like Sienna, who was so deep in flux she'd be lucky to find the horizon, would be an error of gigantic proportions. And yet here he was, wanting nothing more than to join this woman who was struggling to find her place in the world, if only for a few minutes, in the bliss that was his chosen office.

He kicked off his shoes, emptied his pockets and tossed off his shirt. A heartbeat later he stepped to the side of the boat, and before he thought too long or hard about it, dived in with her.

IF THERE WAS one thing Sienna could identify blindfolded, it was someone who thought entirely too much. It had started the second he'd broken off that delicious kiss they'd shared in the kitchen; a kiss interrupted by a traitorous parrot and probably common sense on Monty's part.

She wasn't a fan of common sense. Not currently, anyway, which was why she'd thrown both it and caution out the porthole and jumped into the ocean. *Dream* had indeed become suffocating, and not just because of their forced chitchat and pleasantness. Monty clearly regretted the kiss. Never had a solitary day passed so excruciatingly slow.

She treaded water as she watched him kick off his shoes and dive into the water. A surge of exhilaration had her hiding her smile beneath the surface. She cut through the lapping waves easily and swam toward him, her eyes drawn up to the pilot cabin, where Duchess was watching them as if she'd just found her favorite TV show.

"We have an audience," she said once Monty surfaced. Her heart caught and skipped a beat as he smoothed back his wet hair. He reminded her of one of those models in the fragrance ads, where the men launched themselves off cliffs and into the ocean as if chasing after a siren. She hadn't thought those men were real. Now she knew better.

"We've found the one place she can't or won't go." Monty reached out a hand, brushed against her shoulder as if to confirm she was safe and secure. "You do this often?"

"If you mean swimming in the open ocean? Only at the beach at home," Sienna confessed. "Until I found *Dream*, I…" She paused, wanting to choose her words carefully. "As much as Nana loved cruising and boats, when she was sick, she couldn't take the motion. We settled for sitting for hours next to the shoreline of the Seine, eating bread and cheese and all the things she wasn't supposed to have." The memory was one that lightened her heart, even as it tipped into sadness. She angled her head. "She would have liked you. A lot. She'd have probably called you a pirate."

"And fulfilled my childhood dream," he countered, sounding a bit sad himself. "The pirate and the princess."

She laughed and turned to dive, only to jump in and yelp.

"What?" Monty grabbed her arm and pulled her toward him. It took her a moment to blink the salt water out of her eyes. What she thought was a jumble of seaweed was actually a tangled mess of fishing line and debris clinging to a struggling sea turtle.

"Oh, no." She pulled free and swam forward. "Monty, we need to help her." She moved around the creature, had to duck down a bit to see its face. "She's all tangled."

The turtle blinked slowly, as if exhausted. Sienna was careful when she touched one of its flippers. The line had tightened so much that it had dug into the turtle's skin.

"Don't usually see this breed so far north this time of year." Monty swam up behind her. "Let's get her to the boat." Together they gently maneuvered the sea turtle. "You go first. Easier for me to lift her up."

"I don't want to hurt her."

"She's already hurt. I've got her. Don't worry."

Sienna pulled herself up the ladder and into the boat, returning immediately to take hold of the beautiful and bigger-than-expected reptile.

"Work it, work it." Duchess's commands barely registered as Monty tried to steady the turtle as he climbed up the ladder.

"I'll get a knife to cut away these lines. See if you can loosen the other stuff," he said.

Sienna kneeled beside the turtle, which had gone scarily still. "I'm so sorry this happened to you." She plucked at the kelp and plastic debris until she could see the shell glistening in the sun. "There you are. Aren't you a beauty."

The turtle jerked, flippers flapping as if it suddenly realized it wasn't in the water.

"Monty, she's getting restless. You'd better hurry!"

"Get those knees up! Work it. Work it!"

"Hush, Duchess," Sienna snapped.

"Got a few different ones. Here." Monty dropped down on the other side of the animal. "Cut near the shell if you can."

"Right." She shoved her wet hair out of her face, lifted a section of the line and pried it free just enough to slip the sharp blade under it. When she broke through, other sections of the line slackened. "Shouldn't take too much longer," she said.

They worked as one, moving quickly to cut the turtle free. "When Charlie and Simon hear about this they're going to wonder why we didn't video it." Monty cut another length free.

"Because we needed all four hands to accomplish this! Ah, there." She unwound the last bit of line from around the flipper. The turtle waved it around as if testing that it still worked. "Should we put her back right away?"

"I don't think she's going to give us a choice," Monty said. The turtle was already scrambling toward the ledge. "She's not very old. Doesn't weigh more than fifty pounds." He got to his feet and bent over to pick up the turtle.

"I hope she finds her family," Sienna said softly when he lowered it back into the water. "Can you get your phone?"

"She's going to be gone in—" But he went. Sienna sat on the edge of the boat, watching the turtle relearn how to move, its one flipper not working quite in tandem with the other yet.

"She still here?"

"Yes." Sienna stretched out her arm and pointed. "Just there. Oh."

The turtle stopped and turned, hovered still in the water for a second before paddling over. Tears burned Sienna's throat as their rescue skimmed by, blinked its dark eyes up at them before diving into the depths and out of sight.

"I'd say that was a thank-you," Monty said. "And I got it on film." He touched his hand to Sienna's shoulder. "You're pretty good in a crisis."

"You do what you have to do, especially when someone's suffering."

Monty nodded when she looked up at him, then ducked down into the cabin and returned with some towels.

"You know what I would love for dinner?" she asked when he dropped one next to her.

He stopped drying his hair long enough to glare at her. "If you say kale I'm afraid I'm going to have to throw you back into the water."

"I've been waiting for you to cry uncle." She couldn't stop the grin from forming. "I would kill for a pizza."

Instantly, he looked as if he might drop to

his knees in gratitude. "Unfortunately, I can't think of a place that delivers this far."

"We could stop. How far out are we from someplace?"

"About another hour or so until Santa Barbara. We could stop for the night if I can grab a last-minute slip."

"Grab one. If that's okay with you?"

"That is more than okay. And I even know the best pizza place to go to." He held out his hand and she took it, letting him pull her to her feet. She grasped the towel between them, but could still feel the heat of his body radiating toward her. His thumb brushed against hers for the barest of moments, and for an instant, she thought maybe he'd kiss her again. But he didn't. Instead, he cleared his throat and stepped away, heading up to the wheelhouse to start up the boat again.

"Squawk! Squeeze your glutes!"

Sienna glared at Duchess, who seemed to take her next snack as a given as she soared through the kitchen. "You have the worst timing on the…hey! What are you doing? Stop that!" Sienna ducked as Duchess chucked a measuring cup from an open drawer at her. "Duchess, those aren't toys." She picked up the cup, then almost caught another in mid-flight. Apparently entertained, Duchess stuck her beak into the junk drawer next to the sink and dug in.

She stopped only long enough to demand "guaca-mooleee" and then resumed her pillaging.

"All right! All right." Leaving things where they landed, Sienna grabbed the tub of fruit she had in the fridge and fished out some blueberries and strawberries. For kicks, she tossed in a couple of almonds.

"Yum! Kiss. Kiss." Duchess made a smooching sound and hopped across to the kitchen table to eat.

"Not on your life, Guacamole Breath," Sienna muttered, picking up the paper clips, rubber bands and pencils Duchess had tossed out of the drawer. "We need to bird-proof the place or find you new toys." She scribbled a reminder note to herself, then went into her room to change for dinner.

CHAPTER NINE

WHILE SIENNA TIED down the boat, Monty took advantage of cell reception and made a quick call to Frankie. That his sister hadn't contacted him was a good sign, at least, in regard to Kyle's status.

"Ahoy, wayward traveler," Frankie said by way of answering her phone. "Tell me you're almost back."

"Why? What's wrong?" By his calculations, if they kept going at the pace they were, he and Sienna would hit Butterfly Harbor a little ahead of schedule. Not that his sister knew about Sienna. Somehow he'd managed to avoid telling Frankie about that part of his trip.

"Your sister is losing her mind, that's what's wrong."

"Ezzie again?" Monty winced. Frankie's future mother-in-law must really have been getting on her nerves.

"No. My maid of honor is sick. Brooke's

down with the flu and I've discovered I'm less that competent at multitasking where my wedding's concerned. I might have accidentally ordered the wrong chairs for the reception. It's still a toss-up between chicken à la king or beef medallions for the meat eaters, and I can't get anyone at the party-tent company to confirm when they're delivering and there's absolutely no one to take over. While I love Kendall to death, she can't pull these kinds of things together for me. She agreed to lose her camo pants and tank top and wear a bridesmaid dress and that alone was a hard-fought battle. Roman and I have to be at a conference when all the payments, music and menu have to be finalized."

"And you think I can help?" Monty tried to keep his voice light. Frankie was one of the most composed people he knew; she had to be, given her job as a co-fire chief, but it was clear by her voice that she was feeling out of control. The past few months had definitely given him new insight into his twin.

"No, I don't want you to choose chicken rather than fish for our reception." He could just imagine her rolling her eyes. "I need a sounding board. A neutral party. A voice of reason. That's you."

Monty had to strain to hear her. "Are you whispering?"

"Of course, I'm whispering." She sounded almost manic. "Ezzie is in the next room. I'm not quite that desperate. Yet. I need you to come back fast and convince Roman we should elope."

"I can't do that," Monty said.

"Why on earth not? Montague Elliot Bettencourt—"

Uh-oh. She only used his full name when she was seriously ticked off. Or panicked. "I can't do that because I don't have a death wish."

"Roman won't care. He just needs to hear it from someone other than me."

"Roman does care and you know it. He'll care even more when he realizes it's too late to get all your deposits back. Not to mention what Ezzie and the Cocoon Club will do to you if you cancel on them. You know those senior citizens are planning a big surprise for you both. You'll break their hearts if you don't go through with the wedding in Butterfly Harbor."

"Aw, man. Okay. Talking helped. There's a solution. I just have to find it."

Sienna waved at him from the lower deck,

a bright smile on her face. She'd donned one of the nicer pair of shorts and a clingy pink T-shirt. And she'd left her hair loose and tumbling around her shoulders. Exactly how he liked it.

"Monty, are you still there?"

"I'm here." He leaned his arms on the railing and watched Sienna checking the lines. "Sounds to me like you need a wedding planner."

"Gee, Captain Obvious, you think? Except we've already blown our budget, not to mention the fact that, oh, that's right, Butterfly Harbor doesn't *have* a wedding planner!"

Not yet they didn't. "What if I can find you one?"

"Are you thinking of a career change?"

"Of course not." The only thing he knew about weddings, other than signing his name to whatever gift Frankie purchased, was how to abscond with a runaway bride.

A runaway bride with a penchant for event planning...

"Hey, Frankie, can I call you back? I might have an idea."

"Oh, he has an idea. Awesome. Great. Think away, Boat Boy. Not like I have anywhere else to be." Over the phone, he heard the distinct blare of a call. "Scratch that. I'll check in once I'm back from this call."

And just like that, Frankie was back to being Frankie and hung up on him.

"Hey, everything okay?" Sienna popped up the ladder, expectant eyes shining and happy.

"I'm not sure." But it could be. Oh, this was a bad idea. But it was still an idea. "Let me ask you a question."

"All right." Her brow furrowed.

"Did you plan all your own wedding stuff?"

"Most of it, yeah. I worked with a wedding planner for some, mainly because my father insisted, but I didn't need the help. I was grateful for something to focus on after losing Nana. Why?"

"Well." He wasn't really going to do this, was he? He wasn't really going to ask her to stick around Butterfly Harbor once they arrived so she could help with his sister's wedding. He needed her gone, needed her to find her own life so he could stop thinking about what it would be like to kiss her again. Hold her again. Chase her around his boat in the ocean again.

He needed her out of his life before he fell in love with her.

"Well, what?"

"Remember how not so long ago we talked about you paying me for transport on my boat?"

Her eyes went wide. "You've changed your mind?"

"Not exactly." He mentally crossed his fingers. "How would you feel about giving my sister a hand with planning her wedding?"

"So LET ME get this straight." Sienna wasn't sure what she was more anxious about: the extra-large, double-cheese, extra-mushroom-and-sausage pizza that should be landing on their table any second, or the fact Monty was asking her to help organize his sister's wedding. "You want me to oversee your sister's wedding arrangements. Me? Someone she's never met and who doesn't have the best track record when it comes to successful nuptials."

He suddenly looked as if he hadn't really thought about it from that perspective. "Just because the bride changed her mind doesn't mean the rest of the event wasn't done to perfection."

She smiled. "You're reaching, Monty. What gives? No, wait!" She held up a hand when she spotted their server on her way over.

"Hold that thought. Thank you." Did she sound as grateful as she felt? The pie took up most of the width of the table. Sienna leaned over, closed her eyes and inhaled the fragrant steam rising off the fresh-baked pizza. "We should take a moment and just…hey!" She tried to knock his hands away but he was already lifting a slice to his mouth. "Careful, it's hot!"

"Don't care," he mumbled around a mouthful of food. "I've been thinking about pizza since that salad you made yesterday. And for the record, no more kale. I don't care if it's buried in eggs or bacon."

She chuckled, thinking the kale-and-tomato frittata she'd made for breakfast was delish, but maybe there was a limit to healthy eating. She had, after all, hidden most of his junk food; not to save him from a sugar coma, but to stop herself from self-pity bingeing.

The pizza, she soon discovered, was worth the detour and lost time, not to mention a burned mouth. She loved how Monty seemed to know about all these little hidden gems of restaurants and mentally added this place to her must-return-to list.

"It's really good," she moaned around a

mouthful of spicy tomato sauce and melted cheese.

"It is. You'll have to try Zane's when we get to Butterfly Harbor. It's even better."

"Not possible. For American pizza, anyway," she clarified. "Best pizza I ever had was in this little town in Italy. Nana and I took cooking lessons one summer. Pulled the tomatoes right off the vines on the villa property where we stayed. Now that's an experience."

He glanced away, his jaw tensing. Okay, so maybe he wasn't a fan of the real stuff. Sienna cleared her throat. "Back to your sister's wedding."

"She just needs someone to handle the fine tuning. All the major arrangements have been made. For the most part, I think. We're talking payments, confirming delivery times, getting everything set up for the day of. Jason Corwin's handling the catering, although I'm betting Alethea is going to be helping. She runs his food truck."

The slice of pizza stopped halfway to her mouth. "Jason Corwin has a food truck? In Butterfly Harbor?"

"Yeah. Quick, casual versions of his in-house specialties. Alethea drives that thing around town a couple of times a day, usually landing at the sanctuary construction site at lunch."

"I cannot wait to see this town of yours." She shook her head. "But about Frankie. Are you sure she really needs me?" In her experience, brides often wanted more control over the details than they were willing to relinquish. "This isn't just her having a bride-panic moment?"

"Frankie's not a push-the-panic-button kind of person." Monty reached for another slice and Sienna considered if they should order a second pie. "If she's freaking out, there's a reason. I just want to lighten her load, you know? And you've said you aren't in any hurry to get anywhere and you like projects."

"That's true," Sienna agreed. "Not so long ago you said the sooner we got there, the sooner I'd be gone."

He shrugged. "Things change. I can give this to Frankie as part of her wedding gift."

"You want to give me to your sister as a gift?"

"I want to give her the gift of peace of mind. If you don't think the exchange is fair, tell me how much."

"As you said the night we met, not everything is about money." The way she said it, the sharpness in her voice, had him arching an eyebrow even as she thought about sinking into her ripped upholstered seat. "What I mean is I wouldn't be doing this for money. It would be as a favor to someone who's done me an even bigger one."

"It's a service for a service."

"Here's the thing." She snagged another piece of pizza before he plowed through the rest. "It isn't really up to either you or me. It's up to Frankie. I need to talk to her."

"Talk to her like now?"

"Yep." She pointed to his cell sitting on the table. "Give her a call, tell her what you're planning and what you'd like to do. Then I'll tell her what she can expect. And she can tell me what still needs to be done. When's the wedding again?"

"Twelve days."

She nearly choked. "We've got, what? Another two or three days before we even get there?"

"If we're lucky." He signaled their server, ordered another beer and, to Sienna's amusement and relief, another pizza. "Storm warning came over the radio a few hours ago. It's going to slam the coast before we can get there."

"All right." Was this something she should be worried about? "Get me on the phone with Frankie and we'll go from there."

He picked up his cell and, after an uncertain look at Sienna, made the call. "Hey, Frankie. Yes, I'm calling back. I've got a solution to your wedding problems. But first…" A smile spread across his mouth as he looked at Sienna. "Have I got a story to tell you."

"You do realize that bird isn't ours." Monty stood back as Sienna accepted the bag from the cashier at a convenience store before they headed over to the marina. "What are you going to do with those baby toys when Duchess takes off again?"

"Donate them to an animal shelter or vet's office. Does Butterfly Harbor have either?"

"Seeing as we don't live in the Dark Ages, yes. We have both, actually." She really was disconnected from the real world, wasn't she? "Were those really necessary? We don't want to entice Duchess to stay."

"Maybe not," Sienna agreed in that carefree tone of hers that buoyed Monty's dwindling spirits. "But we also don't want her

ripping apart your boat because she's bored."
She dug into the bag and pulled out the over-
sized plastic ring of keys. She jangled them in
front of her. "Besides, they're so cute!"

"Adorable." Tired of waiting for her to tell
him, he finally asked, "So what did you and
Frankie talk about?"

Sienna turned confused eyes on him. "You
were sitting right there."

"I only heard one side of the conversation.
She didn't prod you too much, did she?"

"You mean about my great escape in a wedding gown? No. Funny enough, it's her own
wedding that's in the forefront of her mind.
Relax, Monty. I found out what I needed to
know and am already on the job."

Considering the number of napkins she'd
scribbled on, it looked to him as if she was
taking on an international trade agreement.
"And what did you need to know?"

"That she's pretty much an overwhelmed
bride-to-be who, despite her claims to the
contrary, really wants the wedding she's
dreamed of to go off without a hitch. She's
going to hand off all the paperwork to me as
soon as we get into town. In the meantime,
she's emailing me a list of tasks she's been
dealing with."

"But you don't have a phone."

"Correction. She's going to email you with the list and you're going to let me see it."

"I'm going to lose control of my cell phone, aren't I?"

"Hmm. Maybe. Oh, and there's this one. I've heard parrots love mirrors."

"Don't get too attached to the bird, Sienna." They crossed the street to the marina, but before they buzzed through the security gate, Monty stopped at the nearby newspaper stand. He scanned the latest selection of fishing and diving magazines, chose a few and was about to pay when once again, the front page of a newspaper caught his attention. The headline sent chills down his spine.

He added the paper to the stack, then hurried to where he'd left Sienna and quickly got them through the gate and almost sprinting toward the boat.

"What's wrong?" Sienna rushed to keep up. "Someone on your tail?" Her laughter died when he glared at her. He waited until they were inside the cabin before he handed her the newspaper. The color drained from her face. "Oh. Oh, no. I can't believe this. It isn't right."

"Since when does right have anything to do

with headlines? You've been promoted from runaway bride to kidnapped bride."

"It says 'potentially,'" Sienna said quietly. "And it doesn't have your name anywhere. It's a fishing expedition, Monty. Not any real truths. If anything, it's spin from Richard's people because he got ditched at the altar. They're trying to repair his reputation and make him the sympathetic character in all this." She looked at him, disappointment mingling with uncertainty in her dark eyes. "If anyone should be angry about this, it's me. Other than saying 'suspected abduction of the bride,' it's totally focused on him."

Monty took the paper from her and scanned the article. She was right. He was so focused on being accused of kidnapping he hadn't stopped to consider what had been written— or in this case not written—about Sienna. Until he read the last paragraph: a statement issued by Sienna's father. "What the—? Did you read this?"

"I read it," Sienna said with a tight smile when he lifted his gaze to hers. "Fatherly concern isn't what it should be."

"How could he say this about you?" The statement sounded so cold. So detached. "Your own father?"

"I told you my father protects what's most important—his business. What I've done threatens it." Sienna turned her back on Monty, but not before he saw the hurt flash across her face. She let out a sharp whistle and called Duchess by name. Monty heard the bird squawk from somewhere above deck.

"Sienna, what he says…" He scanned the paragraph again, trying to absorb the audacity of a so-called father throwing his daughter to the media wolves.

"It's nothing I haven't heard before. I'm troubled, fragile, uncertain and easily overwhelmed. Not always rational and tend to make impulsive, destructive decisions. Granted, I heard him say all that to my grandmother when he didn't know I was listening. Then again, maybe he did. Who knows? Duchess!" She whistled again and rattled the baby keys as an enticement.

"What's this about a hospitalization? Is that true?"

She looked at him over her shoulder. "Does it matter?"

Try as he might, he couldn't decipher her expression. "Of course, it doesn't."

"Nice try." Sienna smirked. "I have to admit, my father played this one pretty well.

He's made me long for the days he ignored me. Now he's planted doubts in your head about my ability to make the right choices, and has you thinking about dropping me off at the next port."

"That's not what I'm thinking at all," he lied. The doubts were there. Doubts he had trouble understanding.

"Really?" She didn't look convinced. "It's what I would be thinking in your place. It's what most people would think."

"I'm not most people."

She lifted a hand to his face, stroked his cheek and offered him the saddest smile he'd ever seen. "You're really not, are you? You're trying too hard."

In the instant before she turned away from him again, Monty didn't see the fun, flirty, trying-to-figure-it-out Sienna who had made a mad dash onto his boat a few days ago. He couldn't hear her laugh or see that smile that lit up her eyes like the stars sparkling in the midnight sky. No. What he saw was a lonely, confused, admirable woman who was searching for the same thing so many others were, including himself. They were all looking for…someone to call home.

Rather than go after her when she went up

the ladder calling for Duchess, he found himself frozen where he stood, his heart breaking for Sienna Fairchild. Possibly forever lost.

CHAPTER TEN

DARKNESS DESCENDED AND Sienna waited, minute after minute, breath after breath, for the worry to cease and the calm to return. One throwaway paragraph in a newspaper story and she was right back in the lonely hole she'd been trying so desperately to climb out of.

She sighed, regret lodged in her chest. How could he not doubt her when there were times she doubted herself?

Duchess's talons clipped along the fiberglass deck as she approached Sienna and dropped her new toy, the plastic keys, into Sienna's lap. Sienna managed a weak smile and drew her finger down the parrot's head. "You're such a pretty girl, Duchess."

"Make it work." Duchess bobbed her head.

"You're also lucky, Duchess. Flying from boat to boat. Nothing to worry about other than who you're going to annoy next. No one to disappoint."

"No one's disappointed in you, Sienna." Monty's voice echoed out of the darkness.

She uncurled her legs and drew them up against her chest, wrapping her arms around her knees as if creating a shell of protection. Sienna waited for him to make a joke, to try to get her to laugh or forget about that stupid headline. How had she thought, even for an instant, that her father would just let her run away when doing so clearly ruined whatever plans he'd had?

"Scoot over, bird." Monty sat down beside her, stretched out his legs and held out a mug topped with what looked like half a can of whipped cream. "My dad's cure-all. Lucky for you I found where you hid the chocolate. Duchess, go entertain yourself."

"Squawk. Pretty bird. Pretty smart bird." She high-footed it across the deck like a soldier marching into battle.

"Sure, yeah, pretty bird. Ah-ah." He pulled the mug back when Sienna reached for it, and set it on the deck beside him. "There's a price you need to pay." Even in the growing dusk, she could see the kindness radiating in his eyes. "Tell me."

"Tell you what?" Sienna pinched her eyebrows together so tight her forehead hurt.

"Tell me what it is your father thinks is going to have me or anyone wanting to help you running for the hills." He caught her chin under his finger, tilted up her head. "I'm not running anywhere, Sienna. We have a deal. You're stuck with me, so you may as well fill me in."

"Maybe I don't want you to know that part of me."

He didn't release his hold. He didn't stop gazing into her eyes. "Maybe it's time someone did."

She liked where they were. Liked how they were with one another. What if…what if she told him and he couldn't accept it or thought her a complete waste of his time? "It's not something I dwell on. It's—it's in the past."

"Obviously it's not, otherwise it wouldn't still hurt. Now spill. Before your cocoa gets cold."

The words welled in her chest before she managed to push them up and out. "It happened when I was twelve. Up until then I'd mainly been raised by nannies. My father traveled a lot, as did my grandmother. About every two or three months she'd whirl in for a visit, this tornado of energy that was exhilarating and terrifying. But between those visits, I spent a lot of time alone. That was the year I got up the courage to ask for a dog for my birthday, but my father said they didn't do anything but make a mess. He had my nanny sign me up for horseback riding lessons instead."

"Not your favorite activity, huh?"

"I hated it. I was terrified of the horses, which, of course, they picked up on. During one lesson, I got thrown. Right over the horse's head. I don't remember landing, but I do recall this odd sensation of flying. I broke my left arm in three places." She stretched out her arm and traced her finger over the barely there scar. "I also had a massive concussion despite having worn a helmet. The doctors told my father the helmet had saved my life. My father's response was to ask how long before I could ride again." Sienna cringed. "I did not react well to that question. I had a bit of a meltdown and needed to be sedated."

"You poor kid." Monty slipped his arm around her shoulders and drew her close. She squeezed her eyes shut, as much to stop the tears as to not watch him look at her.

"Dad didn't know how to respond to that, and pretty much told the doctors to 'fix me.' Translated, that means he ordered them to keep me quiet until I could be controlled. He had me transferred to a private clinic, where I was watched and supervised. One of the board members at the hospital found my grandmother overseas and called her. She was at my bedside within a day." She swiped away an escaped tear.

"I've always felt that stupid horse that threw me ended up saving my life. I spent a few weeks in that clinic, working through a whole lot of stuff I didn't know had piled up. Nana was there for all of it. Once I was discharged, I went to live with her in her house on the beach. She changed everything for me. She stopped going on her trips, backed out of a lot of her obligations. She made me the sole focus of her life. When I wasn't in school, we did everything together. Traveled, read, played." She blinked back tears when Monty's arm tightened around her shoulder. "I know my father's never had any particular use for me, but that he'd exploit what happened all those years ago? It hurts. It hurts so much. And it makes me so angry!" She pounded a fist against her leg. "He knows what people will infer from reading that. He knows! And he doesn't care." How could she have been so stupid as to think marrying Richard would have changed anything where her father was concerned? "How can a parent do that to their child?"

"I don't know." He pressed his lips against the top of her head. "You were right not to go to him after the wedding. I never should have suggested you do that."

She wasn't so sure. Maybe it would have been better…if she'd had the courage to finally stand up to him.

"Did you ever get that dog?" Monty's question caught her off guard.

"No." She shook her head. "Nana had an allergy. And, besides, the older I got, the less time we spent at home. I'm not that twelve-year-old girl anymore, Monty. I'm not fragile. I cracked, but I didn't break. And I won't. Not now. Not ever."

"Of course, you won't." He reached down and picked up the mug. "Now drink your victory drink. We're going to get in a few more hours of sailing before bunking down for the night."

She nodded, relishing the sensation of his T-shirt against her cheek. He felt so good. So warm and perfect. She could smell the ocean on his skin, the spice and citrus of the soap and shampoo he used. This, she thought and squeezed her eyes closed.

This was what feeling cared for, protected and secure felt like.

And she dreaded having to let him go.

"WHAT EXACTLY IS the Cocoon Club?"

Monty glanced over to where Sienna was stationed on the padded bench in the wheelhouse, notes in one hand, his cell phone in the other. She was skimming through the endless list of tasks Frankie had emailed him as a follow-up to her conversation with Sienna.

Keeping one eye on the growing storm clouds overhead, he said, "It's a group of senior citizens. I think there's more than a dozen now in the group. Or maybe *gang* is a better word to describe them. Most of them live together in this big Victorian house that's been outfitted for senior living. Senior shenanigans is more like it. They often nose their way into people's lives, but it's always from the heart. Ezzie, Roman's mom, is what you'd probably call their caregiver. Why?"

"Just going over the table assignments for the reception. Is there a reason why Frankie would not want them all sitting together?"

Monty grinned. "That would be the shenanigans. You remember back in school, there was always this group of kids who, when they got together, trouble seemed to follow? Not malicious trouble, just…things getting a bit out of control? That's the Cocoon Club. Two or three together is usually pretty safe. Any more than that and it's just a matter of time before they make headline news."

Sienna didn't look up from scribbling. "I hope I'm exciting when I get that old. I'll wait on separating them. It looks like instead of one large buffet, Jason's setting up various food tents in the park, is that right?"

"No idea." Monty reached over and clicked on the VHF receiver. He really didn't like the look of those clouds rolling in. And the wind was picking up. Time to check the weather again. "I just wait for Frankie to tell me if she needs me to do anything and I do it. As far as I know, I only have one job."

"Right. You're giving her away."

"Oh-ho-no." Monty shook his head. "I am escorting her down the aisle. No one gives Frankie away except Frankie."

Sienna chuckled. "Noted. According to this, Frankie still hasn't decided on a cake. How is that possible? The wedding's in less than two weeks."

"She doesn't have to." Monty shot a look at his copilot. Duchess, perched on the railing beside him, gazed wide-eyed at the horizon. "Gale at Chrysalis Bakery has this gift for choosing the perfect flavor for her customers' wedding cakes. She's never wrong, so Frankie turned it over to her. It'll be a surprise."

"So, does that mean I shouldn't check in on it?" She nibbled on the end of her pen. "I don't want to step on anyone's toes."

"I'd say checking in on the cake gives you the perfect excuse to visit the Chrysalis and test Gale's gift yourself." He heard the distinctive *beep, beep, beep* coming from the radio and turned up the volume. Sure enough, a storm warning was being issued. Winds tapping out around forty miles per hour. Thunder and lightning expected, along with swells of eight to ten feet. Anxiety prickled his skin. "Great."

"What's wrong?"

"That storm took a turn and is coming right at us." He checked their location. "We're still too far out to slip for the night. We're going to have to ride it out."

"All right." She gathered up her papers and notebook, holding them against her chest. "What do we need to do?"

"We've got a few hours before it gets bad so I'm going to push *Dream* a bit harder than normal for the next little while. See if we can gain us some distance. Go below deck and make sure everything's secured. I might have you take the wheel for a bit so I can double-check the bilge pump and the engine."

"Okay. What about Duchess?"

"Hey, smart bird." Monty glanced over to their other stowaway.

"Squawk. Duchess. Smart bird."

"How smart? Inside or out during a storm?"

Duchess blinked those eyes at him, turned her head to look at Sienna, then threw back her beak and shouted, "Hold that walnut!"

"Um." Sienna frowned. "I'm not even going to try to interpret that one. I'll be fast."

"Great, thanks." He popped open a panel on the dash, pulled out the satellite phone and plugged it in. He'd been keeping it charged out of routine, but he wanted to make sure he had all his bases covered. The radio system was old, but serviceable, although it never hurt to have backup. "You better be okay, Duchess. Don't make me worry about you, too."

"Kiss, kiss, kiss." Duchess spread her feet farther apart to keep her balance.

Sienna returned. The wind had kicked up again and the waves were starting to swell. She'd thrown on one of the sweatshirts he'd bought her and her deck shoes. She'd also tied her hair up and out of the way. "I've got everything as locked down as I can make it. What now?"

"You're going to take the chair." He eased back a little on the speed and got up, then pulled her around him. "You've been watching me, right?"

"Yes." He heard the hint of nerves in her voice even as she wrapped her hands around the wheel. "This is where I follow the direction you've set, right?" She jerked her chin toward the indicator. "Compass is right there. Speed here."

"Right. We're going to veer to the east and try to keep it between forty and forty-five degrees. The swells will come at us from the back, and when they start to hit, we're going to reduce speed by at least fifty percent."

"I do that here." She touched the lever that affected their speed.

"Yes. But I'll be back up by then. You keep us going at the speed we are now. And if you start to feel any big bumps or resistance, slow it down. Speed in a storm only makes things harder and worse."

"All right. Got it. I won't accidentally pass by Butterfly Harbor, will I?" she teased.

"No. I was hoping to get another fifty in today, but we're going to lose some distance."

"Just checking." She grinned up at him.

"Everything's going to be fine. Back in a sec."

A second turned into forty-five minutes, but he wanted to be sure everything he needed to be working was operating effectively. Losing power and drifting could set them miles behind, not to mention the damage that could be done to *Dream*. If they were lucky, they could ride the waves, rather than plowing through them. Nothing was harder on a boat than heading straight into a storm. He closed the hatch to the lower cabin, then double-checked it to make sure it was secure.

His hands nearly slipped as he grasped the railings of the ladder on his way back up. "How you doing?"

"All right, Captain." She was keeping her eyes locked on the windshield as the wipers whipped furiously against the just starting rain. Duchess began singing, bouncing along to the rhythm of the boat rising and falling. "I'm going to have that song stuck in my brain for the next half a century, but we're doing okay. Right, Duchess?"

"Breathe. Inhale. Exhale!"

"Can't she just say yes?" Sienna muttered.

"Want me to take over again?"

"No. I'm getting used to it and I'm feeling like a productive member of this crew. And you'll be able to keep your eye out for anything that might go wrong." She glanced at him. "Nothing's going to go wrong though, right?"

"Hopefully not." He moved to stand behind her, watching as she checked their location, their speed and angled the boat easily into the rising waves. It took a special touch, an instinctive touch, to remain calm and focused while Mother Nature raged around them. He never took anything for granted, but seeing how Sienna kept control didn't make him feel as anxious as he expected. She was an absolute natural. "So your nana taught you how to sail? Ever been in a storm before?"

"A few cloudbursts," Sienna said. "Nothing like this. But she always said the more you fight it, the harder it is to control. A lot like a horse." Her lips twitched.

He dropped a hand on her shoulder. "Did you ever get back on one?"

"I did." She nodded. "In Hawaii a few years later. There was this valley Nana really wanted to see. It had been all she'd been talking about since before we flew over. Only way to get there, of course, was on horseback. Or so she told me."

Monty met Sienna's eyes in the overhead mirror.

"Tricked you, did she?" He grinned.

"Yep. But out of kindness. She knew I would never disappoint her. I spent a good hour with the horse beforehand, working with its trainer, saddled her and talked to her. It did not help that she'd been named Calamity Jane."

The dense gray clouds collided, blocked out the sun and broke open, dumping sheets of rain. Sienna pulled back on the throttle, shifted the boat a few degrees east and kept going.

"I swear that horse understood me," Sienna went on, probably trying to distract herself, or maybe the chatter helped her to focus. "Either that or they sedated her slightly before I climbed onto her. It was two hours to the valley, another two hours back, and there was barely a hitch in the ride. I did, however, wear a helmet."

"What did your father say when she told him?"

Sienna blinked. "What makes you think she did?"

"Because I feel like I'm getting to know her from the stories you've told me. She'd have relayed what happened. If only to prove to him that you'd moved past your fears and issues."

"That and to show him that love, patience and understanding produce better results than intimidation and fear. It made for a very interesting Thanksgiving dinner that year for sure." She was having to shout now as the wind thundered over them. "Any idea how long this storm's supposed to last?"

"Radio chatter estimates a good few hours. Radar is seriously out-of-date on this vessel, so we're going to be winging it." He glanced at Duchess. "So to speak. You let me know when you want me to take over, Sienna."

"Okay." She was looking a little more nervous, but more determined, too. He kept an anxious eye on her and Duchess, and was surprisingly more concerned about the bird. The parrot appeared to be having the time of her life, bobbing and moving in time with the waves.

They continued in silence, the minutes ticking away as night approached.

"It's getting harder to see!" Sienna yelled over the storm.

"Keep your eyes on the instruments. I'll watch the water." Looking for debris and other ships or boats was vital to surviving a storm in one piece.

"She's harder to steer." She shook out one arm, then the other.

"Slow it some more." He reached around her to the throttle, and when he eased it down, he realized they were almost at a full stop. "Okay, that's as slow as we go. Let me take over."

"All right." She kept her hands on the wheel and slid her butt out of the chair. As she stood, she lifted her eyes to the window. "Monty!"

Monty swiveled to see the giant wave crest and slam over the starboard side of the boat. Water exploded into the wheelhouse. Duchess squawked and flapped her wings as the boat rocked violently back and forth. Sienna lost her grip and went flying. Monty let go of the chair and grabbed for her, but she slammed shoulder first into the bulkhead. She hit the deck on all fours, but even as Monty reached for the wheel, he could see she was still moving. "Sienna! You okay?"

"Yes." But her voice wasn't nearly as loud as it had been before.

"Stay there!" As he finally righted himself, he saw another wall of water heading right for them. He managed to grab and yank the wheel another thirty degrees east before he heard the deafening *whumph*.

Then everything went black.

CHAPTER ELEVEN

THE WORLD DROPPED into slow motion.

Shoulder throbbing, Sienna dragged her soggy self across the wheelhouse to grab hold of the railing above her head. Monty was lying prone on the deck, arms and legs splayed. He slid over the slick surface as the boat bobbed in the storm.

Duchess squawked loud enough to wake the dead but not loud enough to bring Monty around. Sienna checked the console. He'd been steering away slightly, not parallel to the storm. The engine continued to rumble and for now the waves seemed to have gotten whatever anger they had out of their system. They were back to the violent eddies she'd been riding earlier.

Before she seized the wheel again, she braced her feet on either side of Monty's hips and grabbed his arms. She wedged him into the corner of the pilot cabin. In the dim light, she saw blood pooling in the water.

She couldn't do anything about that now. She wouldn't be any help to Monty if she couldn't keep the boat moving safely forward. Sienna threw herself into the chair and amped up the throttle just a bit. The engine roared, louder than the storm now, and she quickly resumed the course he'd set. The muscles in her arms strained. Her shoulder felt as if it was on fire. Strands of her hair came loose and stuck to her face. Her clothes were soaked completely through and the rain continued to pour. "Keep going," she whispered to herself. "Just keep going. You know what you're doing. Just. Keep. Going."

"Squawk! Your shoulders are not earrings."

"Not now, Duchess," Sienna snapped and threw every ounce of energy she had into keeping the boat as level as she could.

The rain continued to fall. The waves continued to rise and fall. It was like being on an unending roller coaster, and not the good kind that made you scream with laughter.

"Come on, *Dream*. You can do this. This storm isn't going to beat you, is it?" Sienna kept her tone light, encouraging, as she talked to the boat. She glimpsed the corner, saw Monty hadn't moved. The blood on his head was more visible now, darker around the scalp where he'd taken that hit on the railing. Fear clawed through her, trying to get a hold of her. Whether her hands trembled from the strain, from the stress, or from the cold, she couldn't be sure. All that mattered was getting them to a place where she could finally check on his injuries.

She considered dropping the bow anchor and killing the engine, but there had to have been a reason Monty hadn't done that. She had to trust his judgment and push on with what she did know how to do.

"Forty-five degrees and slow. That's it." She controlled the panic—she'd spent a lifetime learning to manage it. She could freak out later, once she had them at least out of the storm. He'd wake up, she told herself. He'd wake up and be fine. A little dizzy, no doubt a bit cranky, but he'd be fine. He had to be.

She twisted around in her chair when she heard him groan.

Sienna nearly sobbed in relief. Maybe he'd heard her. Maybe he knew… She stopped herself from letting that train move too far along the track. Now wasn't the time to think about how she felt about him; how she'd never felt more alive than when she was with him. More alive. More confident. And happy.

She hadn't been happy since Nana died.

"Oh, Nana. This was all your doing, wasn't it?" Leave it to Winnie Fairchild to have set her on course to meet someone like Monty Bettencourt right when she needed to. Winnie had told her she'd always be watching over Sienna. "How about more of your magic, Nana? I could really use your help with this storm."

Struggling against the pull of the wheel, she thought to herself how she was never going to watch another nautical disaster movie. Never, ever, ever!

Dream's bow arched up and out of the water and slammed down with a thump. Sienna's stomach dropped, her insides churning as she willed the storm to stop, hoped for the strength to keep them all in one piece for just a little bit longer. She needed a distraction. And there was only one thing she could think of to accomplish that job.

"Duchess, how about a song?"

"Squawk! Driver picks the tunes. Shotgun sings along!"

Sienna snorted. "Sing anything."

"Anything!" The trill was amazing and made Sienna laugh, which seemed to impress Duchess, who fluffed her feathers and broke out into an all-too-familiar show tune about favorite things. Amused and relieved, Sienna sang back.

"Squawk." Duchess clicked her beak as if offended at having a partner. But she continued singing. And so did Sienna as they rode out the storm together.

MONTY CAME TO with the strangest desire to see a Broadway musical.

It took a good few seconds for the pain to hit, and when it did, he lifted a hand to his head, not surprised when it came away wet and bloodied.

He righted himself, felt the bulkhead against his back and blinked his eyes open. The dim light of the boat was the only thing he saw. The lapping ocean waves were just about all he heard. Except for the singing. Very distinctive two-voiced singing; one perfectly pitched and the other severely off-key.

"Sienna, let the bird sing."

She gasped and spun around on the captain's chair. "Monty! You're awake!"

"Work it. Work it."

"I take that back," Monty growled. "Duchess, quiet."

"Thank goodness." Sienna abandoned the chair and dropped to her knees next to him, fingers prodding the very sore skin on his forehead. "I didn't know how I was going to get you into the cabin if I had to. Does it hurt?"

"Yes." He caught her searching hands and brought them together. "What happened? How's the boat?"

"Boat's okay. I think. You knocked yourself out trying to get to me. Your foot slipped and blam!" She tried to smack her hands together. "You conked your head on the railing."

"Yeah. That I got. You okay?"

"I'm great!" She beamed at him. "We did it. We rode out the storm. Took a few hours and so Duchess and I covered about thirty years of musicals, but yeah." She sighed and sank back onto her heels. "We're okay. Me, Duchess, *Dream* and now you." She pulled her hands free and caught his face in her palms. Before he knew it, she pressed her mouth against his.

The kiss was everything their first one hadn't been. Quick, searing, surprising. But just as welcome. His hand slipped down to her waist, trying to urge her closer, but she pulled back, shaking her head.

"We need to get you downstairs so I can get the first aid kit."

"Yeah, we'll do that. Help me up first. I want to check our location." The rain continued to fall, but the storm wasn't nearly as tempestuous as it had been. Sienna wedged herself under his arm and together they got him to his feet. It took him a moment to get his bearings, and to stop his stomach from churning. He was going to have a major headache, but Sienna was right about one thing. He was alive. The pain proved it.

She helped him over to the chair and he dropped into it like a wet sack of sand. He blinked, trying to focus his vision. "I can't read this." He tapped the devices on the dashboard. "Read them to me."

"Sure." She read out the numbers and he actually started laughing.

"We barely lost any distance at all." He sank back in the chair. "But for now..." Monty dropped the bow anchor and throttled down. Turned off the engine. And welcomed as much silence as he could get. "For now, we all deserve a bit of rest."

"Good to know." Sienna seemed to be holding him upright in the chair. "I'll get your bed ready. For after. Once we take care of your head, I mean." Her cheeks went bright pink. "Wait here and I'll come back to help you down."

"Sounds good." He closed his eyes, only to blink them open almost immediately for fear he'd drift off again. "Duchess?" he asked and looked over to the bird, who was still singing, but no longer at the top of her lungs. "You good?"

"Pretty bird."

"Geez, bird, sing a different tune." He didn't have a clue how Sienna could help him down the ladder. Instead, he dragged himself across the wheelhouse and when he reached the hatch, he stopped short, finding her on the ladder returning to him.

"What are you doing?" she snapped and immediately locked a hand around his. "You were supposed to wait for me."

"You were hurt." He remembered now, the image of her slamming into the side of the boat almost sickening him. "Your shoulder." He waited until he was down in the cabin before he started probing her shoulder.

"Stop that. I'm fine. Just bruised." But she winced and pulled away.

Before he could protest, she had him sitting at the table. The boat continued to rock under the last vestiges of the storm, but after the past few hours, it felt almost soothing. "You probably won't need stitches," Sienna murmured as she wet a cotton ball with alcohol. "This is going to sting."

"Yep." He nodded. "Just get it over with." His head continued to throb and all he could think about was the bed waiting for him a few feet away. Even with her warning, he sucked in a sharp breath. "Okay, that's not fun."

"I bet." She moved closer as she pushed up his head gently so she could get more light. He had nowhere to put his hands so he settled for resting them on her hips, a gesture that had her freezing. Then she looked into his eyes, and smiled. "Don't start something you can't finish, Boat Boy."

He almost grinned in response until he realized what she'd called him. "That's what Frankie calls me."

"Uh-huh." Sienna nodded and dabbed more alcohol onto his wound. "She told me. She told me a whole lot of things, actually."

"Did she?" He kept his eyes up on her face, mainly because if he looked straight ahead he'd be looking at her... He squeezed his eyes shut. It didn't help. He was still thinking about her…sweatshirt. "You about done there, Calamity Jane?"

Her hand halted. "You did not just call me a horse."

"I'm still working up a nickname for you. After tonight I'm thinking I might have a whole bunch to choose from. Once my brain's a bit unscrambled. Okay, that's enough." He caught her hand. "Bandage me up and call it over."

"All right." She dug out some butterfly bandages and quickly applied them. "You'll probably want to see a doctor once you get home."

He was going to need more than that the way his thoughts were running. There would be nothing less likely, less rational, than for him to fall tail over teakettle for Sienna Fairchild and yet…

Monty took a deep breath. It seemed that's exactly what he'd done. Illusion, he told himself. A few days on dry land, a few days in the real world and not this isolated snow globe of misadventure they'd been on, and his feelings would be back on track: the practical, nonridiculous track.

"All right." She stepped out of his arms and gathered up her trash. "Go get out of those wet clothes. I'll fix you tea and bring you pain pills."

"Then you'll let me get some sleep?"

"Some. I'll stay nearby to wake you up every few hours." She tilted up his chin again with her finger. "Just to be safe."

"Good times." He made a stumbling effort to his room. It took longer than expected, longer than his ego approved of, to change into a pair of wonderfully clean and dry sweats. He was already lying down when she knocked on his door. "Yeah."

"Here you go. It's chamomile, so it should help relax you."

Monty opened his eyes and found she'd changed, as well, and was wearing an oversized T-shirt and what to him looked like skimpy boxer shorts. She sat on the edge of the bed, held out two pills and handed him the mug.

"Awesome. Thanks." He took the pills but nearly choked on the tea. "Gah! Tastes like Calliope's herb garden." Monty set the mug on the narrow shelf by his bed.

Sienna grinned. "The more you say things like that, the more anxious I am to meet this woman. Now." She poked a finger gently against his forehead and pushed his head back. "Go to sleep."

She stood up to go, but he caught her wrist. "Don't go."

"But you need—"

He looked at her, and even though he knew it was a mistake, he couldn't release her hand. "Don't go. Stay. Just…stay."

"All right. Just let me clean up a few things—"

"Now, Sienna." He scooted over, pulled her down beside him. "Just stay with me. For a little while."

He hoped she would. He reveled in being beside her, catching that beautiful fragrance in her hair. "You'll get cold," she whispered.

"Not with you here," he whispered back. "Not ever with you." He closed his eyes, at peace, finally, and let sleep take him.

"And just wrap this around here," Sienna murmured to herself. "Ow!" She jumped when a spark hit her finger. She quickly finished tying off the electrical tape, then tightened the connection. "Got ya."

"Got what?"

Sienna yelped, jerked back and fell on her butt. She glared up at a bedraggled Monty, who was growing a pretty nasty bruise along his hairline. "Warn a girl, why don't you." She raised an eyebrow and he hauled her up. "How's your head?" The second she was on her feet, she was reaching out to examine his bandage.

"Still attached to my body. What were you doing?"

"Double-checking all the connections. I fixed a couple to be safe. A few you'd already taped off, but…" She shrugged. "I figured all that jostling around last night probably knocked a few things loose."

He nodded, then squeezed his eyes shut as if the move had been a mistake. "Mind if I check?"

"Not at all." She scooted past him and returned to the galley. She was spooning up scrambled eggs and dropped two pieces of toast into the toaster when he joined her. "Did it pass inspection?"

"Looks great. Thanks. Not sure I've got the dexterity I need to do that today." He dropped into the seat at the table and rested his head in one hand. "Did you sleep at all?"

"Some." She swallowed hard and did everything she could to prevent the blush creeping up her neck from reaching her face. Truth be told, she hadn't slept much at all. For the longest time she'd lain there, listening to his breathing, relishing the sensation of being so close to him. She hadn't thought she could feel more enthralled than when he'd kissed her, but him putting an arm over her waist at one point meant she couldn't imagine another place she'd rather be.

"How many times did you wake me up last night?"

"Four." She remembered clearly because each time she had, the worry that his head injury was worse faded. By four this morning, she let him sleep through. "Here." She set the bottle of painkillers in front of him. "You're due for some more."

"Thanks." He ran his thumb over the back of her fingers. She watched his gaze flicker across her engagement ring, saw his jaw tense the moment before he released her and reached for the bottle. "You impressed me last night. Keeping the boat in one piece."

She shrugged, focusing on buttering the toast. "I love her, too. *Dream*," she added as if she needed to clarify. "I wouldn't want anything to happen to her. We don't have long before we reach Butterfly Harbor."

"Getting antsy?"

"No." She was surprised to find that she meant it. It hadn't taken her long to get used to life on a boat; this time on *Dream* was bringing back so many fond memories of times she'd spent with her grandmother that it felt almost second nature. Then again, it wasn't just the boat she'd grown accustomed to. "Making a mental note of when I'll have to leave her." *And you.*

She set the plate in front of him, then sat and watched as he ate. Anxiety of an entirely new kind swirled inside her. It was time to ask. "What happens now?"

"More of my enjoying this nice breakfast."

"I don't mean with breakfast." She tried not to tap her fingers on the table. "I mean with…us."

He hesitated, but didn't stop eating.

"Or do you kiss every stowaway who turns up on your boat?" She really hoped not, even as she wished she hadn't asked the question. "There's something going on between us, right? I'm not imagining things?" And, oh, boy had she been imagining things.

He took another bite of eggs, then set down his fork and wiped his mouth. "You aren't imagining anything, Sienna. I think it's safe to say we hold a healthy attraction for one another."

"Could you maybe make that sound more analytical? I don't think my therapist heard you." Safe to say? What was safe with this conversation?

"I bet he or she would say you're deflecting with humor."

She narrowed her eyes. Was he playing with her? "Look, I meant that since I'll be sticking around your little town for a while to help with your sister's wedding—"

"Little town? Could you maybe say that with a little less condescension?"

"I—" She stared at him. What was happening here? What had happened to the affable, playful, fun-to-be-around Monty? Was he picking a fight to deflect from what he was feeling? "Why does it seem as if we're having two separate conversations?"

"Probably because we are. Okay…" He was speaking in very calm, determined syllables. "We need to look at this situation realistically. We are two very different people who come from two very different worlds. That can add a spark or ten to an intense situation."

She tilted her head to one side. "You're saying whatever we're feeling has been the result of close proximity and amplified emotions. That everything registers stronger and more overwhelming because we can't get away from one another."

"See? Not a very different conversation after all." He got to his feet and set his plate in the sink, keeping hold of his toast.

"But, wait." An odd tremor shook her heart. "So there's nothing to our attraction other than circumstance?" That didn't make sense. Last night, when she'd slept beside him, everything had seemed so perfect, so right. He'd asked her to stay. There was no misinterpreting that he had feelings for her—she was certain of it. Head injury or not, no man kissed a woman like Monty had kissed her without a true emotional connection. Or at the least, without wanting to.

"That's what I'm saying. Besides…" His voice fell flat. It was so unlike Monty, she wondered if he'd woken up as someone else entirely. "You're not a free woman, Sienna."

"What?" She jerked her head up when he faced her. "What are you—? Of course I am! I'm not going to marry Richard."

"Tell that to your finger." He inclined his chin toward her hand. "You're still wearing his ring. Other than assisting Frankie with her wedding, you haven't said what your future plans are."

"Well, excuse me for not figuring out my future on your timetable," she snapped and resisted the temptation to try to remove the ring again, this time in his presence. Doing that would only prove his ridiculous theory true and that she was somehow still emotionally attached to Richard.

"Are you on any timetable?" Monty asked in a frustratingly analytical voice. "Don't get me wrong, this whole let's-see-what-happens mentality is a lot of fun, but it isn't real life. Real life is what we're sailing into. It's what's going to be waiting for you at the dock when there isn't an ocean around us acting as romantic inspiration. What does reality have in store for you? A job? Travel? Family? A career? Will it include a conversation with your father? Will you give that ring back to Richard in person or at all? What do you want for your life?" He lowered his voice. "Who are you, Sienna?"

"I don't…know." She frowned.

He peered into her eyes to the point where she couldn't bring herself to look back. "Until you do, this is where we are. I've got a business to run, Sienna. Bills and employees to pay. As wild as this adventure has been, and as much as I may care about you, important responsibilities are about a few days out. And I can't afford any more detours."

He waited for a moment for her to respond. Then he turned and climbed out on deck.

CHAPTER TWELVE

SIENNA SAT IN stunned silence while Monty finished prepping the boat to resume course, unable to do little more than stare at the ring that had absolutely no chance of bringing her a scintilla of happiness.

She hated it; the ring itself and everything it represented. The ostentatious emerald was a statement piece. Not for her, but for Richard. His look-how-much-money-I-can-spend-on-my-future-wife declaration. How had she not seen that before?

She tugged on the band. Just like before, it didn't budge other than to spin in an endless tease. Telling Monty the stupid thing wouldn't come off wouldn't have done any good. It would have sounded like a pathetic excuse and the last thing she wanted to sound like anymore was pathetic.

Sienna glared down at the emerald, sneering at how it glinted against the light. It wasn't even her taste! She liked dainty jewelry. Heirloom pieces that carried tradition along with a simple design, not rocks that could be seen from space. She didn't need loud pronouncements of affection. She needed...

She took a deep breath, her brow furrowing. She wasn't sure exactly what she needed; she only knew what she didn't want.

He's right. Sienna folded her hands in her lap and accepted the truth. It wasn't that she didn't know what she wanted out of life. Nana had taught her to embrace every day as a new possibility; dreams to be chased after, a heart to be filled. It was what Sienna wanted for herself that eluded her. Had always eluded her.

She was always chasing someone else's approval: accolades from her father that did nothing more than push her to clamor after more; the approval of her nana. How many times had she asked herself what her mother would think? And not once had any of those things brought her an ounce of the happiness she felt on this boat with Monty.

Was it happiness? Or was it just different enough to seem enticing?

Either way, what did any of this get her?

He was irritatingly, frustratingly right. She had absolutely no idea who Sienna Fairchild was. That's what she'd seen in the mirror at the yacht club. That's what she'd felt, the empty life she'd been about to jump into nipping at her heels as she'd raced to the marina.

Nana's Dream wasn't the answer she'd been looking for. It was only the means for an escape. An escape that was almost complete now that they were nearing Butterfly Harbor and the end of her deal with Monty.

Monty. Sienna tapped her hand against her heart as if his name was enough to get it to beat steadily again.

Were her feelings for him a result of the fact that he was the utter and complete opposite of the man she'd run from marrying? Or was she just fooling herself? Was she settling because it was easy to be with Monty? Or was she genuinely falling for him?

All those questions whirling in her brain led her to only one conclusion. She would have to find out.

But did she have what it would take to learn the truth?

"STOP IT, DUCHESS." Monty batted away the latest blueberry Duchess sent soaring in his direction. "If you aren't going to eat, leave it alone."

Duchess made a trilling sound in her throat. "Leave it alone. Leave it alooooooone!"

"That's not a song." That he knew of.

In the past few hours, his head had finally stopped throbbing and his vision cleared. He was thinking clearly enough now to admit his conversation with Sienna might have been triggered by his own curiosity about where they went from here.

The closer they got to Butterfly Harbor, the more he wondered if there was any way to fit her into his life. It was an impossible question to answer so long as she remained solidly in flux. It didn't get more flux than Sienna Fairchild.

He wasn't good for her as long as she didn't know who she was or what she wanted for herself.

He could want everything for her, want to be with her, to hold her, kiss her, spend endless days out on the rioting ocean with her, but none of that meant anything if she was simply moving from one life chosen for her into another of convenience and circumstance. He didn't want her by default.

His instincts had been right from the start. Get her off his boat as soon as he could, collect the money she owed him and let whatever happened play out however it was going to. It made perfect sense.

Except for one thing: he was already on the edge of being in love with her.

Frankie had warned him that when the time came and he discovered he was in love, it would be like a life-changing tidal wave hitting him. Life-changing? Didn't he like his life the way it was? He thought so. Everyone else seemed to think so, too. Then again, being alone, with the rest of his life stretched out ahead of him, seemed dull and endless, like the unreachable horizon hovering at the edge of the world. And yet, he could barely wrap his mind around a future that didn't include Sienna Fairchild.

How could he have fallen this hard and this fast? He'd resent her for it if he didn't know none of this had been her fault.

Well, not all her fault. He glanced up at the cloudless sky, considered the fact that Sienna's grandmother might indeed have had a hand in her granddaughter's choice of escape vessels. "At some point you and I are going to have a talk, Winnie." He swung his attention to Duchess, who was pacing along the console, humming to herself. "Not for repetition, bird. Seal those lips."

"Seal those lips. Seal those lips." Duchess clacked her beak and took a little bow.

A flashing light on the dash prevented him from responding. Monty immediately dropped speed when he identified the warning light telling him the engine was overheating. He then realized the voltage meter was dead. He swore, shoved out of his chair and dropped down the ladder to the lower level.

"What's going on?" Sienna poked her head into the hallway. "Why have we stopped?"

"Hopefully not for the reason I'm thinking." He pulled open the panel and saw debris that unfortunately looked like a broken drive belt. "Can you bring me the tool kit?"

"Just a sec." While Sienna retrieved the kit, Monty kept good thoughts. He tried to remember putting in a new drive belt before leaving San Diego; he always carried spares, though. That said, he had been distracted around that time. "Here."

Sienna passed him the box, but it didn't take more than a few seconds for him to admit he was definitely out of luck. "Perfect." He sat back on his heels and looked at her. "We've got a problem."

"OKAY, ERIC. THANKS. Just tell Cal to bill me and I'll take care of the invoice as soon as I'm back." Monty heard the telltale warning that his cell battery was about to die. "Perfect. Bring my main kit with you, too, would you? See you tomorrow." He hit the button to drop anchor and settled in.

"Well?" Sienna sat on the bench nearby, her legs and arms crossed. Monty glanced away. She'd worn those shorts again. The ones that distracted him to the point he all but forgot his name.

"We're stuck here for the night." He sat back on his heels and shut the cover on the engine. "Drive belt's shot and I don't have a spare." He'd never be without one again, however. "My mechanic's bringing it out tomorrow. We're close enough he should be here by noon."

"We're that close to Butterfly Harbor?"

"Half a day at the speed we've been going, but for *Phoenix* it'll only be a few hours."

"*Phoenix*?"

"My speedboat. We usually use it for coast tours for one or two people, small diving groups, but she comes in handy in emergencies. I could send out a stranded signal, but we aren't in any danger and I don't like using up resources that can be focused elsewhere for emergencies."

"No need to explain." She gave him a

quick, tense smile. "Just along for the ride, remember?"

Oh, he remembered.

"You know, there is one thing we haven't done on this trip." The second she finished her thought, her cheeks went pink. "Fishing. We haven't done any fishing."

"I guess we haven't."

"Since it sounds as if we'll be getting into the harbor tomorrow, and we don't have anything on the calendar for tonight—"

"Or any other night," he added and earned a glare of irritation for interrupting. "Excellent plan for dinner. Unless you're squeamish about the fish?"

"Please." Her mouth twisted. "I was scaling and gutting fish before I hit double digits. I'll get the rods. You get the chairs."

As GOOD AS Sienna was about distracting other people, she was horrible at it for herself. She'd spent the morning and half the afternoon going over the notes she'd made about Frankie's wedding, completed a tentative schedule of businesses to connect with as soon as she was in town and decided to leave the seating chart alone until she spoke to the bride and groom face-to-face for their suggestions and ideas.

Why she thought sitting beside Monty on the deck of his boat for potentially hours waiting for the fish to bite would be a welcome respite was clearly an error in judgment. Although, who knew? Maybe she'd suddenly have the epiphany that she was destined for a life of competitive sports fishing.

"Nice reels."

"I found this box of tackle, too. They look handmade." She handed him the metal box, then shielded her eyes and looked up. "This is good timing. Dusk is setting in." Even though it was late in the day, they may still have a chance of catching something. "They'll work, yeah?"

"They'll work." He examined the rod she handed to him. "So will this. Want me to check—?"

"I've got it." She didn't snap, just made the simple declaration. She chose her own tackle from the box and tied it on. A few minutes later she was casting off and taking a seat in the chair beside him.

"You've definitely done this before." He repeated her actions, got a bit more distance than she had and set the pole down in the receptacle on the arm of his chair. "I was thinking about grabbing a beer. You want one?"

"No, thanks. But I'll take some wine."

"Good idea. I'll join you."

Forced politeness, Sienna thought as he disappeared below deck, had its advantages. He'd set new ground rules for his boat. Nothing romantic. Nothing emotional. Until she got her life straightened out, it was all business between them.

Business. Sienna wished she had that wine now. She was not looking forward to having to deal with the real-life stuff that awaited her. The finalization of her grandmother's will next week meant she needed to have a plan of action where her future was concerned. Her days of part-time jobs were over. Her inheritance would give her a cushion, but she needed… No, that was wrong. She *wanted* a purpose. "Here you go." Monty traversed the rocking of the boat with a practiced step. "Depending on what we catch, we should have plenty of food left to supplement."

"Works for me." She accepted her wineglass and leaned back her head, keeping one eye on her line and the other on the water. "Why Wind Walkers?"

"That's what my dad called sailing. Walking on the wind. Seemed fitting."

She envied him, being able to talk about his father with such affection.

He settled in his chair, stretched out his legs. "I was all over the place growing up. Couldn't make up my mind about anything I wanted to do. Drove my father nuts. It didn't help that both Frankie and Sebastian knew exactly what they wanted."

"What's Sebastian do?"

"He owns a bookstore. Cat's Eye. Perfect little shop off Monarch Lane. He opened it about six months after Mandy was born."

"Cat's Eye?"

"Sebastian is also a cat person." Monty chuckled. "Passed that on to Mandy. They've fostered hundreds of cats over the years, most of whom are featured guests in the store. He even rigged these platforms on the walls, above the stock shelves, that the cats jump to and sleep on. They only have two cats now, Tribble and Balthazar. The shelter has been able to keep up and more foster families have stepped in."

"Cats and books. Interesting combination."

"It's his dream come true. Just like firefighting is Frankie's."

"And Wind Walkers is yours."

"I always knew I wanted to make the ocean my office." He drank more wine. "After my dad was killed, and then my mom left, I had to make a living. A local fisherman taught me a lot about boating, let me borrow his vessel when he wasn't using it. Spent a lot of time getting to know the area. I went to work for a tour-boat company out of Monterey. Learned the ins and outs, made note of what I thought worked, what didn't. Eventually I earned enough money to buy my first boat, and on my days off, started running tours out of Butterfly Harbor. Took a while to catch on with tourists, once we got some coming in, at least. For a good while, my business came from town residents, which I was grateful for. That was about five years ago, I think."

"It makes you happy." What must that be like? she wondered. To find fulfillment like that?

"It does. The ocean puts everything in perspective. It reminds you every day how small a place you take up in the world. At the same time, it presents new challenges, allows you to explore, contemplate, discover new things about yourself you can't ignore out here."

"What do you think your parents would

say?" She had to admit, she was curious about his family, especially about the man who raised him. To have lost his father at such a young age and not hold any bitterness about it… She found it confusing. She'd only seen photographs of her mother; didn't have any memory of her at all and she resented having missed out on that relationship.

"My dad would be thrilled. I'm a productive member of society who loves what he does." He glanced over at her. "That's all he ever wanted for me."

"And your mom?"

His smile dipped. "Roxie would probably say I don't make enough money. Although, who knows? Maybe after all this time she's changed. But I doubt it."

They'd each lost their mothers, although in different ways. "You and Frankie don't see her?"

"I ran into her last year. She was dealing blackjack in a casino in Reno. Still waiting for her prince to rescue her from her horrible, mundane life."

"She lost her prince when your dad died."

"Oh, Dad was not her prince. At least not the prince she thought he was. As Frankie puts it, Roxie loved the idea of being married to a firefighter more than the actual marriage. She thought he was going places. It wasn't until they got married that she realized he'd made a commitment to protect Butterfly Harbor and didn't ever want to leave. She left town the day after Frankie and I turned eighteen. She's never been back."

"That's…" Again, he wasn't bitter. Well, maybe a little, but he certainly didn't seem to dwell on it. How did he do that? "That's so sad."

"It is what it is. I considered myself lucky she didn't sell the house first. I got the one Frankie and I grew up in. Frankie inherited our grandparents'. It all worked out for the best." He ducked his chin. "It will for you, too. You just need to find your way."

That was easy for him to say. He'd had a solid foundation. Even with the loss of his father, his neighbors and friends had stepped in to support him. The idea sounded almost fantastical. She'd certainly had her share of journeys with her nana, but she had to think perhaps she was far more sheltered than he'd ever been living in a small town.

"I've always asked permission for everything I've ever wanted to do." What a sad statement to have made. "As if my success depended on the approval of others. What someone else thinks doesn't mean anything, does it? Not if you're happy."

"So long as you aren't hurting anyone else. Absolutely not. It shouldn't." He finished his wine as she looked down at hers. "You're thinking about Richard and your father, aren't you?"

Shame swept over her like a tidal wave. "What must it say about me that even as an adult, getting my father's approval was worth surrendering my happiness?"

"Except you didn't surrender it. Did you?"

"I waited until the last minute, though. Another half hour and I'd have been walking down that aisle to marry a man I know little to nothing about. Because it was the first time my father was proud of me for something. My grandmother must be screaming at me from the afterlife."

"It doesn't matter what you did, Sienna. It matters what you do from here. And by here," he added before she could return them to their earlier conversation, "I mean from the moment you step off my boat. You can't have your life be dependent on what anyone else does, sees or feels. You've given yourself the opportunity to finally find where you belong, what works for you. Don't limit yourself by fooling yourself or settling like my mother did. Believe me, you will end up miserable and alone."

"I'm not alone here, am I?"

"No, you're not." He glanced away and readjusted his fishing rod. "You're with a friend."

"A friend." Awesome. She'd been friend-zoned.

"Doesn't sound as if you've had a whole lot of those, Sienna. Maybe if you did, you wouldn't be in the situation you're in now."

"I could do with a friend," she mused. At least he wasn't cutting her completely out of his life. "If for no other reason than to stop me from making stupid mistakes like getting engaged. I should let Tabitha have him."

"Tabitha?" Now it was his turn to sound quizzical.

"My cousin. Uncle Frank's youngest. She was my maid of honor."

"So you do have family and friends."

"Family, yes. The more I think about it, the more I realize we were never really friends. I always got the feeling she was jealous of my relationship with Nana. Of course, I was always jealous because she had a mom. It's all about perspective, isn't it?"

"I suppose it is."

Sienna's line snapped tight. The reel began whizzing as whatever had caught at the end was making a break for it.

"Grab it!" Monty ordered.

"Got it." Sienna pulled the rod out of its holder, bracing it against her thigh. She pulled back, tightened her hold with one hand and started cranking the reel with her other. "Holy mackerel, this thing is heavy." Her arms strained as she struggled.

"You've got it!" Monty got to his feet, moved behind her, but he didn't touch her; didn't even try to help her. "Just keep it steady, nice and even. There you go."

Sienna laughed in the moment and then nearly lost her grip. When the flapping fish slammed against the hull of the boat, she yanked up hard. The fish dropped onto the deck, flipping and flopping, its silvery scales glistening in the dimming sun. She blinked, set down her rod and walked around to examine it. "What is it?"

"It's a fish."

She rolled her eyes.

"Dinner?"

She laughed.

"It's a sablefish," he told her. "Black cod."

"Oh, a butterfish. Excellent."

"So you've cooked one before?" He bent down and removed the hook from the fish's mouth and set her future meal into a bucket.

"Nope. I've eaten one, though." She grinned. "Your turn." She pointed to his line as it whizzed free. "Need some help?"

"No, thank you." Monty retrieved his rod and a few minutes later had another fish landing on the deck. "Halibut. Excellent."

"Tonight, we shall feast." This time it was Sienna who made quick work of the hook while Monty gathered up their equipment.

Contentment slid through her. They really did make a good team and the quiet fishing time gave her new insight into the man who had inadvertently ridden to her rescue.

"Hang on!" Monty held up a finger, then disappeared downstairs, only to return a few minutes later with a tape measure.

"Really?" She folded her arms across her chest and waited as he studied each one. "Well?"

"Doesn't matter."

She beamed. "Ha! Sure it does. 'Cause mine's bigger. For the record and between *friends*." She moved him aside and grabbed the handle of the bucket. "That wasn't a question I needed an answer to."

He smiled back and chuckled. "Noted for future reference."

CHAPTER THIRTEEN

THE SOUND OF muted conversation and unfamiliar voices drew Sienna out of her sleep. She blinked awake, a bit startled to find sunlight streaming into her cabin at a higher point than she was used to.

She sat up, pushing her hair out of her face, and took a moment to get her bearings. Her and Monty's dinner conversation had stretched far into the night; long enough to welcome the moon and bid farewell to the ocean bounty they'd caught earlier in the day. She'd finally fallen into bed sometime after one, happy, well-fed and utterly and completely content.

A contentment that was none too thrilled with Monty's loud speakerphone conversation at… Sienna glanced at her watch. Oh. She bit her lip. It was after ten. Oops. She'd slept through breakfast.

When she popped open her door, she expected to find Monty in the galley, but the entire interior was empty. Whomever he was talking to was up on deck. Taking quick advantage of her solitude, Sienna jumped into the shower, got dressed and headed toward the voices. A smile curved her lips as she passed the table and found a thermos of coffee waiting for her, along with a bagel and cream cheese wrapped in plastic. She grabbed them both and a banana and climbed the ladder… only to stop short when she found Monty buried in the engine compartment, being observed by a woman in a loose-fitting T-shirt, jeans and a black baseball cap with BHFD embroidered on it. One look at the long red ponytail sticking out from the back of that cap would have identified the woman immediately had she not turned amused, friendly and familiar sparkling green eyes in Sienna's direction.

"You must be Frankie," Sienna said. After setting down her breakfast, she offered her hand in greeting. "I didn't realize you'd be making the trip out with Eric."

"She made the trip out instead of Eric," Monty's muffled voice said from inside the hatch.

"There was an issue with one of the tour boats. Had to take precedence," Frankie explained. She sat on the padded bench and scooted over to make room for Sienna. "And seeing as I have the next forty-eight hours off, I thought I'd do a few favors and come help this pirate find his way home. I grabbed a few hours sleep, then took a boat. Sorry if we woke you up."

"Don't be." Sienna felt a tinge of guilt at having neglected her morning duties. She'd begun to enjoy the schedule she and Monty had established together. "I'm not clearheaded just yet. Give me a minute." She quickly poured some coffee. Two sips later, she felt the day shift into focus. "Okay, that's better." She sighed in a way that had Frankie grinning.

"Oh, yeah," Frankie said. "You and I are going to get along fine."

Any unease Sienna might have felt at meeting Monty's sister melted away.

"Hey, Man!" Monty yelled. "Where's that kit already?"

"Man?" It took Sienna a minute to connect the name to Monty's goddaughter. "Oh, Mandy. She came with you?"

"Not willingly, exactly," Frankie muttered under her breath. "Kyle begged me to get her out of the hospital. She's been living there since he was admitted."

"How's he doing?" Sienna peeled the banana and ate.

"Better than expected. It's still going to be a long recovery, though, and he doesn't do that great with all the attention. Between his mom and Mandy, he's going a bit stir-crazy."

"He'll have to get used to the hovering." The young woman who climbed up the side of the boat and dropped onto the deck aimed a look at Frankie that would have stopped Sienna from arguing. "Hi. You must be Sienna." Mandy set a green metal toolbox down near Monty, then wiped her hand on her cut-off jeans. "I'm Mandy."

"It's nice to meet you, Mandy. I've heard a lot about you."

"I'll bet." Mandy grinned and flashed a quick look to Frankie. The teen wore her blond hair in the same manner as Frankie, but Mandy's baseball cap displayed her dedication to the 49ers, as did the black-and-red T-shirt she wore. She stood at about Sienna's height and displayed more curves than angles—a testament, no doubt, to the amount of time she spent in and on the water. "And I know very well Kyle asked you to kidnap me, Aunt

Frankie. Lori and I took bets on which one of us he was going to try to get rid of first." The young woman's smile widened, but Sienna could still see a trace of concern in her brilliant blue eyes. "I won twenty bucks for the shelter fund."

Sienna recalled Monty telling her about all the work Mandy did for the local animal charity. Sienna sipped her coffee and listened to the ensuing banter between Mandy and her godparents. The affection among the three was obvious and it was clear Monty had been right when he'd said Mandy was fifteen going on thirty-five. There was a maturity about her that made her comfortable to be around the adults in her life.

"Squawk! Pretty bird. Pretty bird. Guacamooleeeeee!"

Frankie and Mandy both jumped. Monty jerked and bashed his head on the compartment ledge. Amid the cursing echoes, Sienna laughed. "I was wondering where she'd gotten to. Good morning, Duchess." Sienna grabbed her banana, broke off a piece and stood up to offer it to the parrot. "Duchess, this is Frankie and Mandy. Duchess found us after one of our stops."

"You didn't mention the bird," Frankie said

in a tone so identical to her brother's, Sienna thought she was hearing double. "You starting a collection or something?"

"Or something," Monty muttered.

"She's so pretty," Mandy whispered, sticking close to Sienna who offered up a chunk of fruit. Duchess grabbed hold with one foot and began nibbling the offered banana. "Oh, look! That's so cute. Look at how she eats."

"You may not have a bird, Man," Monty said as he slipped free of the hatch and sat back on the deck. "Tribble and Balthazar would not approve. Neither would your father."

"I wasn't going to ask for one." Mandy watched as Sienna drew a finger down the bird's back. "Yet," she mumbled under her breath.

Sienna shared a secret smile with the teen. "She's been pretty friendly, but go slow with her. And no matter how much she asks, no guacamole or avocado."

"Hi, Duchess. I'm Mandy." Mandy moved a bit closer. "You're very pretty."

Duchess stopped eating, blinked assessing eyes at Mandy and inclined her head as if making a life-altering decision. She clicked her beak, ruffled her throat and said, "Get your knees up!"

Mandy and Frankie laughed. Monty groaned. "Don't encourage her."

"Are you bringing her home with you?" Mandy asked and took the rest of Sienna's banana that she offered and continued to feed Duchess.

"I doubt anyone decides anything for Duchess," Monty said. "But so far she's along for the ride. If that storm didn't frighten her off, I doubt anything will."

"What's the verdict with the belt?" Frankie asked.

"Going to take more work than I thought to get it running again." Monty dug around in his toolbox. "There's a lot of rust that needs scouring off, otherwise this will happen again and maybe do more damage next time." He looked up at Sienna. "It's going to be at least another day before I can get her going again. Maybe it's best if you head back with Frankie and Mandy. I'll get in when I can." He leaned into the engine as if she'd been dismissed.

"Oh." Disappointment crashed through her. It might have at least been worth a discussion. "I guess that makes sense."

He hadn't mentioned this idea to her yesterday; then again, he hadn't known Frankie was the one coming out with the parts he needed. Or that the belt would need more work. Had he? Sienna hadn't considered going anywhere near Butterfly Harbor without Monty. She wasn't entirely sure she wanted to. But it seemed she didn't have a choice. "Is that okay with you, Frankie? Are you ready to trust me with your wedding?"

Frankie's gaze shot from her brother to Sienna, and only then did Sienna see the relief and gratitude shimmering. "I was ready the second Monty suggested it and so was Roman. I have to leave the day after tomorrow for that conference. If I can get you in touch with everyone before then—"

"Don't worry. We'll get it taken care of." Sienna found dropping into wedding-planner mode delayed the emotions she'd have to deal with later. She was saying goodbye to Monty. Today.

Sure, she'd see him again, but the time they'd shared on *Dream* was over.

"I'll need to make a few phone calls and figure out where I'm staying." Sienna had thought she'd have time to figure out her arrangements. Now, everything seemed to be moving in fast-forward mode.

"Luckily, you have a couple of choices," Frankie said. "Roman and I can arrange a room at the Flutterby—"

"That gorgeous inn on the cliffs?" Sienna's heart soared. "I've only seen pictures, but it's stunning."

"Pictures don't do it justice," Frankie agreed. "Or there's an apartment over the Butterfly Diner you can use. It's unoccupied now that Brooke moved out."

"Brooke's my mom," Mandy explained. "She and my dad got married last month. On my birthday," she added with a radiant smile. "It's a cute little place. She fixed it up while she lived there."

"How about you let her decide when she gets there?" Monty said. He'd finally looked up. "And you and Roman aren't footing any bill for this. This is all on me, Frankie. She's my wedding gift to you, remember?" His face went red when the three women on the boat all looked at him with the same expression. He pointed a wrench at them in turn. "You know what I mean. Every single one of you. Sienna and I have a deal." Finally, he met her gaze. "No money changes hands between the two of you, understood?"

"What kind of deal do you two have exactly?" Frankie asked Sienna, turning away from her brother.

"It's a really long story." Sienna cringed.

"Well then." Frankie slung an arm around Sienna's shoulders and squeezed. "It's a good thing the boat ride to Butterfly Harbor is a long one. How about Mandy helps you get your stuff together."

MONTY STAYED WHERE he was and avoided his sister's probing gaze as Mandy and Sienna went below deck. He didn't have time for the regret surging through him. He'd known from the moment he'd kissed the runaway bride that he needed to find a way to get her off his boat. Leave it to Frankie to unintentionally give him the out he needed.

"Hold up there, baby bro." Frankie stooped down and grabbed his arm before he could resume his repairs. "What's going on, Monty?"

"You need your wedding planner operational and I need to work on my boat," Monty explained, but there was no point in trying to hide anything from Frankie. His twin knew him almost better than he knew himself.

"Please. You'll have this thing up and running in a few hours. You're trying to get rid of her. Why? You two not getting along?" She narrowed her eyes. "Or maybe you're getting along too well."

He and Frankie had only one rule between them. They didn't lie to each other. That meant, at this moment, it was better to stay silent. Better, but not easier. Whatever feelings he had for Sienna couldn't go any further than this boat. Because beyond this boat was a reality Sienna needed to deal with. But not answering only gave Frankie the answer she'd clearly been expecting. She sank back on her heels and let go of his arm.

"Oh, man." She looked toward the open hatch, then back at him. "Oh, man. You finally did it, didn't you? She's it, isn't she?" She let out a whoop of laughter.

"Keep your voice down," he snapped.

The teasing light vanished from Frankie's look. "Oh, Monty. I don't mean to make fun. It's just so…unexpected. Or maybe not, considering you dated Leah for a while last year. She wasn't your usual type, either."

"My usual type?" Monty echoed. "I don't have a *type*."

"Oh, please. Of course, you do." She gave him her men-are-so-dumb-sometimes look. "You like women who are settled, low-maintenance and content. I've only spent a few minutes around her, but I can honestly say I don't see Sienna as any of those things."

"She's also not available," Monty reminded her. "Did you see the rock on her hand?"

"Hard not to." Frankie shrugged. "Doesn't mean anything. She didn't exactly drag him along like an anchor. It hasn't even been a week since she dumped her fiancé—what was his name again?"

"Richard Somersby. And she didn't exactly dump him. More like she…abandoned him." And that, he had to admit, was what continued to gnaw at him. She hadn't told Richard she didn't want to marry him. She hadn't told Richard anything, nor did she seem particularly inclined to at any time in the near future. "Whatever might be going on with the two of us—"

"So there is something going on?" Frankie pressed.

Monty glared at her. "Whatever is going on with the two of us, there's no moving forward until she makes an effort to clean up her past. She needs to deal with what she left behind if there's to be anything going forward."

"You are such a romantic." Frankie wiped away an imaginary tear.

"Knock it off, Frankie."

"Oh, please," she snapped back. "You need to get over yourself. Maybe if she knew you were waiting for her on the other end of whatever she has going on it would make it easier for her."

"I can't be the reason she cuts ties with Richard." He wasn't about to be anyone's escape plan. "She needs to do it for herself. Not for anyone else. Not for me."

Frankie opened her mouth as if about to say something more, then closed it again. "All right. I won't disagree with you there." She pushed to her feet. "Oh, one thing." She snapped her fingers before he started to resume his repairs. "Have you told her how you feel about her?"

He pretended not to hear her.

"Monty—"

"Stop." He lost his grip on the wrench. "Please, Frankie, just stop." He glanced up and found his sister watching him with surprisingly concerned eyes.

"Not until you tell me why."

"Because." He shook his head. "Because women like Sienna don't stay. She might be adrift now, but she won't be in a few days when she gets her inheritance. Once that money hits her bank account, she'll be off on new adventures, just like she was with her grandmother. She wouldn't be happy with me, Frankie. Not long-term. And when people aren't happy, they die. Maybe not for a while, but inside, a little every day."

"A bit melodramatic."

"We saw it happen, Frankie. We lived through it with Mom. She fell for the romance of it all with Dad. She married the heroic fire-fighter thinking she was getting one thing and then reality hit and it turned her into someone else. Someone neither of us even recognizes." He looked back at the engine. "Or wants anything to do with. I won't do that to Sienna. She needs to discover things for herself, on her own. I can't have anything to do with whatever choices she makes from here."

"Sienna isn't Roxie." Frankie's voice sharpened. It always did on the few occasions they'd discussed their mother. "I never once saw our mother look at Dad the way Sienna looks at you. Roxie didn't want to be happy, Monty. You know how I know? Because we ceased to matter the second Dad was gone. The second the life she pushed him toward vanished, so did she. It just took her a couple more years to actually leave." There wasn't anger in her voice, just disappointment. And it wasn't just aimed at Roxie. "I don't think it's Sienna feeling trapped that has you worried, Monty. You're scared of finally having everything you've always wanted."

"Ooooh, this is gorgeous!" Mandy scooped up Sienna's wedding gown from the twin bed and held it in front of her as she twirled and twirled. She held out the long skirt and sighed like Cinderella in front of her fairy godmother. "You actually got to wear this?"

Sienna wrapped her wedding necklace in a T-shirt before placing it in one of the store bags for transport. "I really did." That fateful morning felt like weeks, even months ago. And it had only been several days. "Don't be fooled by how it looks. It's very uncomfortable."

And after the time she'd spent on *Dream*, she doubted she'd fit into it any longer. In more ways than one.

"It's a princess dress," Mandy whispered.

"I suppose it is." But she hadn't felt like a princess wearing it. She'd felt like a prisoner. "I'm not sure it's really my style." She wasn't entirely sure what her style was.

"How can this not be anyone's style?"

Mandy whipped off her baseball cap and let her long blond hair tumble free. "Is there a mirror on the boat? Do you mind if I go see?"

"Knock yourself out," Sienna said. "There's one on the inside of the bathroom door."

"Cool." She ripped open the cabin door. "Oh, hey, Aunt Frankie. Look at this dress! Isn't it the ult?"

Frankie's eyes went wide before she trailed a reverent hand down the tight sparkling embroidery. "That is positively stunning." She shifted disbelieving eyes on Sienna. "That wasn't enough, huh?"

"If I got married because of a dress I really would be an idiot," Sienna said and took a step back as Frankie joined her. "Is something wrong?"

"My brother's being stupid, so nothing new." Frankie sat on the edge of the bed. "You good with all these decisions being made for you? Going back with me and Mandy at Monty's behest, I mean?"

"You need my help with the wedding and the sooner I get to Butterfly Harbor, the better." Sienna combined bags and did a final check to make sure she hadn't missed anything. There wasn't much to miss. Clothes and books mostly, along with her bathroom stuff, which was already packed. "I just didn't expect to leave *Dream* so soon." It felt as if she was saying goodbye to a friend.

"Or Monty?"

Sienna shrugged. "I'm not exactly in the right frame of mind to be able to say one way or the other." When Frankie didn't respond, Sienna asked, "What?"

Frankie shook her head. "Nothing."

"I've known you for less than an hour, but that expression is something." Sienna took a steeling breath. "We've got a long ride ahead of us so maybe it's best to get it out of your system now."

"Does what I think matter?" Frankie tilted her head. "Does it matter what anyone thinks?"

Had Monty been sharing their conversations? "It shouldn't." But after a lifetime of trying to please the unpleasable, the habit was difficult to break. "I suppose if I still cared about what people thought I wouldn't have run out on my wedding, would I?"

"No," Frankie responded. "I don't suppose you would have."

Which meant Monty was wrong. While she might not know who she was, she was definitely on her way to finding out. And Butterfly Harbor sounded like the perfect place to do that.

"YOU HAVE EVERYTHING?" Monty wiped his hands on a rag and followed Frankie, Mandy and Sienna over to where Frankie had tied *Phoenix* to the side of *Dream*. Mandy's arms were full. A large plastic bag that no doubt contained Sienna's wedding dress. And Frankie carried the books.

"I left you the book you started. And a few others." Sienna shrugged. "If I missed anything else I guess I'll see you in a couple days." He didn't miss the detached tone in her voice. "I appreciate you taking me this far."

"We'll go wait on the boat." Frankie gave Mandy a substantial push to wipe the curious expression off the teenager's face. "Move it, Man."

"No fair. It was just getting good."

Sienna tucked a strand of hair behind her ear and looked at Monty. "This is because I asked you where we go from here, isn't it?"

"Me sending you off with Frankie?" He could lie to her. He probably should, if for no other reason than he didn't want to think about her leaving with that sad and disappointed look in her beautiful eyes. "Partially. You need to get unstuck, Sienna."

"Who determines when that's happened?" she challenged. "Me? Or you?"

"I'll be back in Butterfly Harbor soon. We can talk then."

"Right. Okay."

She turned to go, and he caught sight of his sister and Mandy suddenly busying themselves with the knot securing the boats together. He shoved his hands in his shorts pockets and glared.

"Just…one thing," Sienna said, and swung around.

"What's that?"

"This." Sienna slipped her arms about his neck and brought his head down to hers. The kiss she gave him made his brain smoke hotter than *Dream*'s engine had a day earlier. Before he could think, he pulled his hands free and clasped her hips. In his heart, he knew he wasn't going to have any peace of mind once she was gone. When she pulled away, she waited, forehead pressed against his, as their breathing returned to normal. "Figured I'd give you something to think about while I'm gone. Duchess?"

The bird squawked and flapped her wings from her perch on the upper railing.

"Take care of him, okay, Duchess?"

"Sailing, sailing…"

Monty stood there, on his boat, and watched as Sienna Fairchild climbed into the *Phoenix* with his sister and goddaughter waiting. He was still watching long after the cruiser disappeared into the distance.

CHAPTER FOURTEEN

"THERE SHE IS!" Mandy yelled over the roar of *Phoenix*'s engine.

Sienna pushed her hair out of her face and looked up to where Mandy pointed and saw the Flutterby Inn standing strong at the top of the cliffs of Butterfly Harbor. The bright yellow structure, with glistening white trim and shutters, looked like something out of a storybook, with its Victorian turrets and gingerbread accents. The line of thick cypress trees and redwoods protected the Flutterby from the elements even as they added to the picturesque quality of the California coastline.

"That look on her face is all the answer we need, huh, Man?" Frankie called before she slowed down and let the *Phoenix* idle while Sienna got her fill of the view "Abby keeps a few rooms held back for special guests," she said. "If that's where you want—"

"Oh, I want." She most definitely wanted. "But I don't want Monty paying for it," she added. Now that she'd be back on dry land, she'd be able to straighten things out with her bank. "Our deal was for transportation and basic necessities, not for my housing." Besides, she already owed him far more than money. Whether he believed it or not, he'd given her the space she'd needed to take those first steps not just of independence, but clear of grief. For that, she'd never be able to repay him.

The fact that she already missed him—now that could cause a few unexpected problems. Then again, maybe kissing him before she left hadn't been the best idea. She pressed her lips together as if she could still feel the warmth of his mouth. She'd meant to show him what he'd be missing.

She hadn't expected what her own reaction would be. "Is there much more to see?"

"From out here, not really," Frankie said. The *Phoenix* bounced gently against the waves. "Your best views, aside from this, are going to come from town. Don't worry. We'll play tour guide and make sure you have the lay of the land before setting you loose."

"I told Lori I'd be back at the hospital around three so she could pick Leo up from school." Mandy tapped her watch. "It's two now."

"All right. You want to stop and get Kyle some lunch before going to the hospital?" Frankie looked to Sienna. "I bet you're hungry by now, huh?"

"Lunch would be great. I'd like to be sure to get settled in the hotel in time to call my bank and finally get a cell phone."

"No problem. The diner's pretty quick." Frankie sped up and angled in closer to shore. "So the marina's in sections. The main marina is where Monty keeps the boats for Wind Walkers. Tourists hang out there and folks dock in those slips if they go out on the water frequently. Out here—" she pointed to the smaller cove area separated by an outcropping of rocks and trees "—it's sort of residential. We have people who live on their boats all year round and some who stay for long stretches. A few rentals and houseboats. Good afternoon, Mrs. Yamishimi!" Frankie yelled and she and Mandy waved to the small, dark-haired woman watering a colorful array of flowers in window boxes. "The only person in Butterfly Harbor who can give Lori Knight or Calliope Costas a run for their money where gardening is concerned. Her late husband used to be caretaker for the town's parks and golf course before he passed away."

Mrs. Yamishimi waved back before stepping inside the two-story houseboat. The structure was charming, painted in grays and blues, with lots of windows and stained glass and a back-deck patio filled with greenery and what looked like comfy furniture.

"We don't lock off the marina. It's open twenty-four seven. The sheriff's station is on the hill there, about halfway between the main thoroughfare and the Flutterby." A small group had clustered around a shedlike building at the top of the dock. Laminated posters listing the various tours and activities Wind Walkers offered shone against the afternoon sun. "Looks like there're two boats out now, right, Man?"

"*Star Dancer* and *Sun Catcher*," Mandy confirmed. "David has a dive group today and Faith was scheduled for a round trip to San Francisco."

"Busy season?" Sienna asked.

"Not by half," Frankie confirmed as she slid *Phoenix* effortlessly into the slip and killed the engine. Mandy hopped out and tied them on. "Summer's the busiest, of course, but we're pretty steady during the year. Gotta love California weather. Another boat's going to be great. Especially one with extended overnight potential. It's what Monty's been wanting to do for a while. Why don't you leave your stuff here for now. We'll get it after lunch."

"All right." Sienna set down the bags she'd been gathering and followed Frankie and Mandy up the gangway and onto dry land. Within minutes she found herself standing behind a waist-high stone wall that divided the street on the other side from the marina and the beach. She shielded her eyes, looked up one way, then down the other, enjoying the beautiful view of ocean mingling with small-town life.

"So this is Monarch Lane," Frankie told her as they headed for the street. "It can pretty much get you anywhere you need in town. Up that way is the Flutterby." She pointed to the right. "A little beyond is Calliope's farmer's market and her home, Duskywing Farm."

"You have to go there on a Friday or Saturday for the market," Mandy gushed. "Well, anytime, really, but the market's amazing. And it's the best place this time of year to see any butterflies. It's off-season right now, but Calliope always has some." She shrugged as if the information was a given. "That's where I have my birthday party every year."

"And if you keep going up that road about another half mile or so, that's where they're building the sanctuary."

"That's where the accident happened," Sienna said.

"Yeah," Frankie replied with a quick glance at Mandy. "So you can see here, it's what we call downtown. Lots of stores and places to eat. Touristy and local businesses. Go down two blocks and turn right and you'll find the bookstore."

"My dad owns that," Mandy added. "And right nearby is Chrysalis Bakery."

"They're doing your cake," Sienna remarked.

"Yep. I've left it in Gale's very capable hands, but she'll understand if you want to check in. Okay, enough of me playing tour guide." Frankie clapped her hands together. "Let's eat."

Sienna checked the traffic before they crossed the Lane. A smattering of cars were parked along both sides of the road. She spotted people down at the beach, enjoying the cool but sunny day. There was no missing the Butterfly Diner, with its bright monarch butterfly decorations around the metal and glass doorframe. It looked as if the 1950s had plopped one of its iconic diners right in the middle of town, except the decor was done in white, black and orange. The second Frankie pushed open the door, Sienna took a deep breath and nearly passed out in delight.

Suddenly she wanted anything and everything on the menu.

"Take a seat wherever, Frankie!" A tall woman with a long ponytail called as she passed with a pot of coffee in each hand. "Mandy, you staying or going?"

"Going, please."

"See Twyla at the counter with your order."

A bell clanged from the kitchen. Sienna liked the crowded diner instantly, seeing faces of all shapes, hues and ages happily engaged in conversation or eating.

"There's a booth at the window." Frankie steered Sienna to the right. Pretty soon Sienna had a mug of steaming hot coffee in one hand and a laminated menu in the other. "I know it sounds typical, but everything's good. Especially the pies. Holly makes them from scratch every day. Hey, Holl." She smiled up at the woman who had greeted them upon their arrival.

"Finally got a day off, huh, Frankie?"

"Yup. This is Sienna Fairchild. Sienna,

Holly Saxon. She's been running this place for years."

"I'm thirtysomething, not eighty." Holly greeted Sienna warmly. "You'd be Frankie's wedding planner."

"Ah, yes. That'd be me." She gulped. "How did you know?"

"Small town," Holly said, as if that explained everything. "Feel free to meet anyone you need to here. Happy to set you up with a booth if you want them to come to you. Anything we can do to make Frankie and Roman's wedding easier."

"I appreciate that," Sienna said. "The food smells amazing." The combination of hot oil, sizzling meat and fresh-baked pies reached out and caught her by the nose.

"Thanks," Holly said. "We try. You want a minute with the menu?"

"Ah, no, actually." She ordered the chicken-salad sandwich while Frankie got a burger and a side of onion rings.

"To share," Frankie said when Holly left with their order. "You're going to save me from myself, but I can't resist those rings."

"Is everyone so…friendly?" Sienna asked.

Frankie shrugged, then waved to Mandy, who was looking around for them. She slid over when Mandy joined them. "We try to be. Just a quick rundown that might help. If you want the most reliable information in town—"

"Gossip," Mandy corrected.

"Tomato, to-mah-to," Frankie said with a grin. "Then you go to the hardware store. Harvey Mills knows everything that goes on with everybody."

"Everything?" Suddenly Sienna wasn't so sure about how she was going to fit in, what with her recently hightailing it out of a yacht club wedding.

"It'll be a good few days before people know about…well." Mandy leaned across the table. "How you ended up on Monty's boat."

"As far as anyone knows, you're a friend who's come to give me a hand with my wedding," Frankie said. "That won't last, of course, so just be prepared. Especially once… wow." Frankie sank back in her seat and stared over Sienna's head as the door chimed. "I swear that woman's got radar. She knows when I'm even thinking about her."

"Who?" Sienna turned as Mandy leaped out of her seat to hug the woman who approached. Given the age and description she'd heard from Monty, along with the slightly sucker-punched expression on Frankie's face, there was only one person this could be. Frankie's future mother-in-law, Ezzie Salazar. Ezzie wasn't that much taller than Mandy, but her teased black hair added a good few inches in height. With an oversized handbag that could probably supply an army infantry division, this was a woman who looked like she could take on any situation and win.

"Oh, my girl." Ezzie rocked Mandy back and forth until Mandy laughed. "How are you doing? I heard Kyle's doing better. How about you?" She released Mandy but clasped her face between her hands. "You hanging in there?"

"I'm good, thanks. I'm going to the hospital now and taking him one of Holly's mocha shakes. Ezzie, this is Sienna."

"Nice to meet you." Sienna held out a hand that was promptly ignored as Ezzie dropped into the seat beside her. The next thing Sienna knew, she was wrapped in a hug so tight she couldn't breathe.

"You are going to make my boy's wedding come off without a hitch." Ezzie patted her on the back. "Thank you so much. Frankie's told me everything. I don't want you to worry about a thing." It was Sienna's turn to have her face caught as Ezzie looked at her as if assessing her. "I am here to assist in any way you may need."

"Ah, Ezzie?" Frankie reached across the table to grab the older woman's arm. "Please don't scare Sienna off her first day on the job."

Sienna found herself laughing and waving off Frankie's concern. "It's fine, Frankie, don't worry." It wasn't the caterer or the cake or the wedding arrangements Frankie needed the most help with. It was Ezzie. "I'm so glad I met you first. I'm sure I'll have to have help getting acclimated and figuring out the logistics and details. I bet you're the perfect person to help with that."

"Oh, I am, I am. What can I do?"

"Let's talk first and go over the list Frankie sent me. How's your schedule tomorrow morning?"

"I'm with the Cocoon Club in the morning. At their place. Would you mind coming there?"

"I'll probably need a few hours with you. How's eight?"

"Eight is perfect. I'll fix breakfast. Oh, this is perfect, isn't it, Frankie?"

"So far," Frankie agreed, looking a bit shell-shocked. When Ezzie focused again on

Mandy, Frankie leaned closer to Sienna. "I can give you a white flag when you're ready to surrender."

Sienna shook her head and smiled. Granted, she hadn't worked with Roman's mother yet, but she loved the enthusiasm. Not to mention the open affection Ezzie Salazar had for her future daughter-in-law. She'd worked on enough charity committees with her grandmother that she knew how to manage even the most demanding and difficult personalities. At least Ezzie led with a smile.

"We'll do fine, don't worry. Oh, wow. Is that my lunch?" She watched Holly set down the plate filled to brimming with her sandwich and fries, and then Frankie's burger. The onion-ring tower practically reached Sienna's shoulder. She plucked one of the small rings free and popped it into her mouth, earning a smile of approval from Ezzie. "If the town is in need of a new fitness instructor, have I got a bird for you."

FRANKIE HAD SPOKEN the truth. Monty had overestimated how long the repairs to the boat were going to take. He tended to overestimate how long anything was going to take so as not to disappoint anyone, just in case.

The fact that he had the engine humming better than ever a few short hours after Sienna had left on *Phoenix* did seem a little like the universe was giving him a solid kick.

He closed up the hatch, grabbed his toolbox and headed to the electrical panel. He'd been postponing a more intense inspection until he had the time and the right instruments. Now it seemed as if he had both in abundance.

He could smell jasmine in the air when he stepped into the hallway. The scent of Sienna's skin and shampoo clung to what felt like every molecule on the boat. So much for being alone. Sienna remained all around him. He could hear her laugh and sense her presence as if she was quietly reading. He could, he supposed, pretend she was in her cabin, behind that closed door.

Irritation prickled his skin. What was wrong with him? He loved being out on the water, on his own, with only the ocean and sky as his companions. It was his refuge, his happy place. His reminder that all was right in his world. She couldn't have replaced that peace in only a few days.

Could she?

"Not if I don't let her," he muttered, then started when a streak of green soared in through the open hatch. Duchess settled on the counter, talons gripping the edge of the Formica, and watched him. "What's up, bird?"

"Squawk. Guaca-mooleee!"

Monty flipped open the metal panel and shone his flashlight on the connections. "You're supposed to be self-sufficient. And I'm not the new guy, remember. No guaca-mole for you."

"Nice flat back."

"I can't believe I'm spending my evening conversing with a bird." But he did just that as he examined the wiring, replacing what he could, making note of what needed to be addressed once he was in Butterfly Harbor.

Once he was satisfied with the job, he closed the panel and faced Duchess, who had fallen asleep where she was perched. She woke up, though, when he latched his tool-box and stashed it on the floor by the cabinet.

"Guaca-moleeee."

Monty snorted. "All right. Let's see what we've got for you." He bent down to check the refrigerator's contents. Something inside him tugged when he noticed the vegetables had been neatly arranged into containers, with a few salads already made up. He pulled one out, a smile playing across his mouth as he read the note Sienna had left.

"Eat before junk." Monty set the salad on the counter.

"You got this." Duchess clicked her beak.

"Don't worry." He pulled out another container, popped open the lid and set it on the counter by the bird. "She didn't forget you." Duchess lowered her beak into the fruit-and-nut selection, then gobbled down the blueberries and cut-up strawberries one by one.

He made himself a sandwich to go with the salad, eating at the table, unable to concentrate on his book. Easily distracted, irritatingly frustrated, he carried his beer back up on deck, where he sat down to watch the end of the sunset.

Even that didn't bring him much calm. He missed her.

Far more than he expected. Exponentially more than he wanted to. And so much that he considered turning on the engine and heading for home while it was still dark.

He wouldn't. Not yet. As much as he wanted to see Sienna again, they needed this time apart. She needed to see what the world had to offer outside the bubble of *Nana's Dream* and he needed to distance himself so that when he got back to his town, his home, it wasn't tainted by memories of her.

Things would be different once he got to town. As welcoming as Butterfly Harbor was, the novelty and shininess would wear off for her soon enough. A woman who had seen so much of the world wouldn't be content in his little corner of it.

One of those lies Frankie predicted he'd tell himself, Monty supposed. But it was one he could live with. It would soften the blow for whatever was going to happen.

He settled in on the deck of *Dream*, sipping his beer, Duchess perched on the railing beside him, and drifted off to sleep beneath the rising moon.

And dreamed of going home to Sienna.

CHAPTER FIFTEEN

"NANA, YOU ARE most definitely looking out for me." Sienna stood at the giant window in her room at the Flutterby Inn admiring the ocean in all its sun-setting glory. She'd thought that first morning she'd awoken on *Dream* had been the start of something new, but she'd been wrong. Today, this moment, watching the end of her first day in Butterfly Harbor, was her new life starting.

She'd stayed in countless hotels and inns all over the world, most of them the best money could buy. But few had the cozy, homey atmosphere of the Flutterby Inn. The beacon of Butterfly Harbor was the perfect mix of old-fashioned hospitality outfitted with all the markings of a contemporary, comfortable escape.

Sienna unlatched and pushed open the window, then stretched as the cool evening air hit her. There was so much she wanted to see tomorrow, so many people to meet and talk with. She had a two-page list that had to be dealt with before Frankie left for her conference or, more importantly, felt more at ease.

But first, she had to make a call.

She picked up the pay-as-you-go cell phone she'd bought at one of the stores after lunch and made the only call she could think of to get her life back on track. Her hands trembled as she dialed. And waited.

"Hello?"

"Tabitha? It's Sienna. I'm sorry if I'm calling during dinner."

"Sienna?" Her cousin shrieked so loud Sienna had to hold her phone away from her ear. "Where are you? Are you all right? Are you hurt?"

"Tab, I'm fine." To prove it to herself, she leaned against the window frame and continued to look out at the ocean. "I promise. I haven't been kidnapped or any of those ridiculous claims they ran in the paper. I am safe and sound." More importantly, she was happy.

"But your father…" Tabitha trailed off. "If you aren't in any trouble, why would he tell us—?"

"To save Richard any embarrassment, I'm sure," Sienna said. "And before you say anything, I know I shouldn't have handled things the way I did. Running away like that was wrong. I just… I couldn't breathe, Tab. Marrying Richard wasn't the right thing to do. I don't love him." She didn't much like him, either. When Tabitha remained silent, Sienna took a deep breath. "You don't understand, do you?"

"No," Tabitha said, as if coming out of a trance. "I don't."

"Well, the good news is, you don't have to." Sienna was determined to keep this conversation positive.

"If everything's fine, why are you calling me?"

"Because I'm hoping you'll do me a favor. I need a few things from my house, including my purse and cell phone. Can you overnight them to me if I give you an address?"

"Sure, yes. I guess. But…" She trailed off again, as if distracted.

"Tab? Is everything okay?" When Sienna heard what she thought were other voices in the background, she could have kicked herself. "Are you alone, Tabitha? Or is someone there with you?"

Another delay. "No, I'm here. What all do you want me to send you?"

Sienna told her the items, then added the Flutterby's address. "One more favor, Tab?"

"Uh-huh."

"Please don't tell anyone where I am. I'm not ready to see people, especially Richard or my father. It's important, Tab. Promise me you won't tell." When Tabitha didn't answer, Sienna pushed harder. "Tabitha? Please."

"All right. You swear you're all right? That man didn't hurt you, did he?"

"Monty could never hurt anyone," Sienna assured her. "In fact, if it wasn't for him, I don't think I'd know which end was up. I'll be back in San Diego soon. In time for my birthday."

"In time to claim your inheritance," Tabitha said with her usual touch of disdain. Sienna didn't have time for Tabitha's attitude. "I guess I'll see you then. I'll get this stuff sent out in the morning."

"Thanks, Tab. You're a lifesaver. I have to go. I'll talk to you later."

"Bye." Tabitha clicked off before Sienna could.

"Strange, that cousin of mine," she whispered at her phone before she headed into the bathroom to change for bed.

"I BROUGHT YOU a surprise." On time the next morning for their appointment, Sienna held up a pink bakery box to show Ezzie.

She'd found the town's oldest Victorian

home as easily as expected thanks to the morning desk receptionist. Willa McNeill gave excellent directions. The added bonus of a walk up and down the side streets of town only elevated Sienna's already cheery mood. It was an architectural fan's dream with a variety of design structures mingling among one another. One of her favorite houses was most definitely the bright yellow English-inspired cottage with a large carved wooden door and a stained glass window of a monarch butterfly above it.

Her morning had gotten off to a brilliant start when she'd met chef Jason Corwin at breakfast at the inn. Their quick discussion about the catering for Frankie's wedding was a good intro and an excellent first step in getting her wedding ducks in a row.

She'd even made Chef Corwin blush with her fangirling, something that had delighted his sweet and very pregnant wife to no end. Abby Corwin, the manager of the Flutterby, was anxious to hear if the inn had met Sienna's expectations. Sienna had been thrilled to let her know they'd been exceeded. Monty hadn't been wrong. His town was charming, as were the people who lived here.

As positive a start as she'd had, even more

progress was made at the Chrysalis Bakery. Hence the box in her hand.

Standing on the front porch of the home of the infamous Cocoon Club, Sienna's smile grew brighter when Ezzie looked suspiciously at the box. "You didn't have to bring anything, Sienna." Ezzie stepped back and waved her inside. "I've taken care of breakfast, remember?"

"Oh, this isn't breakfast." She lowered her voice and glided the box in front of Ezzie's nose. "It's a wedding cake sample."

"It is not!" Ezzie gasped. She reached for the box, but Sienna snatched it away. "How'd you ever do it? I've been begging Gale to tell me what she had planned for weeks!"

"So I heard," Sienna said with a sly grin. "I'll just say I can be very persuasive when I need to be. Oh, hello." As she looked down the hall, she spotted two women, both on the far side of seventy, with curious albeit suspicious gazes pinned on her.

The *clomp, clomp* behind her was accompanied by the distinctive sound of a rubber-footed and squeaky-wheeled walker. She shifted and smiled at the elderly stooped man standing behind her. "And hello to you, as well."

The old man's eyes narrowed as he moved closer. He inched up his chin so he could see into her face. "You'd be this runaway bride we've heard about then?"

Sienna's face went hot. "Um."

"Oscar, behave yourself," Ezzie ordered and patted him on the shoulder. "Oscar Bedemeyer, this is Sienna Fairchild. And you know very well she's helping Frankie with her wedding."

"What was wrong with the groom?" One of the women came forward, her bright orange hair striking a match of color in the room. "He some kind of doofus?"

How did she answer that? "Ah, not really."

"All of you, behave," Ezzie ordered, only to be interrupted by the whizzing of a wheelchair exploding out of one of the side rooms. "Alice, now remember your speed limit!"

Alice brought her wheelchair to a screeching halt right at Sienna's toes. Alice's slight frame shook with what Sienna recognized as Parkinson's tremors. "It's nice to meet you, Alice. Oscar." She nodded to each, then to the redheaded woman. "And you are?"

"Myra. This is Eloise," she said and pointed to the woman behind her. "And that's Harold.

Over there's Elliot and Penny. You can remember her because of her big boo—"

"All right, that's enough," Ezzie called
over her shoulder. "Sienna, you can join me
in here. We have work to do," she told the
others. "Interrogation may commence once
we're done."

"Interrogation?" Sienna swallowed hard
and clutched her bakery box to her chest.
"Oh, that won't be necessary, I'm sure."

"I'm betting he was a doofus," Myra declared and led the others away. "Come on,
Alice. Your speedway awaits! Ezzie, we're
going to take our morning constitutional."

Alice gave Sienna a shaky smile. "Nice to
meet you."

"You, too." Sienna stepped back so Alice
could join the rest of her group as they put
on their jackets and scarves. Not that they
needed them. The weather had been nice
enough for Sienna to leave her sweater back
at the inn. When the door closed behind her
and Ezzie, she breathed an unexpected sigh
of relief.

"They're exhausting, I know." Ezzie waved
her forward. "Come on. We've got work to do.
And you have an escape to make. They won't

return until close to eleven. They're going to the diner for breakfast."

"On their own? Are they—?"

"One thing you never tell the Cocoon Club is that they're too old to do anything. If they can't make the walk back, Holly will call me and I'll run down in the van. Now." She clapped her hands together and licked her lips. "Let's open that box and see what Frankie and Roman are getting for their cake."

"WHAT DO YOU mean all my accounts have been frozen?" It took all of Sienna's control not to yell at the bank manager on the other end of the call.

After a productive morning that had her marking off half her to-do list, she'd picked up lunch from the diner and headed to the marina. Catering, check. Cake, double check. Seating arrangements, in progress, and in Ezzie's capable hands since she was better acquainted with the residents than Sienna. The confusion about the cost of the rental tables and chairs had been remedied, but she still had to confirm a schedule with the linen suppliers and the backup tents in case of rain. She also needed to check in with city hall to verify the park had been blocked out for the wedding and any permits they might need were securely in place. After that, it was the little stuff, including helping a still flu-ridden Brooke Evans with the upcoming bridal shower in a few days. Frankie Bettencourt's wedding, it seemed, was coming along great.

Just as Sienna's life continued to fall apart.

She'd hoped for peace and quiet out by the water and instead was becoming a noise hazard herself. "Who authorized freezing my bank accounts?"

"It was by court order, Ms. Fairchild."

Sienna could tell by the way the bank manager said her name he wasn't entirely convinced that's whom he was speaking to. "Well, unfreeze them."

"I'm afraid I can't do that, ma'am. Not until we have an order reversing the request."

"I'm the only one on the accounts," Sienna insisted. "How can anyone have the authority to…?" The thoughts spinning through her mind came to a skidding halt. "My father." The kidnapping report in the paper suddenly made so much more sense. "Okay. Okay." She took a cleansing breath, pinched her nose and stepped to the side as she spotted Mrs. Yamishimi headed in her direction. "Tell me this. No one else has been given access to the account, have they?"

"I'm afraid I'm not able to discuss this matter except in person."

"Oh, for the love of frogs, it's me. You're talking to *me*. Me. Sienna Fairchild." She rattled off her personal information much to the disapproval of Mrs. Yamishimi, who seemed apparently in no hurry to get home. "You're telling me you can't discuss my own account with me?"

"Not at this time, ma'am. Not without visual confirmation of your identity. Or a certified letter from your legal representative. You may call back once you have all that lined up."

Sienna let out a growl and stomped her feet as the line went dead. Just as her independence had started taking shape, she had the financial doors slammed in her face. Her father. Again. Why was he so determined to keep her in check now?

Now, when she wanted to be able to at least pay back Monty for the expenses he'd incurred since she'd stowed away on his boat. She didn't like the idea of being beholden to anyone, let alone someone…

"Oh, boy." Let alone someone she'd fallen

in love with. "Why, oh, why do I always have the absolute worst timing on the planet?" She pressed a hand to her cheek and faced the only person nearby. Mrs. Yamishimi. The Asian woman with silver-streaked dark hair tilted her head and offered an understanding smile. Mrs. Yamishimi patted the paper bag in her hand. "Come with me. We'll have tea."

"Oh, no, thank you, but I can't. I have—" Errands to run. People to meet. And she needed to catch up with Frankie before dinner and give her an update.

"You have time to accept that which you're afraid of. Come along." With her bright white athletic shoes, baggy sweatpants and matching pink hoodie, she headed down the curving road to the private residences located at the marina. "Come, come."

As if caught under some spell, Sienna did as she was told and soon found herself enchanted once again by the sight of the houseboat Mrs. Yamishimi called home. "It really does look like a house."

"My late father-in-law designed and built it for a wedding gift for myself and my husband. Shoes off, please."

"Oh, yes, of course." Inside the sliding glass door, she quickly slipped out of her shoes. The two-story structure was both spacious and cozy, with several windows to allow for a generous amount of natural light. Decorated in soft creams and grays, there wasn't a lot of furniture that wasn't service-able, and it was all practical and neatly ar-ranged. Clutter was kept to a minimum and the framed photographs along one shelf de-picted a full life well lived. A collection of potted orchids lined a narrow path between the entryway and kitchen.

"Tea is already steeping," Mrs. Yamishimi told her as Sienna wound her way into the kitchen.

She stopped almost immediately, trans-fixed by the view in front of her. The entire back of the house was glass. A sliding door was the only break and led out to the lush patio Sienna had seen from the *Phoenix* yes-terday. Tears burned her eyes and she blinked them back.

"Your home is stunning," she whispered. More than stunning. It was perfect. "I'm sorry," she said at Mrs. Yamishimi's inquisi-tive look. "I was thinking about a trip I took to Japan with my grandmother. There was a village on the coast. About the size of But-terfly Harbor, I think. The entire shoreline was filled with homes just like this beside the ocean. Not quite as many windows, but the feel..." She pressed a hand against her chest. "I'd forgotten about that trip. Thank you for the memory."

"You are most welcome." Mrs. Yamishimi led her to a table. "I have many memories, too. My husband and I raised three children in this house. They've all moved on. Have homes and families of their own." Where Sienna expected sadness she found only joy on the older woman's wrinkled face. "Lives are for living, are they not?"

Sienna nodded. "Yes, I've come to understand that."

Tea was poured. The paper bag Mrs. Yamishimi was carrying was opened and cookies were put on plates retrieved from the cabinet. "Gale makes me special tea biscuits once a week. We will share."

Touched, Sienna smiled. "Thank you." She opened her takeaway box from the diner and offered the same. "Where do your children live now?"

"My youngest is in Seattle. In a house not too dissimilar to this one. He and my daughter-in-law are expecting their first baby in June."

"That's wonderful." Growing up, she'd

been one of those girls who had an entire nursery filled with baby dolls. Probably because she'd been so lonely as an only child. She wanted kids. At least, she thought she did. Did Monty want them?

The image of him leaped to her mind. Monty. That lump in her throat was back; the one that had formed while she'd been on the phone with the bank. It had only been a day since she'd left him out on the boat, but she missed him so much she ached. "How long were you married?"

"Forty-three years." The misty expression in Mrs. Yamishimi's eyes had Sienna swallowing hard. "There's not a day that goes by that I don't miss him. He is a part of me." She tapped a hand against her chest. "I knew, from the moment we met, that he was for me."

"I thought that only happened in storybooks," Sienna said softly.

Mrs. Yamishimi smiled. "When you know, you know. Life gives us signs. They lead us where we need to be at just the right moment. My Henry." She shook her head. "We did not have enough time together. But maybe…" She looked around her home, a smile curving her lips. "I think perhaps I've been given another sign. Thank you, Sienna."

"You know who I am?" She set down her half sandwich and reached for her tea. "How?"

"Small town," Mrs. Yamishimi laughed. "It will take you time to get used to it, but soon all will settle down. Yes." She lifted her sandwich. "All will settle down for you very soon."

THE SOLITUDE OF Mrs. Yamishimi's houseboat almost had Sienna forgetting there was a world outside. Few places had ever brought her as much peace; the only other being her nana's beach house in San Diego.

At Mrs. Yamishimi's urging, she'd accepted another cup of tea, and brought out her wedding-planning notebook on the deck, where she now sat surrounded by a forest of planted fauna that reminded her of the cantina in Plover Bay. The water lapped gently and beneath the scent of the ocean, she inhaled the calming aromas of jasmine and lavender.

Reorganizing and updating her notes for Frankie's wedding, Sienna found herself feeling quite at home in the little town. Whatever effort or stress she felt over the meetings and details faded away, and she found she was truly enjoying the prospect of bringing

Frankie and Roman's nuptials to fruition. Problems were a challenge, not an obstacle, and she liked the idea of rising to them.

"You look at home here."

Sienna glanced up as Mrs. Yamishimi joined her. "I feel at home. The tea is delicious."

"Would you like more?"

"No, thank you." Sienna closed her binder and sat back, gazing at the calm ocean. "I don't know how you don't just sit here all day. It's lovely."

"This was Henry's and my favorite place in all of Butterfly Harbor." She offered a sad smile. "And it was just for the two of us. Tell me something." Mrs. Yamishimi sat in the chair beside her. "What do you see out there?"

Sienna smiled. "Endless possibilities."

Tears glistened in the older woman's eyes. She reached over and laid her hand over Sienna's. Not so far away, the blare of a police siren broke the peace.

"Well, that doesn't happen very often." Mrs. Yamishimi rose and peered toward the marina's entrance. "And that's not any of our sirens."

"Maybe the sheriff or fire department has a new vehicle?"

"Doubtful. That would cost a fair amount of money," Mrs. Yamishimi said with a twist of her mouth. "Our mayor isn't exactly generous when it comes to things like that. You've heard about our mayor, Gil Hamilton, I suppose?"

"Monty mentioned him." And she'd gotten an earful just from smatterings of conversations she'd overheard at the diner. "He seems popular, but for the wrong reasons."

"I always thought he had promise. With all these shenanigans lately, I'm not so sure anymore. I voted for him. Believed he got a raw deal because of who his father was. But now, with this horrible collapse at the sanctuary building site and the recall election, I don't know what to think."

"There's someone running against him in the recall election, isn't there?"

"Leah Ellis, yes." Mrs. Yamishimi sat up, but the frown was still in place. "She's a terrific young woman. Lawyer, who took over her uncle's practice a couple of years ago. Do you know, she helped me rewrite my will? Barely charged me enough for the ink in her printer. She's got that mayor of ours in her sights. And I don't mean for anything good.

She wants him gone just as much as the rest of us."

"Too bad you have to wait until November to vote."

"Oh, it's all but decided. Gil knows it. He's just pretending he doesn't. That's not to say he hasn't done some good for the town. He has. But he's also added to the damage his father did. Hamilton Senior had his hand in more tills in this town than the tax man. Dozens of families had to walk away from their homes because of him calling in loans and refusing to refinance when the housing market began to tank. Just turned a blind eye. Nasty business that was."

"But the town's doing better now, isn't it? Monty said a lot more businesses are open and homes are selling again. Surely some credit has to go to Gil?"

"I suppose." Mrs. Yamishimi didn't look convinced. "Have you met him yet? The mayor?"

"I've not had the pleasure."

"Well, you make certain not to let him charm you too much, Sienna. That boy." She shook her head. "The sooner he's out of office, the better, if you ask me. Now, look there. There's a new one." Mrs. Yamishimi shielded her eyes and turned her attention to the horizon. "She's a beauty, isn't she?"

Sienna's heart skipped a beat as she followed her new friend's gaze to *Nana's Dream* making her way slowly toward the marina. Inching out from behind the cliffs to the Flutterby, the gleaming, polished white wood looked like history moving across the water. "That's Monty's new boat. He's back."

"Well, don't just sit there. Go welcome him home. Go on. It's time for my afternoon nap, anyway. Just promise you'll come back and see me again."

Sienna stood. "I promise. Thank you for inviting me into your home. It's beautiful. And so are you." She bent down and kissed the old woman's cheek.

She retrieved her shoes, then quickly made her way up the dock and along Monarch Lane to the commercial area of the marina. She stood there and watched as Monty steered *Dream* into an empty slip at the far end. A group of men headed directly toward him, some she didn't recognize. Her stomach dropped. She twisted around and saw a state police vehicle parked askew, lights still spinning. No one was inside.

Because two officers were standing ready. Their hands on their weapons.

Just as Sienna moved to follow them, an SUV with Butterfly Harbor Sheriff's Department written on the side stopped and parked far more carefully. The two men who stepped out were tall and impressive, and had all-business expressions that sent more warning bells off in Sienna's brain.

"Excuse me, what's going on?" Sienna asked as she hurried over to greet them.

The taller of the two men pushed up his baseball cap that had BHPD embroidered on the front. "Nothing dangerous, ma'am. Just responding to a request for jurisdictional assistance with regard to one of our residents."

Sienna looked over to *Dream*. "You don't mean Monty Bettencourt, do you?"

The other officer leaned against the SUV and folded his arms. "Do you know Monty?"

"I do. And you do, too. You're Holly's husband, Sheriff Saxon, aren't you?" She addressed the man in the baseball cap. "I'm Sienna Fairchild."

"Sienna Fairchild." He offered his hand even as he grinned. "I'd heard you were in town. I can't tell you how good it is to meet you. And to see you. Deputy Fletcher Bradley, this is Sienna Fairchild."

Bright blue eyes sparkled when Fletcher smiled. Sienna blinked quickly. Goodness. The men in this town were certainly... She blew out a breath. Well, they were all something to look at, that was for sure.

"I've never seen a kidnapping victim look so good," Deputy Bradley said. "Or so free. You have perfect timing, ma'am. I'm pleased to meet you."

What on earth were they talking about? "What's going on?" Sienna asked again.

"Well, normally I'd say I couldn't talk about it, but seeing as you're involved with all this, I can. It's best you come with us. After you, ma'am."

"Sienna, please, Sheriff."

The sheriff nodded. "And you can call me Luke. Now, let's go see what mess Monty's gotten himself into."

CHAPTER SIXTEEN

"Four, three, two, one—"

"Stop the clock, Duchess." Monty felt *Dream* knock gently against the dock and breathed a sigh of relief. He was home. After wiping the back of his arm across his brow, he turned off the engine and jumped off to tie down the boat. Duchess followed, hopping from railing to railing and, of all things, humming to herself in much the same way Sienna did.

Sienna. He'd missed her. Missed talking with her, laughing with her. He missed looking at her. Not long ago, he'd treasured his time alone out on the sea, just him and the ocean tangling together as he rode the waves. But the last day of this trip had definitely felt…well, empty without her. Maybe he'd been wrong to push her away. Or maybe he was simply anxious to see how she'd settled into his little town.

Could she be happy with him? With the

life and business he already had mapped out for himself? Couples should have shared dreams, couples like Frankie and Roman. But Sienna loved the ocean and being on the water. Maybe that was enough?

Footsteps pounded on the dock. Half expecting Sebastian or Roman, he shielded his eyes and stood up. Finding Vincent Fairchild and Richard Somersby flanked by two uniformed officers immediately darkened his homecoming. "Gentlemen. I'm getting a sense of déjà vu." Monty moved back onto the boat, but stepped forward to greet them. "Get that court order did you, Richard?"

"Mr. Bettencourt, if you'd please join us on the dock?" One of the state patrol officers gestured to him. "We have a warrant for your arrest."

Monty almost laughed. Until he saw the second officer's hand resting on the butt of his sidearm. He did as was requested, but not silently. "What's going on? What's the charge?"

"Kidnapping, to start with," Richard said with a smug expression of satisfaction. "I'm betting we can come up with a few more charges yet."

"You have got to be kidding me." Monty

sighed. "Seriously? Oh, no, come on." Monty's temper flared as the click of handcuffs echoed in his ears as the metal cinched around his wrists. Duchess squawked loud enough for Monty to wince. "I've got friends and neighbors watching this, not to mention customers." Sure enough, he could see people streaming out of shops and the diner and heading for the dock. Forget the charges. With the way the Butterfly Harbor rumor mill ran, he'd be the topic of discussion for the next decade.

"Sergeant O'Brien."

Monty wanted to cheer at the sound of Sheriff Luke Saxon's voice. "Luke, you gotta tell these guys what a crock this is. I didn't kidnap anyone."

"Of course, you didn't." The female voice snapped through the air and had Monty alternately thankful yet groaning silently. "Take those cuffs off him."

"Sienna…"

"Don't 'Sienna' me," she growled, pushing herself between Luke and Sergeant O'Brien. "There's been no kidnapping."

"Sienna! You're all right." Richard lunged for her and wrapped his arms around her to the point that she almost disappeared. "I've been so worried about you."

Sienna stood stiff in her fiancé's arms, her gaze flicking to Monty first and then to her father. "I saw your concern splashed all over the local papers. Your concern, too, Dad."

"Sienna." The flash of relief in Vincent Fairchild's eyes took Monty by surprise. He must have really thought Sienna was in danger. "I'm glad to see you are unharmed."

"Certainly, I'm unharmed. I can look after myself." She wedged her hands against Richard's shoulders. "Wasn't it clear that I wanted a break? I didn't attend my own wedding! Let go of me, Richard. I'm perfectly fine." She shoved him away. "I went with Mr. Bettencourt on my own volition. If anything, he has a case against me for hijacking his boat."

"Sienna," Monty warned. "This isn't a joke. Don't make this worse."

"I told you to take those cuffs off him," Sienna ordered. "Luke, they have no right—"

"Begging your pardon, ma'am, but we have an arrest warrant right here." The second state officer faced Butterfly Harbor's sheriff. He held out a piece of paper.

"I don't care what that says," Sienna said. "I wasn't kidnapped. And if the supposed victim isn't willing to press charges, how can someone else?"

"Can we maybe do this someplace a little less public?" Monty asked from between gritted teeth. "Luke?"

Luke's lips twitched as he glanced over his shoulder and eyed the crowd that was gathering. "Since you probably don't want to be perp-walked through Butterfly Harbor, I think we can settle this now. Sienna, you are denying the charges that have been made against Mr. Bettencourt?"

"I am," she replied.

"You don't have to protect this man, Sienna. You're safe now," Richard urged and ran a hand down her hair as if trying to soothe her. "I'm sure Bettencourt had it all planned. Kidnap an heiress and make some fast cash. It all makes sense. Why else would you have disappeared before the wedding?"

"Get your hands off her, Richard."

The cool restraint in Monty's voice spoke to Sienna, who finally felt free of whatever obligation she might have been holding toward her fiancé.

"I ran away because I didn't want to marry you, Richard." Sienna lifted her hand and tugged at the ring on her finger, but it merely spun and didn't budge. "I ran away because I don't love you. I don't want a life with you.

Heck, I don't even like you. I know I should have said something sooner, and I am sorry about that. But I…" She looked to Monty. "But I wasn't brave enough then. Now I am." She grimaced and pulled harder on the emerald. "Oh, for crying out loud. Anyone have something to cut my finger off with?"

Monty chortled. Luke and Fletcher both grinned. The out-of-town officers looked… confused while Richard sputtered. Sienna's father, on the other hand, hadn't even blinked.

"That can't be right," Richard protested, his pale cheeks going drunk red. "You've let this man twist your feelings and thoughts, Sienna. Your father told me about what happened all those years ago, how fragile you are. Easily manipulated. Let's get you somewhere where you can think more clearly, away from other…*influences*."

Monty had never wanted to deck someone more in his entire life. "She's the least fragile person I've ever met!" Monty declared and earned a glance of appreciation from Sienna. Easily manipulated? Please. She might not know what direction she was headed, but she was certainly capable of figuring out how to get there. Richard was a fool. He didn't have the first clue about the woman he was supposed to have been marrying.

"Sienna, listen to reason." Vincent Fairchild's voice took on that placating, gentle tone Monty often associated with parents who were trying to hold on to their patience. "Richard and I only want—"

"I don't care what Richard wants," Sienna said, but Monty could see the hurt and disappointment in her eyes as she addressed her father. "I'm sorry, Dad. I know you needed this marriage to happen to save your business. I'd give anything not to throw you a curve any more than I always have, but you're asking me to give up my future to save a business. I can't—I won't marry Richard. Not ever. You just have to accept that."

Sienna shifted her attention to the state officers who had accompanied her so-called rescuers. "For the last time, get those handcuffs off Mr. Bettencourt," Sienna demanded, her glare sharpening as she stared at Sergeant O'Brien. "I'm the only one who can file a complaint and I won't. No harm was done to me. He was helping me get away from a difficult situation. If anything, he saved my life. Now let him go."

"Ma'am." Sergeant O'Brien gave her a short nod and unlocked the cuffs.

"This is so going in the town's newspaper," Fletcher Bradley laughed. "'Do-No-Wrong Monty Bettencourt Almost Arrested for Kidnapping a Runaway Bride.' I can see the headline now."

"Sergeant O'Brien, why don't you and your officer come back to the station with me?" Luke Saxon said. "We'll get this straightened out paperwork-wise and you can have a break. I bet you're needing one about now."

"Wait a minute!" Richard lunged at Sienna and grabbed her wrist, yanking her toward him.

Monty didn't have time to move. A flash of green and yellow exploded off the boat as Duchess squawked and shrieked. The parrot swooped in and locked her talons on Richard's shoulder, flapping her wings hard in his face.

"Grab the walnut!" the bird yelled as Richard let out what Monty could only describe as a cry for help. He released Sienna's hand and tried to bat away the bird. The man spun in circles, tripping over his own feet as he frantically tried to escape the bird. Twirling along the dock, he inevitably lost his footing, and as Duchess finally flew off, Richard toppled into the water.

"Oh, no!" Sienna ran ahead, skidding to a stop just as Monty caught up to her. They and the officers looked down to where Richard struggled to dog-paddle.

"Ah, man." Fletcher threw an irritated look at his boss when Luke gestured for him to help out Richard. Fletcher kicked off his shoes, dropped his belt and handed over his cell and wallet, then dived in in an attempt to save Richard and his dignity.

"That's pathetic," Monty muttered as Duchess returned to the boat, where she began humming to herself. Feeling partially caught up in an out-of-control Hollywood camp comedy, Monty let out a breath. "Sienna? You all right?"

"Fine." She nodded stiffly without looking at him. "I'm so sorry for all this, Monty. I hope you know I had nothing to do with it." She glared at her father, who seemed shocked.

"I do know that." Monty reached out for her, but she stepped away. "Sienna?"

She offered a weak smile. "If you don't need me for anything else, I'd like to go back to my room, Sheriff. Luke," she added when he started to correct her.

"That's fine. I know where to find you if I need any information."

She nodded.

"Sienna—" Vincent Fairchild caught her arm as she passed. "We need to talk."

Sienna looked down at his hand, then back up at him, and for the first time, Monty didn't see any emotion on her face at all. "There's nothing left to say, Dad."

"Wait, Sienna—" Vincent started after her, but Monty put himself between them.

"Let her go, Mr. Fairchild."

Now it was Monty's turn to seem shocked. What he saw was the face of a man coming to terms with what he'd nearly done to his only daughter. A man who looked, for want of a better term, lost.

"All right…" Fletcher grunted as he sloshed up onto the dock and dragged a waterlogged Richard Somersby behind him. "What are we doing with him?"

"Bring him to the station. He can dry out in one of our cells," Luke said. "We'll check with Sienna in a few hours to see if she wants to file assault charges against him."

"Assault? I didn't—" Richard's protests were cut off by a chest-deep coughing jag. He bent over, braced his hands on his knees and tried to breathe in and out slowly. "I want my ring back. And I want to call my lawyer."

"Mr. Fairchild?" Monty wasn't so sure he liked the older man's pale color. "Are you feeling okay?"

"Yes, yes." He wrapped his right hand around his upper left arm. "I'm sure I'm fine. Just need to get away from all this… excitement." He winced but not before panic flashed in his eyes.

"Luke!" Monty yelled. "I need some help here."

"No, it's fine," Mr. Fairchild wheezed. "I'll be okay. This isn't the first—"

"What's wrong?" Luke took one look at Vincent and pulled out his phone, then dialed 911. "Sir? Mr. Fairchild?"

"It'll pass. It always does. I just need to sit down for a moment," Vincent insisted, and motioned to the nearby bench.

Monty helped him while Luke spoke to Dispatch. "Frankie's coming. Ambulance will take longer. Budget cuts, remember," he added at Monty's wide-eyed stare. "It comes from the next town.

Monty looked back at Vincent. The man began to wheeze again and his complexion went grey. "I don't think we can wait. You've got a siren in your cruiser. You drive."

SIENNA DIDN'T DO as she'd said she was going to. She didn't return to the Flutterby. Instead, she found herself wandering up the hills of Butterfly Harbor, wedding binder clutched against her chest as if she was a wayward schoolgirl.

How did she even process what had just happened? Her father and fiancé had chased her down, labeled her confused and needing their direction, *still* wanting to marry her off. How…why? Did her father hate her so much that he didn't care she didn't want to marry Richard? Had her running away not given him pause that the marriage wasn't in the same stratosphere as a good idea?

What had she ever done to make her father dislike her so much?

She stopped to take a breath. The hill wasn't steep, but it was long and she wasn't exactly wearing walking shoes. To her left sat winding streets with those charming, unique houses, their yards exploding with spring colors and life. But the grove of thick eucalyptus and cypress trees to her right promised a forest of quiet.

It was all she could do not to dive into the trees. To hide. To try to come to terms with the lengths her father had been willing to go to get her out of his life, and into one he'd deemed suitable.

A sleek gray cat walked along the edge of the road. It stopped at the end of a wooden fence, hopped onto one of the posts and sat there, watching her. Welcoming the distraction, Sienna approached, slowly, so as not to spook her. She could hear the cat's purr before she even slid a hand down the feline's silky fur and in the distance, a soft tinkling of bells chimed in the air. "You're stunning, aren't you? What's your name? You're not a runaway." Sienna moved closer and the cat bumped its head against the binder. "Oh, no. You're well loved, aren't you?"

"She is most certainly that."

Sienna jumped.

"My apologies." The woman beside her offered a small smile. "I didn't mean to startle you. I thought perhaps Ophelia was coming to fetch someone, so I followed. You must be Sienna, Frankie's wedding planner."

"I, um, yes." Sienna offered her hand and found hers clasped between warm, gentle ones. "Sienna Fairchild." The woman's smile widened. She was extraordinary to look at. Tall, and curvy, with hair the color of fire done up in curls and braids with tiny bells and shells woven through. Her dress reminded Sienna of the endless green mountains of Ireland, and how it twirled around her legs exposed bare feet adorned with delicate chains and braided twine. Sienna found herself grinning. "You must be Calliope Costas. Monty told me about you."

Calliope inclined her head to confirm. "My sister, Stella, will be home from school soon and Xander is up at the construction site. I'd love the company." She didn't wait for Sienna to agree, but turned and wove her arm through Sienna's, leading her up the rest of the hill. "You come from the ocean. I can feel it in you. In your soul."

She…what? "I, well, I've been on Monty's boat for a few days. His new boat. *Nana's Dream.*"

"I cannot wait to see it." The dense trees behind the fence gave way to an abundant farm. Rows upon rows of fruits and vegetables were growing among one another. "You've had a difficult day. A rest and some organic lemonade will help."

"Oh, I don't want to impose."

"New friends are never an imposition." Calliope motioned for her to enter and called for Ophelia to proceed them through the swinging gate. "My door is always open. I have some lovely hibiscus lemonade my sister and I made last night."

Sienna had never stepped foot in a fairy world before now. The entire setting was picture-perfect. The stone cabin that sat at the end of the path was nestled among the fields, a beautiful herb garden and a neat yard filled with picnic tables and benches. Ribbons and lace tied to the posts of the front porch billowed in the breeze. Wind chimes rang, while crystals and bits of glass spun against the sunlight. The bright red door of Calliope's home solidified Sienna's suspicion about the woman's Celtic ancestry.

No wonder Frankie had decided to hold her bridal shower here. It was the perfect setting.

"Let's stay outside," Calliope suggested, and gestured to a small black iron table along the side of the cabin. "Please, sit. I'll be out in a moment."

Ophelia let out a soft meow and pranced on.

"Does anyone ever say no to her, Ophelia?"

Ophelia meowed again, then looked up into

the sky before darting off after a stray butterfly streaking through the air.

Sienna set down her purse and binder and sank into the padded chair. What had taken her so long, she wondered, to find the courage to stand up to her father? Doing so felt both exhilarating and exhausting, and left her with an almost hopeful buzz.

"Home is where you make it." Calliope had come around the corner with a wooden tray in her hands. "In case you're hungry. I have scones left from this morning. Rosemary and orange. And one of our first jars of honey." She poured Sienna a glass of lemonade, then sat.

The tart drink made her mouth tingle, but there was that faint hint of hibiscus and the ever-so-light touch of sweetness. "It's delicious."

"Stella is experimenting with her flavors. Lemonades and teas. She's hoping to sell lemonade this summer at our weekend market."

"Is she? You know, I was talking with Jason Corwin this morning about the catering for Frankie's wedding." How nice to have a distraction after the chaos at the marina. "He still hasn't decided on the drinks to serve beyond the open bar. Would you and Stella mind if I suggested this?" She drank more. "I know Frankie and Roman would like to include contributions from as many people as possible on their day."

"What a lovely thought. You can ask her yourself in a few minutes. Stella is very fond of Frankie."

"I assume the feeling is mutual since Stella is one of Frankie's flower girls. Oh, that reminds me. You're hosting Frankie's bridal shower this weekend, aren't you?"

"I am indeed. And I must admit, that was my real motive for seeking you out. I would very much appreciate your input on the event. And your help."

"Oh?" Sienna's eyebrows knitted. "But you don't even know me. Why would you—?"

"I believe people always find the right path for themselves. Eventually."

"Their path?" Sienna didn't understand.

"It's not always the one you expect to find, is it? Sometimes it simply presents itself."

Sienna pondered that and drank more of her lemonade. After drizzling her scone with honey, she said, "You certainly have an interesting communication style. You make it sound as if I've always been on my way here."

"Perhaps you have." Calliope settled in

her chair. "Butterfly Harbor is many things to many people, Sienna. But most of all, it's given so many a home, a place to belong. We're more than neighbors and patrons of businesses. We're a family. And we recognize one of our own." She frowned and touched a hand to her temple. "I'm sorry. Your difficult day is about to get more trying. Your phone."

"I turned it off," Sienna admitted. "After my bank hung up on me." The bank. She supposed she was going to have to hire an attorney.

"Yes. You need to turn it back on." Calliope sat forward and motioned to Sienna's bag. "Please."

"All right." She pulled out her phone and did as Calliope said. It started ringing immediately. The number wasn't familiar, but at Calliope's silent urging, she answered. "Hello?"

"Sienna, it's Frankie."

"Oh, hey, Frankie. I'm not late, am I?" She glanced at her watch. "I thought we were meeting at the firehouse before you left for San Francisco."

"Where are you? You need to get to the hospital."

"I'm at Calliope's. The hospital?" She

didn't like the tone in Frankie's voice. "What's going on?"

"It's your father. Monty took him into the ER with chest pains."

Sienna's ears roared. She tried to speak, tried to ask questions, but the fear that descended robbed her of anything other than panic.

"Sienna?"

"Yes." When she looked down at her shaking hand, she saw Calliope had taken hold and was squeezing tight. "How…?" She swallowed hard. "How bad is it?"

"I don't know. I just think you need to get over there fast. Now, Sienna."

MONTY STOOD JUST outside the curtained partition in the ER of Butterfly Harbor Memorial Hospital. He listened as Vincent Fairchild answered all the questions posed to him by nurses and then the attending physician, and Monty found himself wondering if Sienna was aware of her father's previous health issues.

He stepped back as they wheeled a cardiac monitor into the cubicle, then found himself shaking his head at Vincent's vociferous protests that soon died when the beeping on the monitor began sounding.

Paige Bradley, Deputy Fletcher Bradley's wife and the supervising nurse on duty, stepped out from behind the curtain and motioned for Monty to follow her to the desk.

"Is he going to be all right?"

Paige tucked a strand of hair that had escaped her blond ponytail behind her ear. "I don't want to speak for the doctor, and you're not family, Monty. I'm sorry."

He understood. He didn't like it, but he got it. "His daughter should be here soon."

"Then if she wants, I can talk to the two of you together." She picked up her clipboard and rested it against the slight swell of her belly, pen poised to scribble. "Did he lose consciousness at all during the drive here?"

"No. No, I kept him talking. I should have given him something, shouldn't I? An aspirin. I have it on my boats for emergencies like this. I just didn't think—"

"There's nothing to blame yourself for, Monty." Paige gave his arm a reassuring squeeze. "I recertified you myself for your CPR and first aid training. You did the right thing, getting him in here."

"So what's happening now?"

"We're going to monitor him for the next few hours. Once we get those results and the lab work back, we'll have more information for you."

"I'm sorry to interrupt." A young man in scrubs joined them. "Monty, Mr. Fairchild is asking to talk to you."

"Me?" Monty couldn't have hidden his surprise if he'd tried. "Is that okay?" he asked Paige.

She nodded. "Just try not to get him excited. We want those readings as clear as possible. Keep in mind, we have given him a shot to help him relax, so he might not be as coherent as you'd expect. You know where the coffee station is, right?"

"Oh, I know. Spent too much time there on Christmas Eve," Monty said, recalling spending a good portion of his holiday in the hospital when Frankie had been injured in that fire. "Thanks, Paige."

"You bet."

Given one didn't knock on a curtain, Monty pulled back on the edge and peered around. "Mr. Fairchild?"

"Ah, good. Mr. Bettencourt—"

"Monty, please. And stop trying to sit up." He placed a hand on the older man's shoulder and kept him in place. "They need you to relax so they can get an accurate reading on what's going on with your heart. You wanted to talk to me?"

"Yes." He sagged back against the pillows, his skin still pale and blotchy. He tried to catch his breath. The beeps on the machine were erratic. Then, as he seemed to focus on his breathing, he finally calmed down. "This stupid heart of mine hates me. Always has." He turned his head on the anemic pillow and offered a weak smile. "I bet, after spending some time with my daughter, you're surprised to learn that I have a heart."

Monty's lips twitched. "I did wonder." In truth, he was more surprised to discover Vincent Fairchild had a sense of humor. "You've hurt her. A lot."

The man seemed to be aging in front of Monty's eyes. "A lot of things go through a man's mind when he thinks he's about to die. None of them are good. I've been a selfish man my entire adult life. Building up the business, making something lasting that would continue on after my death—it's all that's been important to me for as long as I can remember."

Monty bit the inside of his cheek.

"You disapprove," Vincent said without looking away from him. "You think I'm a stupid fool who should have realized the only thing that mattered was Sienna."

The old man got it in one. But rather than piling on, Monty shrugged. "It's not my place—"

"It has to be someone's place. After my wife died, it was my mother who tried, but since she's been gone, I don't know." Vincent shook his head. "I don't think Sienna was the only one to lose her tether. I know you'll find this difficult to believe, but I do love my daughter, Monty."

"All right." Monty was willing to humor him. For now.

"I know it doesn't seem so. All the damage I've done. I thought I was making her strong, making her a survivor. Someone who could take on anything life threw at her."

"She is all those things, sir," Monty replied, unable to resist pointing that out. "She's an incredible woman, with a big heart and a thirst for adventure. She's smart and funny and embraces life with her entire being." She was, in Monty's eyes at least, perfect. Perfect for him. "She's amazing."

"Yes, well, all that's thanks to her grandmother, I assure you." He took a sharp breath, held it for a moment and closed his eyes. "After I lost Sienna's mother..." He trailed off for a moment, grief clouding his gaze. "Do you know what it's like to love so deeply, so completely, that everything else ceases to exist?"

An image of Sienna drifted through his mind and he ducked his head. "I have an idea."

"When Sienna's mother died, part of me went with her. She was my anchor. My guiding light. She kept me focused on what was important, and for me, that was her. She wanted a child so desperately, despite the doctors telling her she shouldn't risk it. From the moment she discovered she was pregnant, it was as if her life, our life together, ceased to matter. All she wanted was to bring Sienna into the world. And all I wanted was to make her happy. The fear of losing my wife..." He pressed a hand against his chest that was currently covered in adhesive monitors and wires. "The fear of losing her overshadowed everything else. And then the anger after she was gone, I let it consume me. Now look what I've done to my life. To my daughter's life. I withheld my affection, my approval, using it as some kind of reward because I couldn't bear to love anyone else as much as I'd loved her mother. I deserve whatever is happening to me now." Vincent's eyes began to droop.

Monty saw the curtain flutter lightly.

"You should be saying all of this to Sienna, Mr. Fairchild," Monty said.

"All of that…" Vincent waved his hand as if he could dismiss his confession. "On the dock." He swallowed, licked his lips, as he tried to stay awake. "Sienna said she was sorry because she thought my business needed her to marry Richard to survive. That's…not true." He blinked, as if trying to focus on Monty. "He needs my money. My capital. And I needed to know…to know Sienna was settled and safe. For when…this happened." He gestured to his heart. "I didn't want my little girl to be alone. I thought Richard was the man to give her all the things she needed, but…now I fear…"

Monty rose to his feet as Vincent's voice dropped. "Fear what?"

Vincent dropped his hand onto Monty's. "Tell her I love her. That I've always loved her if I'm not…" His head lolled to the side. Alarms went off.

The curtain was ripped open. Sienna stood

there, face pale, eyes wide with terror as she looked at the two of them. "Dad?" Tears welled in her eyes. "Daddy?"

"We need you two gone. Now!" Paige ordered, as she gently pushed aside Sienna and waved Monty out of the cubicle. "Paddles! Set charge for—"

Monty's ears buzzed as Paige and the other nurses' voices faded into the background. He pulled a struggling Sienna into the hallway, and when she tried to pull free and dive back to her father's bedside, he wrapped her in his arms and held her as she cried.

"THIS HAS GOT to be the worst coffee I've ever ingested." Sienna stared down at the sludge in the paper cup.

"Well, we could get some paper and draw pictures with it." Monty's continued attempts to bolster her spirits both amused and irritated her. "Or maybe the hospital has some spackling that needs doing?"

"Stop it." She laughed, swiped at another tear she couldn't believe she hadn't already shed. They'd been in the waiting room for over two hours. Paige Bradley had popped in long enough to tell them her father had been stabilized. He was unconscious, but still alive, and surgery was looking more probable.

Monty reached over and took her hand. "How much did you hear?"

She dabbed at the corner of one eye. "You mean what my father said? Almost all of it. I've never heard…" She had to clear her throat. "I've never heard him talk about my mother. Ever. I guess now I know why. Even if I can't understand it." To think that all these years had gone by and her father still couldn't let go of the love he'd had for his wife. "I wish he'd told me. Talked to me about her. The only things I know are what my grandmother told me and they weren't that close. If something happens to him, I'll never know. Even worse, I'd be alone." She tipped her head back. More tears.

"Sienna—" Monty began.

"We got here as fast as we could!" Ezzie Salazar called out. The explosion of energy that had burst through the doors to the waiting area had Sienna jumping in her chair. Ezzie led the way, arms loaded with paper bags and trays of coffee.

Sienna slowly rose to her feet, mouth dropping open at the parade of people filing in behind Ezzie.

"Logistics and transportation held us up. Plus, we had to stop and get food obviously. And gracious, Sienna. Give me that garbage. You, too, Monty." Ezzie plucked the paper cups from their hands and dropped them into a bin. "Here. Real caffeine. Unless you want a milkshake?" She handed Sienna a cold paper cup. "Holly's mocha shakes make everyone feel better."

"Ezzie, what are you doing here?" Sienna stared at the straw sticking out of the cup, then watched as Myra, Oscar and Eloise from the Cocoon Club pulled up chairs around the coffee table and produced a deck of cards. "What are all of you doing here?"

"Supporting our friend," Myra announced as she pushed the cup closer to Sienna's lips. "Now drink up. You look frightful. Sugar. That'll help. Drink."

The elevator dinged and Mandy appeared, pushing a wheelchair in front of her that contained a young man who had to be Kyle Knight. The couple emerging behind them looked familiar, as if she'd seen them in passing, but Sienna had yet to meet them.

"We heard about your dad," Mandy said when she reached them. She parked Kyle nearby and made the introductions. "Kyle, this is Sienna Fairchild. Oh, and these are Kyle's parents, Lori and Matt Knight."

"You're one of Luke's deputies," Sienna said, remembering.

"Guilty as charged. My luck I had to take today off. Totally missed my chance to arrest this guy for kidnapping." Matt slapped Monty hard on the back. Sienna laughed, liking the big man immediately.

"How is your dad doing?" Lori, nearly as tall as her burly husband, asked.

"Stable for now," Sienna said. "Thank you all for coming. You really didn't have to. I know Kyle probably shouldn't be moving—"

"Kyle's ready to make a break for it," Kyle told her. He had a collection of butterfly bandages on his forehead and temple, and the bruising around his face was significant. His leg was in a cast from toe to thigh and braced straight out like a lance. "Believe me, I was grateful for a reason to get out of that room. Hey, Ezzie, please tell me you brought burgers."

"I did! Help yourself. Lori, you and Matt, too. And don't you worry about Leo. Holly said Charlie is going to bring him to the diner after chess club at school. You can pick him up on your way home."

"Thank you, Ezzie." Lori gave her a quick hug. "You're a lifesaver."

"You really are." Monty gave her a hug too. "But you're still not getting your hands on Roman's bachelor party."

Ezzie raised an eyebrow. "The day isn't over yet. Sienna? How are you doing? Okay? Holding up?" She rested her hands on Sienna's shoulders. "You haven't said much."

Because she couldn't. She couldn't utter a word. Her heart, her soul, was too full.

"She's okay, Ez." Monty slipped an arm around Sienna's shoulders and squeezed. "She's just realizing that she was wrong." He pressed his lips to her forehead as she burrowed into him. "You're not alone, Sienna. Not even a little."

CHAPTER SEVENTEEN

"HEY, MONTY." Sheriff Luke Saxon dropped a file on Fletcher's desk as he walked from his office with his eight-month-old daughter, Zoe, balanced in one arm. Monty stepped to the counter and peered over to see if he could peek into the holding cells. "If you're looking for Richard Somersby, we had to let him go."

"Figured." Monty didn't even try to hide his disappointment. "Sienna didn't want the hassle of filing charges against him. He leave town?"

"As far as I know." Luke looked to Fletcher.

"Saw him heading for the highway yesterday in a red Mercedes convertible driven by a petite blonde who looked a bit dazed."

"Good." Hearing Richard was long gone was at least one piece of inspiring news.

"How's Sienna's father doing?" Luke asked as Zoe drooled around her fist.

"Better than expected. It was a pretty significant heart attack, but they've mitigated the damage. Another couple of days and he should be released." What happened after that remained to be seen. "I came by to ask you for a favor."

"Name it. Does this have to do with Roman's bachelor party?"

"No. Everything's set for Sunday. Six a.m. at the marina. Jason's providing the food."

"Man, six a.m. on a Sunday?" Fletcher groaned. "That's inhuman of you."

"I could call Sheriff Brodie from Durante and tell him we won't need him or his deputies to cover for us if you'd rather," Luke suggested.

"Nope!" Fletcher held up his hands. "Six is good. It'll be the best bachelor party ever. Since mine," he added with a grin.

"Did you by any chance do a deep dive on Richard Somersby while he was in custody?"

"No. Why?" Luke's eyes flashed with interest. "Should we have?"

"Something Sienna's father said to me the other day in the ER. Sienna told me she was marrying Richard because it would solidify some new deal between him and her father. She thought it was to save her father's business, but according to Vincent, that's not true. It's Richard's company that needs…"

He trailed off, looking between the sheriff and his deputy. "What?"

"Sometimes I just love being right," Fletcher said as he kicked his feet off the desk and dropped to the ground.

"Fletcher might have mentioned he got wonky vibes off him." Luke grimaced. "Like that's even a thing."

"Apparently it is. Here." Fletcher dug through one of the baskets on his desk, pulled a file free and gave it to Luke, taking Zoe in exchange. "Richard Somersby. Originally from Shrewsbury, Connecticut. Youngest of three sons born to Kingston and Ermetrude Somersby."

"Ermetrude?" Luke asked. "Boy, she must have had a hard time in the schoolyard with that one." He flipped open the file and began to skim. "Go on."

"Oldest son is a neurosurgeon," Fletcher said as he settled Zoe against his shoulder. "Middle son is lead counsel for an oil corporation overseas. Both megasuccessful, pillars of the community, yada yada. Richard, however, appears to be the family screwup. He's started up multiple businesses, all of which have gone straight down the drain within six to twelve months. His latest attempt, RS Consultation, supposedly has clients ranging from mega-media groups to investment and real estate ventures."

"Clients like Sienna's father's business?"

"Uh-huh. Which had me reaching out to Fairchild's CFO, who informed me that Vincent set aside over three million dollars as an investment in Richard's business once Sienna and Richard's marriage was a done deal."

"Three million dollars is a lot to lose, especially for someone like Richard," Luke said.

Monty nodded. "Yeah. Guess that explains his desperation to get Sienna to the altar. Are there any other investors putting in that much cash?"

"None that I could confirm, despite the claims on Somersby's website," Fletcher said. "Nobody's talking or admitting to any deal with Somersby. Add to that, Somersby's father has apparently cut him off from the family fortune."

"So he has no backup plan. Boy." Luke let out a low whistle. "She really dodged a bullet with that marriage. You want us to keep digging?"

"Nah." Monty shook his head and thought Fletcher was going to be a great dad to the baby he and Paige were expecting this summer. Either he didn't notice the puddle of drool collecting on the shoulder of his uniform, or he didn't care. "Richard's gone and Sienna has enough going on—she doesn't need to add this to the load."

"You going to tell her?"

"That Richard was only marrying her for her money? Depends. It's better than her thinking her father tried to pawn her off with a dowry. Thanks, guys. See you Sunday morning."

"THANKS, CALLIOPE. I'll drop off the decorations at your place on my way back to the inn. Gale's delivering the cake for the shower Sunday morning, right?" Phone to her ear, Sienna glanced over her shoulder. "Perfect. Nope. He's doing a lot better, thanks. I'll talk to you later. We're ahead of schedule for the shower, so nothing to worry about. Thanks. Yeah, bye." Sienna clicked off her phone. "Sorry, Dad. I didn't mean to wake you."

"Don't be. I'm starting to bore myself in my dreams." Vincent sat up straighter in bed. Sienna hurried over to help secure his pillows. "You're enjoying all this party planning, aren't you?"

"I am." Somehow, in the days since his

heart attack and ensuing surgery, they'd found common ground on which to tread. "It's fun. And I get to help people I really like. It feels, I don't know, almost like a calling. I bet that sounds stupid."

"It doesn't sound stupid at all. You seem happy, Sienna. Happier than I've ever seen you. Not that we've spent a lot of time together." He sighed in regret. "I'm sorry for that."

"It's the past." She didn't want to ruin the peace they'd found. She knew he'd never be the father she wanted, but she could see he was trying. And that, at least, was progress. She pushed her notes back into her binder. With Frankie's shower the day after tomorrow and the wedding the Saturday after that, time was getting tight. But so far she was keeping on top of everything. And thriving. "How are you feeling?"

"Pretty good. Honestly, better than I have in months. It's good to have energy again."

"It's good to have access to my bank accounts again. Thank you for that." It had been such a relief to finally be able to pay her own way. Thankfully Tabitha had done as she'd promised and sent Sienna's purse and phone to her. Sienna had picked up the parcel at the front desk after her father's surgery had been completed.

"The bank must have seen fit to do it themselves. I haven't made any phone calls since I've been here, Sienna. You have my cell phone, remember?"

She did remember. She also remembered teasing him that he wouldn't get it back until he walked out of the hospital on his own two feet. She had, however, contacted her father's attorney, physician and CFO to tell them about her father's condition and that she expected them to keep the business going until he was ready to come back. Thankfully her father had capable and responsible employees, which meant he could take an extended sabbatical without much impact on the company. They must have taken care of the bank issue.

"I just assumed." She shrugged. It didn't matter how it had happened. She had her finances again and she had a check already written out to Monty for what he'd spent on her during their journey.

"I've been in a fog for a while, I'm afraid," Vincent admitted. "I never should have agreed to Richard's idea to talk to the press. That article in the paper was garbage. And

I don't know how they found out about your time in the hospital. Attributing that quote to me is something I'm going to have my lawyer look into just as soon as I'm at the office."

Sienna was glad she was sitting down because she felt her legs shake. "You didn't tell them?"

"I didn't. I wouldn't. Never mind the fact that it happened when you were a child. Your grandmother would come back from the grave and never let me live it down if I ever did anything so despicable." The horror on his face had Sienna rethinking almost every moment of her childhood. "But you thought I did it."

"I…yes." She didn't want to lie or pretend anymore. "Yes, I did."

"And it didn't surprise you." He shook his head and glanced out the window for a long moment. "Monty was right. We should have put this behind us years ago, but I thought I was too late. I thought if you were settled and comfortable with Richard, I wouldn't have to worry about you anymore."

"I heard what you told Monty the other day, Dad." She managed a quick smile. "I was standing on the other side of the curtain. You don't have to worry. And about you and…

Mom." She tried to hold back the tears. "I've wanted to talk to you about her for so long. I want to know her, Dad. I want to know the woman you knew. The woman you loved."

He looked at her and then reached out his hand. When she took it, for the first time in her life, she felt wanted. She felt heard.

"First of all, to get rid of the notion that your party-planning abilities are silly. Your mother..." He cleared his throat. "Your mother had the same talent. Birthdays, weddings, showers, vacations—she could make all the complicated arrangements and plans look easy. Her friends were always asking her to plan for them. I used to tease her she should make a business of it, but she wouldn't hear of taking money for doing something she loved. You are like her so much, Sienna. So much. But I think, most of all, you have her heart. Which means she's never been very far from me at all." He squeezed her hand. "I'm only sorry it's taken me so long to see it."

Sienna smiled through her tears. "So you'll tell me about her?"

"Where would you like to start?"

"I FEEL LIKE I've been cooped up for weeks. Thanks, Lori." Sienna sank into one of the upholstered high-back chairs in Flutterby Dreams, the inn's recently designated four-star restaurant, and resisted the urge to kick off her shoes. Dinner overlooking the ocean with a man she didn't want to be away from? Everything in her life seemed to finally be falling into place.

"Good to see you out of the hospital," Lori said. "Your dad's doing okay, then?"

"They're discharging him on Monday. I have strict orders to stay away until then."

"Good thing, since Frankie's shower is tomorrow," Monty said as he joined her. "Sorry I'm late. Finishing up the last of the plans for Roman's bachelor party cruise."

"Kyle's so upset he can't go." Lori handed them each a menu. "He was really looking forward to it. But at least he's home now. Leo's keeping him entertained with video games. And now he has a lot of time to study for his contractor's exam."

"What is going on with the sanctuary project?" Sienna asked. "I've been so preoccupied with Dad and the shower plans I keep forgetting to ask."

"Investigation is wrapping up," Lori said. "It's looking like there was something shady going on with one of the suppliers. The good news is the town council stepped in and hired a new head of construction, who will be here in a few weeks. The site should be cleared by then and ready for a clean start, so to speak. Anyway, you two enjoy your dinner. Wine's on the house."

"Thanks, Lori." Sienna waited until the hotel manager left before she leaned over the table. "Fair warning, if I drink wine tonight, I'll be asleep in twenty seconds."

"Coffee it is." He glanced around the room, his gaze hesitating on a couple of other customers for a second before he smiled.

"What?" Sienna noticed the young couple at a table in the corner. They were holding hands and whispering, and completely wrapped up in each other.

"That's Willa O'Neill and Kevin Pine."

Willa, she knew from the inn, but Kevin was a new face.

"Willa is one of the shyest people you will ever meet. Kevin's had a crush on her for years."

"Obviously one of them made a move," Sienna said with a smile.

"At Brooke and Sebastian's wedding, it was Willa who asked Kevin to dance. They've been inseparable ever since. It's nice to see."

He shifted his attention back to her. "You're nice to see, too."

She smiled, felt her cheeks flush. "Thanks. Um, how's Duchess?"

"Duchess has declared *Dream* her new home. At least for the time being."

At her raised eyebrows, he chuckled. "Like I'm going to chuck her overboard after what she did to Richard. That bird deserves a reward."

"I guess she does. Speaking of rewards." Sienna pulled the check out of her purse and set it on the table. "I was finally able to get back into my account. I know checks are old-fashioned, but…" The relief she felt at finally being able to repay him surged through her.

He looked down at it, the smile fading from his face. "You're kidding, right? I told you I don't want your money."

"Sure you do." She rolled her eyes. "And all that was back when I couldn't get to my money. Now I can. And I want to show my appreciation. Put it toward *Dream*'s refurbishment."

"I don't know why I have to keep saying it." He pushed the check back to her. "I'll find the means to pay for *Dream*'s upgrades myself. In my own time."

"Don't be ridiculous."

"Don't be condescending." He kept his voice low and aimed a look at their server that had the young man detouring from their table.

"What on earth is wrong with you? Bring him back here, I'm starving, Monty." She waved her menu only to have Monty's hand lock around her wrist. She looked down to where his fingers tightened. "Ow."

He eased up immediately and sat back with a sigh. "I'm sorry, but I need to make something very clear to you, Sienna. I'm not now, nor have I ever been, interested in you because of your money."

"Even if that were true, it just makes things easier for both of us. Think of all the upgrades you can do with *Nana's Dream* with that money."

"Even if that were true?"

Realizing what she'd said, she tried to backpedal even as she shivered against a sudden chill. "You know what I mean. It's okay if you like the fact I have money. Everyone always does. It's just part of my life."

"So even though I'm sitting here saying I don't care about your money, you don't believe me."

"It's not a matter of…" Why was this such

an issue? "Monty, why are we having this conversation? If you don't want to take the check, fine. I can have my attorney deposit it into your business account."

"You're not hearing me at all, are you?" He shook his head. "I don't know who you suddenly think I am, but I am not your fiancé. I'm not Richard Somersby."

She smirked. "I am well aware."

"Are you? Because he's the one who wanted you for your money. I fell in love with you, Sienna Fairchild. You. Not your bank account, not your inheritance, but you. The woman who showed up on my boat without a dime in her pocket or a change of clothes."

"You...what?" She could barely breathe. "Did you say you're in love with me?"

"The universe seems to have an unlimited sense of humor, yes. That's exactly what I said."

"But..."

"But?" he pressed.

"But I don't know..." Her head spun. The words, the sentiment, the emotions swirling around inside of her—nothing could settle long enough for her to process how she was feeling. "I've had a lot happen in the last few weeks, Monty. This is a lot to take in." Even more than the realization of her own feelings for him.

"Is it?" Monty's voice went cold. "Are you sure you're not just scared?"

"Darn right I'm scared." But how could she be when she knew deep down that she loved him, too? "I heard that part at the hospital, about Richard only marrying me for money. He lied and kept secrets to get it. It's nothing other people haven't done to me in the past. Everyone always wants something. Even when they say they don't."

"That might be the saddest thing I've ever heard about someone."

"I would really love to stop having this conversation in public if you wouldn't mind?" She glanced around the room and noticed the other guests had stopped speaking. "I'm sorry I tried to give you a token of my appreciation. If you want, we can forget about the check and move on."

"That wasn't a token. It was the annual budget of a small country. And move on to what? To you thinking I love you because you come with a hefty bank account?"

"Some women come with a big house, others a ready-made family." As quickly as she held a future with him in her grasp, she felt it slipping away. "I don't see the difference."

"The difference is I'd love you no matter

how much money you have. I don't want you thinking you have to pay me to stay."

"Pay you to… That isn't what I was doing." Was it?

"You don't have to buy people things or pay for dinners or throw around bonus checks because you're afraid someone's going to leave you, Sienna."

"That's easy for you to say. You've got people to spare in your life, don't you? You never have to worry about why they're spending time with you."

"No." A light went out in his eyes. "No, I guess I don't. But the very idea you can't accept someone might love you just for you makes me wonder if there's any kind of future for us."

She watched, horrified, as he pushed back his chair and stood up.

"I've lost my appetite. You enjoy your evening, Sienna. And your money. Since it seems to be what you're determined to hide behind." With that, he walked out of the restaurant and didn't look back.

"Is that straight?"

Sienna listened half-heartedly to Stella Costas's question. "What?"

"The sign? Is it straight?"

Sienna blinked, realized what she was being asked and did a final check of the Congratulations, Frankie sign stretched across Calliope's back patio. The effort brought a smile to her lips and she nodded. "It's perfect, Stella. Go ahead and tie it off."

"Thank goodness." Charlie Bradley, Paige and Fletcher's ten-year-old redheaded daughter, sagged against her friend's legs as she continued to steady her on a step stool. "I can't feel my arms anymore."

"All right. The rum punch is definitely punching." Holly, taking one of her rare days off from the diner, rushed out of the house to check on her twins, Zoe and Jake, who were hanging out with their honorary aunts and godmothers. The group of women who were already in attendance had swooped in like mama birds to help with the shower for one of their own.

Sienna had more than enough assistance to finish the final preparations. Paige, who was expecting her first baby with Fletcher this summer, was arranging the table display for the potluck lunch that would start in less than an hour. Lori, along with Willa O'Neill, Calliope and Abby Corwin, who had been relegated to a very comfortable chair with cushions, were finishing the balloons and streamers.

Now that Stella, Calliope's young sister, and Charlie were done with the sign, they raced off to the gate to wait for their fellow musketeers Marley and Phoebe, who would be arriving with the bride-to-be and her maid of honor, Kendall Davidson. Mandy and her mother, Brooke, Frankie's maid of honor, who had finally overcome her bout with the flu, would be arriving with the rest of the guests.

With a significant portion of the female population of Butterfly Harbor scheduled to attend, Sienna did a quick check of the picnic tables and made certain there was enough nonpunchy hibiscus lemonade to be served.

"I believe you may stop fussing now, Sienna." Calliope joined her, juggling an obviously teething Jake Saxon in her arms. "Everything looks beautiful."

"With this backdrop, that's not hard to do." Sienna sighed with approval. "I can see why so many people celebrate the milestones of their lives here, Calliope."

"I've been considering opening it up to events for folks outside Butterfly Harbor. Maybe joining forces with the Flutterby. Destination weddings. That kind of thing. What do you think?"

"I think it's a wonderful idea. Low-key, intimate gatherings, but also larger events." Sienna nodded. "You'll probably want to do a little landscaping. Evening out areas here and there. Maybe designate a space for a dance floor. Something easily removable for the winter. Not that you get snow or anything."

"I was thinking the exact same thing." Calliope handed baby Jake to her so she could pour herself a glass of punch. "This is merely to do a little quality control, of course."

"Um. Hey there, little fella." Sienna accepted the baby with as much calm as she could muster. She hadn't been around a lot of infants before and couldn't remember the last time she'd held one.

"Careful. They sense fear," Abby said as she waddled by. "Did you ask her yet?" She adjusted Sienna's hold to support Jake's butt more securely. Jake responded with a giggle and dropped his head onto Sienna's shoulder. Sienna's heart fluttered.

"I was getting to it," Calliope replied.

"Ask me what?"

"Running the farm is a full-time job, and I'll be hiring new staff to help with that,"

Calliope said. "Abby and I were thinking we could both use an event coordinator. Someone who could organize events at the inn and the farm."

Sienna looked between the two women. "You want to hire me?"

"We do," Abby confirmed. "I'll be pretty busy with the new baby. Lori's great at the inn, but she's opening a new flower shop, so I'll have to hire someone to work with Willa. Taking events off her plate would make her life easier. And you're a natural at them." Abby pressed a hand against her back. "We don't expect an answer right away. We know you have a lot to figure out for yourself."

"We hoped maybe knowing your options would help with that," Calliope added.

"Speaking of options, how are things going with Monty?" Abby's knowing gaze told Sienna she already knew exactly what had happened at dinner at the Flutterby.

Sienna's face went hot. "Fine." She shrugged. "Just...yeah. They're okay." She distracted herself with Jake's teeny fingers.

"Sienna." Abby touched her arm. "Small town, remember? Not to mention I run the place where you and Monty had your argument."

Sienna swallowed around her too-tight throat. "Let's just say I pretty much blew things up. I didn't mean to. It…happened." Somehow she'd known she would. She always messed up a good thing.

"I'm sorry, honey." Abby looked to Calliope. "You have any special herbs or life wisdom for a broken heart?"

"Her heart isn't broken," Calliope assured them. "Merely misguided. Monty is one of the best men I know, Sienna. You can trust him."

Sienna couldn't help it—she laughed. "It's not that simple."

"Isn't it?" Calliope set down her drink and took Jake in her arms. "If you give yourself time, you'll realize it's exactly that simple. Whether you want to admit it or not, he passed your test. The test you didn't even realize you'd given him."

"I…" Sienna blinked. After a sleepless night and replaying their argument in her mind, until this very moment… Calliope was right. The check had been a test. She hadn't been able to believe he'd meant it when he'd said he didn't want her money. "All right. Think on this later, okay?" Abby turned to the front gate, where arriving cars were beginning to pull in to park. "This party's about to get started. Oh, no games, right? Because Frankie—"

"Frankie hates bridal-party games," Sienna finished for her. "First thing Frankie told me. And speaking of Frankie, there she is. All right, everyone." Sienna clapped her hands for attention. "The guest of honor is here! It's time to celebrate. Charlie? Hit that music."

"On it!" Charlie tapped the speaker that was set up by the gift table. As the sound of Aretha Franklin's "Respect" drifted through the air at Duskywing Farm, Sienna set aside thoughts of Monty and focused on her new friends.

"CAN I JUST tell you that your crap-tastic mood today is the one storm cloud hanging over this boat." Sebastian Evans sidled up to where Monty stood at the bow of *Star Dancer*. His long-time childhood best friend, business partner and cocaptain for the day cast him an uncharacteristically accusing look. The boat rocked and swayed to its familiar, calming rhythm while the sound of friends—men he considered brothers—cheered and bantered through the end of the celebration. "You look positively miserable, Monty."

"Sorry." Monty sipped the bottle of root beer he'd been nursing for the better part of an hour. "Had a really bad evening last night."

"So we heard. How much was the check for?"

Monty grimaced. "Sometimes I loathe small towns." He tried to avoid an answer, but Sebastian knocked his shoulder with a fist. "I could have bought three *Dream*s with change to spare."

"Well. As your friend, I can absolutely understand why you turned her down." Sebastian took a long drink. "As your business partner, I'll say you're a class-A idiot."

"Awesome." Monty leaned his arms on the railing and lowered his head. "Thanks for that."

"My pleasure. So you want my take?"

"More than I want air to breathe."

"You're a reverse snob."

"I'm a what?"

"You heard me." Sebastian rested his arms on the railing. "You're a practical man. Always have been. You've worked for every dollar you've made and turned it into two. Hard work equals profit. The idea of anything coming easy to you feels like a swipe against your pride. But here's the thing. The more you cling to your pride, the further away she's going to be. You told me about her, remember? You said she spent a lot of years being the friend everyone wanted because of what she could give or bring them. That's a lot of emotional baggage for her to be dragging around. Never knowing why anyone is in her life. Waiting for them to approach her with their hand out. Having a fiancé nearly drag her down the aisle for a payout couldn't have helped the situation or her mindset. It's what she knows, Monty. It's up to you to show her there's another way."

"She wouldn't listen to me."

"And you didn't hear her. That check was a preemptive strike."

That check was a slap in his face. "I love her, Sebastian. Not her money."

"You can't hate something that is so much a part of her. And you shouldn't walk away from something you have no understanding of. You want a future with her? Try compromising. Trust me, that's what's going to save you in the end."

"You've only been married a month." Monty drank more of his root beer. "You can't possibly have gotten this smart about relationships so quick."

"Sure I can. Because I married the right woman. Albeit almost two decades late. So, had enough fun in the sun for one day?"

"Ready to head back?"

"If it means you'll go talk to Sienna? You bet."

Only then did Monty notice the rest of the noise on the boat had stopped. He stood up, turned and found the entire bachelor party standing behind them.

"Tell me we're going back so he can talk to her?" Roman pleaded. "While I'm grateful for the party and the load of fish I'm taking back to the station house, I am begging you, for all our sakes, please make up with her."

"We're going back," Monty confirmed to cheers and groans. "And strap in, 'cause we're going fast."

CHAPTER EIGHTEEN

SIENNA STOOD WITH clipboard in hand, as Frankie opened her bridal gifts. Sienna accepted each gift card as it was presented, wrote down the gift received and any special notations needed for forthcoming thank-you notes Frankie would have to find time to write. Sienna made a note to herself to pre-address envelopes so all Frankie had to do was just fill in the details.

"Sienna?"

Sienna had to take a moment to identify the voice. She turned and found her cousin. "Tabitha? What on earth are you doing here?"

Tabitha's hand shook as she tucked her blond hair behind her ear. "Your phone's turned off. I came up to visit Uncle Vincent. I need to talk to you. Please. It's important."

"Is it about Dad? Wait. Hold on." She searched for Calliope and waved her over. "I need to get to the hospital."

"Of course." Calliope frowned. "Who is

that?" She looked beyond Sienna to where Tabitha was hurrying off.

"My cousin. She came to get me. Can you finish writing down the gifts? I'll be back to clean up. I just need to make sure he's all right."

"Certainly." Calliope accepted the clipboard and pen. "Sienna," she called after Sienna had grabbed her purse. "Be...careful." She glanced up at the sky, where storm clouds began to gather. "In fact, why don't you call the hospital first. Just to make sure—"

"No time. I'll be back, I promise." Sienna ran to catch up with Tabitha. She slid into the passenger seat of the Mercedes and held on as her cousin sped away from the farm.

"What happened? Did he have another heart attack? Is he conscious?"

"It's important we talk," Tabitha assured her, then took a sharp left and headed into town.

"You're going the wrong way. Tab, the hospital's..." Her voice faded as an uneasy sensation slid over her. "Tabitha, where are we going?"

"I told you. To talk." She floored the accelerator.

Minutes later they reached the marina. Before Sienna could confront her, Tabitha was out of the car and headed to where *Nana's Dream* was docked.

"Tabitha!" Sienna shoved out of the car. What was happening here? And what was Tabitha doing in Butterfly Harbor, of all places?

"Sienna!" Mrs. Yamishimi called to her from farther along the dock.

"Mrs. Yamishimi." Sienna detoured to greet her friend. "We missed you at the shower."

"I had a call from my son at the last minute. My daughter-in-law's been put on bed rest, so I'm heading up to Seattle tomorrow. I just wanted to say goodbye." She glanced toward *Nana's Dream*. "Who's that on Monty's boat?"

"My cousin, Tabitha. I guess she wants a tour." Sienna's laugh seemed strained even to her own ears.

"Oh?" Mrs. Yamishimi's eyebrows shot up.

Fat raindrops plopped onto Sienna's head. "I'd better give it to her before that storm comes in. I'll stop by for tea as soon as you're back," she assured the older woman.

"All right."

Sienna reached *Dream*, but couldn't see

Tabitha. Her cousin must have disappeared below deck. "Tabitha?" Sienna shouted.

Duchess squawked above her. The bird seemed flustered on her perch on the railing.

"Hey, there. I've missed you." Sienna reached out, but Duchess reared back, stretched out her wings and let out a screech that had Sienna wondering if the bird was injured in some way. With a frantic flapping, she tried to prevent Sienna from ducking inside to join her cousin. "Duchess, stop it! Just stop!"

She'd never spoken so harshly to the parrot before and she felt bad, especially when Duchess flew off toward the cliffs of Butterfly Harbor. "Great. Now I'm going to have to earn a bird's forgiveness. Tabitha? What's this all about? I need to get back to the shower."

"It'll just be a few minutes, I promise." Tabitha's voice echoed from the bow of the boat.

"What are we even doing here?" Sienna demanded. "You hate boats."

"I wanted someplace private to talk." Tabitha's voice echoed from Sienna's old berth. "And I wanted to see what was so appealing you chose this wreck over marrying Richard."

Sienna rolled her eyes. "Forgive me for not

wanting to marry someone who was only interested in my money." She stepped into her former room. "Tabitha?"

"We're going to need more privacy," Tabitha said, coming forward and shoving Sienna hard.

By the time Sienna caught her footing, Tabitha slid the berth door closed and locked it.

The next thing she knew, the engine rumbled to life and they were headed out to sea.

"FASTEST DOCKING IN the history of nautical arrivals," Roman Salazar announced as the bachelor party disembarked. "For the record, it was a slam-dunk day, best man." He slammed a hand on Monty's shoulder. "Good friends, fishing, beer and fun. My mother could not have done better."

"High praise, indeed," Monty muttered as he finished tying off the boat. The men headed off to meet up with their significant others at the shower or to go home. Luke, Ozzy and Sebastian stayed back to help Monty clean up.

"Where did this come from?" Luke yelled when the rain began to fall. Not just in sprinkles, but in huge drops.

Monty glanced up at the angry gray sky. The hair on the back of his neck prickled. He heard someone calling his name, faintly, carried on the wind. Finding Calliope Costas racing toward him had him jumping off the boat and rushing to meet her. Calliope rarely came down to the docks.

"Sienna's in trouble," she said.

"Where is she?" Monty demanded.

Calliope shook her head. "I don't know. She drove off with a woman in a red sports car."

A red sports car? Monty's mind raced. Fletcher said Richard Somersby had driven off in a red Mercedes convertible.

Mrs. Yamishimi was pushing through the wind, her arms braced in front of her. Calliope reached out for her and drew her into the safety of her hold.

"Have you seen Sienna?" Calliope yelled over the storm.

"A little while ago. She was showing her cousin Tabitha your new boat, Monty." She pointed to the now-empty slip.

"Tabitha?" Monty tried to remember Sienna mentioning the woman.

"What's going on?" Luke demanded as he joined them.

"That woman who picked Richard up at the sheriff's station. He said she was blonde, right?"

"Yeah. Petite. Blonde. Attitude."

"That's her," Mrs. Yamishimi confirmed. "I did not like her."

"Monty, Sienna's out there. In this storm." Calliope grabbed his arm. "You've got to find her."

"Squawk! Pretty girl trouble." Duchess struggled against the gusting wind and landed on the railing of *Star Dancer*. "Help pretty girl."

"Duchess!" Monty could have kissed the parrot. "Do you know where she is? Can you find her?"

"You mean like Lassie?" Luke asked.

"Squawk. Follow Queen Duchess."

"Unmoor us!" Monty yelled at Ozzy Lakeman. The former sheriff's deputy turned firefighter was well versed in emergency situations.

"Get inside, both of you," Monty ordered as Luke raced up to the wheelhouse and started the engine. No way was he going to lose his chance. Not when he finally knew what he wanted. Not when he knew he didn't want to live this life without Sienna. "This storm's turning nasty."

"Monty?" Calliope yelled and he heard the fear in her voice.

"Don't worry. I'll bring her home." Seconds later he gunned the engine and followed Duchess as she led the way.

THERE WASN'T ANYTHING for Sienna to do except pace and wait for Tabitha to let her out. The pacing soon became impossible as the storm and rolling waves battered *Dream*. "Hang in there, girl," Sienna whispered and rested her palm against the hull. "Whatever it is my cousin's doing, she won't hurt you."

She tried to keep track of how long they had been moving, but a sense of time seemed to disappear when on the ocean. Tabitha… really? Sienna got up and pounded on the door, jiggling the handle hard enough to make the wood panel whine. "Tabitha! Let me out of here! You don't know how to control this boat!"

As the accusation left her mouth, the engine went silent. The door flew open and Sienna was shocked to find Richard standing on the other side.

"You have got to be kidding me!"

"Sienna, I need you to listen to me."

"I don't think I do." She raced past him and up the steps to the deck. Wind and rain pelted the boat, tossing it up and down, back and forth. Her hands slipped as she grabbed onto the railing. Sure enough, Tabitha was behind the wheel, but looking back at her with accusing eyes.

"I need you to marry me!" Richard shouted over the howling noise from the top step of the entryway. "I need that money your father promised me!"

"Oh, come on, Richard. You can't be serious!" Sienna had had enough. She hauled herself up to the wheelhouse. Her pretty, flower-patterned summer dress, specially chosen for today, was soaked and plastered against her body. "Tabitha! What's happened to you? You've teamed up with this…with this…" She swung around as Richard followed up behind her. "This doofus?" The Cocoon Club's description suddenly seemed apt. "What's wrong with you, Tabitha?" she yelled.

"I love him," Tabitha yelled back with just enough of a whine that, for an instant, Sienna felt sorry for her. "I believe in him. All he needs is the three mil your father promised."

"That's not going to happen," Sienna said. "My dad knows everything, Richard. Everything." She stared daggers at her ex-fiancé and wondered if he'd told Tabitha the truth about everything he'd done. "Unless you're holding me for ransom. Is that the plan?" She looked at Tabitha. "You're willing to commit a felony for him?"

"I—" Tabitha's eyes went wide, as if she didn't understand what was going on. "We just wanted to talk to you. You don't have to marry him for long. A few months would do."

Enough for the check to clear. Sienna gaped, gripped the back of the passenger seat and shook her head as the waves continued to churn. "You thought by bringing me out here you'd somehow convince me to marry a man who only sees me as a bank account? What reality show are you living in Tab?"

"Give me enough money to disappear," Richard said.

She looked at him, unable to feel anything for him but pity. "No."

"You don't understand," Tabitha wailed. "He's got people after him. He's in terrible trouble. If you don't help us—"

"Us?" Sienna winced. "Tab, tell me you aren't dumb enough to think anything Richard is doing is for anyone but himself. This is all about him and his greed."

"That's not true. He was worried about you. Even before the wedding he—"

It wasn't that Tabitha stopped; it was the expression on her face. As if she'd revealed something she wasn't supposed to. The last piece of the confusing puzzle Sienna couldn't quite put together suddenly fell into place.

"You were in on this from the start." Sienna stared, heartbroken at her cousin's betrayal. "You knew why he was marrying me and you still pushed me into it. Why?"

"Because someone had to love me best," Tabitha spluttered. "Gran adored you. Doted on you. She left you that house. She gave up everything for you and forgot I even existed and when she died, I got nothing."

"Because she thought you had all you needed. You had the love of two parents—at least, she thought you did. You can have the house, it's not important!"

Tabitha opened her mouth as if to say something, but then shut it and clutched at the wheel as another swell hit the side of the boat. It occurred to Sienna that her cousin's pain was there, the same pain Sienna had spent a lifetime pushing down. The rejection, the hurt. All this time… All this time her cousin had let her resentment fester, preventing them from being anything more than distant relations.

"So you're going to throw everything away over *him*?" Sienna shouted. "What makes you think he won't chuck you overboard the second he doesn't need you anymore? Because he doesn't need you, Tab. Not now. Not now that you're the one people saw luring me onto this boat. You came to get me from the shower. He can vanish and you'll be left to deal with the consequences of what could constitute a crime."

"I—" Tabitha shook her head, but the doubt was there as she looked between Sienna and Richard. "That's not true, is it? After everything I've done, you wouldn't do that to me, would you, Richard?"

When Richard hesitated, Sienna faced him. "Well? Would you, Richard?"

He still didn't answer. Tabitha let out a shriek that had Sienna shrinking back as her cousin flew out of the pilot's chair. She knocked her fists into Richard's chest and sent him stumbling. "You lied to me! You were setting me up this whole time!" She hit him again and he came up hard against the side of the hull.

"No, Tabitha! Don't!" Sienna dived for her cousin, but she was too late. Tabitha struck out one more time and sent Richard flying overboard into the ocean.

Sienna cursed and raced down the ladder to grab the life preserver. She searched the dark swells for where he'd gone in. When he broke free of the surface, gasping for air, she launched the preserver and hauled him back to the boat.

"I can't believe I'm dragging your soggy butt back onboard," she grunted. He choked and gagged and seemed to spew up half the sea. "You keep Tabitha out of this, you hear me? Not a word about her being involved or I'll find a way to throw you back in."

Wheezing, flailing and lying beneath the pelting rain on the deck of *Nana's Dream*, Richard nodded.

She climbed into the wheelhouse, waved a shivering Tabitha out of the captain's seat and turned the engine back on. Seconds later, she was heading home.

Home.

Her heart swelled to where she could barely breathe. Butterfly Harbor...no, Monty, was home. In a short time, she'd found friends, a new family, people to belong to. She had the promise of a future, a job, something that would make people happy. Something she was good at. She'd found the father she'd spent a lifetime longing to connect with.

And she'd found a man she loved. Loved to the absolute core of her being.

The wind slammed into *Dream* like a vicious whip and for an instant, the boat seemed to hover between staying upright and going over. When it slammed back down into the water, she hit the throttle. "I'm not going out this way." She gritted her teeth. *Dream* strained against the pressure of the storm, but continued to move. She crested wave after wave. Behind her, she heard Tabitha wretch. Sienna searched the gray sky for a hint of color—a hint of light that would show a break in the weather.

"Get me home, Nana," she whispered like a prayer. "Please get me back to him. Get me back to Monty."

Her hands cramped. Her fingers went numb as they clenched the steering wheel. She heard her name. A whisper on the wind. Faint. And in the air, she smelled roses and jasmine.

"Nana." Sienna closed her eyes, released the fear tightening her muscles, that was making her body ache. Her grip eased and for a moment, she gave herself over to the storm.

"Squawk! Guaca-mooleeee!"

Sienna's eyes shot open. She gasped as Duchess landed and blinked those beautiful black eyes at her. Sienna laughed and settled into her chair. As she eased her hold on the wheel, she felt something slide off her finger.

She looked down as the engagement ring clattered onto the deck.

The sky began to clear, the clouds blowing through as if a wind pushed from behind. The waves continued to surge, but they were lighter now. Easier to navigate.

Tabitha gasped, leaned over the railing and threw up. Richard clawed his way across the cabin, his eyes widening with greed as he reached for the engagement ring that continued to slide out of his grasp as the boat rocked one way and then the other.

Sienna turned the boat into the waves and caught sight of another craft heading right for them. She knew, even before *Star Dancer* was fully visible, it was Monty. The seconds to reach him seemed innumerable.

She switched off the engine and popped out

the key, sliding down the ladder to be there the instant he jumped boats. When she was in his arms, she didn't cry. She laughed. And held on as if she'd never let him go.

"You okay?" Monty tilted her head back and looked into her eyes. Then he kissed her. Hard. Quick. And again. "Did they hurt you?"

"I'm fine. *Dream* saved us. Well. I helped." She smiled at him as the sun streaked through the parting clouds and erased the last of the darkness. "I don't know where that storm came from, but it arrived just in time. I knew exactly what to do."

"That doesn't tell me what happened, but I don't care right now." He drew her close again, wrapped himself around her so completely, she knew she'd found exactly where she belonged. "Luke and Ozzy are with me."

"Did they bring handcuffs?" Sienna asked. "For Richard," she said, looking seriously into his eyes. "Just Richard."

His hands dived into her hair. "You sure?"

She nodded. She didn't want Tabitha suffering any more than she already was. A broken heart was bad enough, as was having to come to terms with the fact that for so long she'd hated Sienna when they'd had so much in common. She touched Monty's face, traced the features she'd spent the past few days memorizing.

"What's this?" He caught her hand, curled her fingers. "Where's the ring?"

"It fell off." She chuckled. "That means I'm officially unengaged."

"Not for long, you aren't." He brought his mouth down on hers.

"You cannot be serious." Luke's voice meant they quit their kiss, although reluctantly. He stepped forward, shaking his head. "This has got to be the craziest darn thing I've seen in a long time. You said the bad guys are around here?"

"Yes," Sienna murmured against Monty's lips and pointed upward.

Luke hesitated. "You pressing charges against Richard this time?"

"Absolutely. Kidnapping works. For now."

"Got it. Carry on, Monty." Luke slapped him on the shoulder and headed up to the wheelhouse.

"Sienna?"

"Yes?" She blinked innocent eyes at him, as if she had no idea what he was going to say next.

"You going to marry me or not?"

"Only on one condition." She looked over

her shoulder and smiled at Duchess, who was pecking against a yelling Richard's arm. "We get to keep the bird."

He kissed her again. "Deal."

EPILOGUE

"You're sure you haven't seen her?" Sienna asked the three covering firefighters standing frozen in the Butterfly Harbor station.

Two men and a woman, all looking confused, shook their heads.

"Ah, geez." Sienna's calm evaporated as she paced.

It was T minus two hours until Frankie and Roman's wedding. The groom and his groomsmen were at the Flutterby Inn getting ready. The park was in full decor mode. The food tents were gearing up for service and populated with guests. Prewedding snacks were being distributed as music flitted out of speakers all around the area. Even from a distance Sienna could hear the celebration beginning.

And yet the bride was missing.

Sienna stopped when she heard the familiar roar of the fire department's SUV outside the station. She'd been prepared for anything and everything. Apart from a runaway bride.

"Thank goodness." Sienna sighed. "I bet that's her now. Frankie?" Sienna raced for the door. "Is that you?" She skidded to a sharp halt and nearly screamed when she saw the bride. "Oh, Frankie."

"Where have you been?" Ezzie Salazar shrieked from the doorway as Frankie walked slowly into the firehouse. "What happened? What have you done to yourself?"

Sienna's heart broke at the sight of her friend's tearstained face.

"I forgot to pick up a thank-you gift for Sienna." Frankie looked like a wilted, drowned daisy. Her hair, which had been done to perfection earlier this morning in cascades of curls and loops, hung in limp, damp ropes around her soot-covered face. Beneath her firefighter jacket, her wedding dress was in tatters, singed at the edges and drooping off her body as if it had surrendered in battle. "On the way back, there was a car accident. Not me," she added in a detached tone. "A family just outside town. There wasn't time to call 911. I only meant to stop and see if they…needed help. Someone had to get into the car—there was a baby—then it went up in flames and I didn't get completely out of the way…" She took a wobbling step toward Sienna and her soon-to-be mother-in-law. "I'm ruined." She flopped her arms up and down, sending droplets of water into the air. "I had to stop. They needed… I'm so sorry."

"What are you sorry for?" Ezzie demanded, shocking both Sienna and Frankie. She marched up to Frankie and cupped her face in her hands, love and admiration shining in her dark eyes. "Is the family all right? The baby, too?"

Frankie nodded. "They're fine. But I'm a mess. I can't get married today. Look at my dress." She lifted the destroyed satin between two fingers. "It wasn't all that special. I mean, I found it at a thrift store, but I liked it. And what's even worse? I sound like such a girl!" Tears pooled in her eyes.

"Now, there'll be none of that. There's always another dress. And there's a shower right here at the station that you can use and we can easily do your hair again." But even as Ezzie lifted a strand of Frankie's normally bright red hair, she didn't look convinced.

"Time to call in reinforcements," Sienna announced, dialing her cell phone. "Frankie, into the bathroom. Strip and get in the shower.

Now. Ezzie, get Sandy in here to do her hair again. Tell her I'll pay her double."

"Yes, ma'am." Ezzie was punching buttons on her phone as she pushed Frankie down the hall. A half hour later, the firehouse had been overrun by bridesmaids, a hairdresser, a makeup artist, a photographer and one in-control wedding planner. Kendall, the maid of honor, was keeping the children in the wedding party under control at the park. "I've got someone getting you another dress." Sienna walked up behind Frankie, who was sitting at a makeshift dressing table in the kitchen of the Butterfly Harbor Fire Department.

"What about shoes?"

"Those, too. Hey." Sienna moved around to look into her friend's eyes. "You wouldn't be Frankie if you hadn't stopped to help that family. I also have no doubt you could have walked down the aisle looking exactly as you did and Roman would have thought you the most beautiful woman in the world."

Frankie managed a smile, sniffed at her tears. "Yeah. He probably would have. He's such a good guy." She laughed. "This isn't what a wedding day is supposed to be like."

"There's nothing predictable about anyone's wedding day," Sienna said. "Trust me on that."

"Hey, Sienna! Special delivery!"

"My hero," Sienna whispered at the sound of Monty's voice. "Don't worry," she ordered a panicked-looking Frankie. "He hasn't said anything to Roman and no one will until you two are successfully married." Which she'd make happen if it killed her. She backed up to give Sandy the hairstylist some room for final touchups.

Sienna hurried out of the kitchen and snatched the garment bag out of Monty's hand.

"Hey!" He grabbed her arm when she darted away. "Don't I even get a thank-you kiss?" He puckered his lips and stretched out his chin.

Sienna rolled her eyes, kissed him quickly, then backed away. Only then did she get a full view of him in his best-man tux. "Hmm-mmm, Monty Bettencourt. You do clean up nicely."

She patted a hand on his chest and felt his heart flutter to the beat of her own. "How's Roman?"

"Ready to get this thing started. She okay?"

The concern for his sister reminded Sienna of what was really important.

"She's fine. You want to stick around to see the final product?"

"Nah. I'm good. Do me a favor. Just make sure… She's probably missing our dad. I offered to give her away, but she belted me for it. Still." He shrugged.

"I'm already way ahead of you." Sienna kissed him again. "Go on back and be ready. We'll be on time. Don't worry."

Sienna whipped the garment bag into her arms and propelled herself into the kitchen. "The dress is here. Let's get you wired in." She unzipped the bag and pulled out the dress.

"Oh, Sienna." Frankie rose to her feet as if in slow motion. "Oh, I couldn't. It's yours."

"Like I was going to wear it again," Sienna said with a grin. "You loved it when you saw it that first day on the boat. All we have to do is make sure it fits."

It did fit. More perfectly than it ever had on Sienna. Tissues stuffed into the toes of the shoes made those fit, as well. With minutes to spare, Frankie Bettencourt was princess-perfect and ready for her big day. Again.

"You are a picture." Sienna stepped back

to admire the bride. The photographer continued to snap pictures. Pictures that in a few weeks would make Frankie laugh rather than cry. "Now, one more thing."

"We need to get in the cars," Ezzie said. "All of you." She shoed Calliope, Paige and Lori out of the station. "Hurry up, the rest of you!"

Sienna opened the refrigerator and pulled out the bouquet she'd had specially made for Frankie. Her personal gift to the bride. When she handed it to her, she made sure Frankie could see the small silver frame woven into the stems. "I can only imagine how much you're missing your father today, Frankie." She opened the hinged clasp to reveal the photograph she'd found in one of Monty's old photo albums. It was one of Frankie and her father when she'd been about five, held in her father's arm, his firefighter helmet perched on her too-small head. She could almost hear the laughter ringing out from the photo. "I wish he could be here today to walk you down the aisle, but maybe this will help ease the pain a little."

Frankie's chin wobbled. "Oh, Sienna." She reached out and hugged her. "I've never received a more perfect gift. And I'm so happy you're going to be my sister-in-law."

She stepped back, held out her hand.

"Me, too," Sienna whispered. "Now let's get you married."

MONTY STOOD BACK and watched as his family and friends celebrated into the late hours. Hundreds of strings of lights brought Skipper Park into full view, casting shadows against the growing darkness as guests danced and laughed and toasted the happy couple and their new life together.

The entire town had shown up; or at least it seemed that way. Sebastian and Brooke Evans mingled around the dessert bar that featured a chocolate fountain and an endless supply of marshmallows and strawberries. Their daughter, Mandy, spun a still wheelchair-bound Kyle around the edge of the dance floor, while his parents, Matt and Lori, took turns dancing with their son Leo. Paige and Fletcher mingled with the guests, as Charlie Bradley and her troupe of friends spun in dizzying circles to the beat of the band.

The bride and groom glowed, as did his sister's fairy-tale wedding gown, which he'd first seen not too long ago stuffed into the closet of *Dream*. And there, in the middle of the dance floor, Sienna and her father shared a slow, careful dance.

The smile of contentment on Sienna's face sank into him, leaving him with a feeling of contentment he couldn't describe. Her grandmother's estate was finally settled. After much deliberation, Sienna had donated more than half of the money to various charities, including a wild-parrot sanctuary in Southern California. And the beach house? Sienna had decided to give that to Tabitha. It had, after all, been something Nana would have approved of.

Kidnapping was the least of Richard Somersby's worries. The FBI had recently opened an investigation into his business dealings and chances were he'd end up serving enough time Sienna would never have to give him another thought. As for Vincent, Sienna's father had decided to take early retirement and was in the process of ending his tenure at his company. He was, finally, in his own words, putting Sienna first. He was already looking at property in Butterfly Harbor for the many visits he planned to make in order for them to spend more time together.

"It's been a good day." Mrs. Yamishimi slid

her arm into Monty's and offered him an un-derstanding smile. "It's been a good week."

"It's been a busy one, that's for sure. How's your daughter-in-law doing?"

"Better, thank you." She offered a sad smile. "They've asked me to move in with them. To be part of their family."

"You're leaving Butterfly Harbor?" He couldn't imagine this town without her.

"I told myself I'd know when the time was right." She patted Monty's hand, then slipped something out of her pocket. "I hope to come back for the wedding, but in case I'm not able." She pushed the envelope into his pocket. "My gift to both of you. May you have more happy years than I had with my Henry."

Monty felt himself tear up as she moved off to find a glass of champagne. When he caught Sienna's curious gaze on him, he smiled. And joined her on the dance floor. "May I cut in?"

"You may indeed." Vincent handed off his daughter. "You did a wonderful job, Sienna." He stepped in and kissed her cheek. "Your mother would be so proud of you. As proud as I am."

"Thank you, Dad." Sienna's face turned pink with happiness. When she stepped into

Monty's arms, she sighed and sagged against him. "I'm going to sleep for a week after this."

"He's right. Everything went off perfectly."

Sienna giggled. "With only a few detours."

"I like detours in weddings." He pressed his lips to the top of her head. "They can provide some very entertaining results."

"What did Mrs. Yamishimi give you?"

"Saw that, did you?" He chuckled and wasn't surprised when she slipped the envelope out of his pocket. "Go ahead. Open it. She said it was an early wedding present."

Sienna pulled out a folded document, shock blanketing her face. "I don't believe it."

"What? What is it?" He took the papers and scanned them.

"She's given us her house. The houseboat in the marina. She's transferred the deed and everything. But why...?" She searched the crowd for the old woman and when she found her, she sent her a smile of thanks.

Mrs. Yamishimi closed her eyes in acknowledgment.

"I have everything I've ever wanted. Ever dreamed of," she whispered. "And all because of *Nana's Dream*." She looked up as a wide-winged parrot soared overhead, demanding guacamole. "I'm home."

"And you're loved."

She was loved. She knew it. Love was everywhere in Butterfly Harbor. Her eyes met Monty's and she smiled, touched her hand to his face. She was home. He knew it.

He drew her close and they finished their dance.

* * * * *

For more great Butterfly Harbor Stories from acclaimed author Anna J. Stewart, go to www.Harlequin.com today!

Get 4 FREE REWARDS!

We'll send you 2 FREE Books plus 2 FREE Mystery Gifts.

Love Inspired books feature uplifting stories where faith helps guide you through life's challenges and discover the promise of a new beginning.

FREE
Value Over
$20

Get 4 FREE REWARDS!

We'll send you 2 FREE Books plus 2 FREE Mystery Gifts.

Love Inspired Suspense books showcase how courage and optimism unite in stories of faith and love in the face of danger.

FREE Value Over $20

Get 4 FREE REWARDS!

We'll send you 2 FREE Books plus 2 FREE Mystery Gifts.

FREE
Value Over
$20

Both the **Romance** and **Suspense** collections feature compelling novels written by many of today's bestselling authors.

YES! Please send me 2 FREE novels from the Essential Romance or Essential Suspense Collection and my 2 FREE gifts (gifts are worth about $10 retail). After receiving them, if I don't wish to receive any more books, I can return the shipping statement marked "cancel." If I don't cancel, I will receive 4 brand-new novels every month and be billed just $7.24 each in the U.S. or $7.49 each in Canada. That's a savings of up to 28% off the cover price. It's quite a bargain! Shipping and handling is just 50¢ per book in the U.S. and $1.25 per book in Canada.* I understand that accepting the 2 free books and gifts places me under no obligation to buy anything. I can always return a shipment and cancel at any time. The free books and gifts are mine to keep no matter what I decide.

Choose one: ☐ **Essential Romance**
(194/394 MDN GQ6M)

☐ **Essential Suspense**
(191/391 MDN GQ6M)

Name (please print)

Address | Apt. #

City | State/Province | Zip/Postal Code

Email: Please check this box ☐ if you would like to receive newsletters and promotional emails from Harlequin Enterprises ULC and its affiliates. You can unsubscribe anytime.

Mail to the **Reader Service:**
IN U.S.A.: P.O. Box 1341, Buffalo, NY 14240-8531
IN CANADA: P.O. Box 603, Fort Erie, Ontario L2A 5X3

Want to try 2 free books from another series! Call 1-800-873-8635 or visit www.ReaderService.com.

*Terms and prices subject to change without notice. Prices do not include sales taxes, which will be charged (if applicable) based on your state or country of residence. Canadian residents will be charged applicable taxes. Offer not valid in Quebec. This offer is limited to one order per household. Books received may not be as shown. Not valid for current subscribers to the Essential Romance or Essential Suspense Collection. All orders subject to approval. Credit or debit balances in a customer's account(s) may be offset by any other outstanding balance owed by or to the customer. Please allow 4 to 6 weeks for delivery. Offer available while quantities last.

Your Privacy—Your information is being collected by Harlequin Enterprises ULC, operating as Reader Service. For a complete summary of the information we collect, how we use this information and to whom it is disclosed, please visit our privacy notice located at corporate.harlequin.com/privacy-notice. From time to time we may also exchange your personal information with reputable third parties. If you wish to opt out of this sharing of your personal information, please visit readerservice.com/consumerschoice or call 1-800-873-8635. **Notice to California Residents**—Under California law, you have specific rights to control and access your data. For more information on these rights and how to exercise them, visit corporate.harlequin.com/california-privacy.

STRS20R2

#363 CATCHING MR. RIGHT
Seasons of Alaska • by Carol Ross
Pro angler Victoria Thibodeaux is this close to landing the industry's top spokesperson contract. Then she meets Seth James, the smooth-talking finalist who is looking to both outfish and outcharm her!

#364 THE LITTLEST COWGIRLS
The Mountain Monroes • by Melinda Curtis
Former child actress Ashley Monroe needs Wyatt Halford as the star in her Western movie, not as her wedding date! That is until a mix-up ties them together in a way they never could have expected.

#365 A VALENTINE'S PROPOSAL
Cupid's Crossing • by Kim Findlay
The future of Carter's Crossing hinges on a Valentine's Day proposal between Nelson and Mariah. Will the reformed groomzilla and wedding planner make this a night to remember, or jeopardize the whole town?

#366 COMING HOME TO TEXAS
Truly Texas • by Kit Hawthorne
A reckless mistake drove Dalia Ramirez away from the Texas ranch she loves and the boy who broke her heart. Is a disaster enough for her to return to her hometown and face Tony Reyes?

YOU CAN FIND MORE INFORMATION ON UPCOMING HARLEQUIN TITLES, FREE EXCERPTS AND MORE AT HARLEQUIN.COM.

HWCNM0121

Visit
ReaderService.com
Today!

As a valued member of the Harlequin Reader Service, you'll find these benefits and more at ReaderService.com:

- Try 2 free books from any series
- Access risk-free special offers
- View your account history & manage payments
- Browse the latest Bonus Bucks catalog

Don't miss out!

If you want to stay up-to-date on the latest at the Harlequin Reader Service and enjoy more content, make sure you've signed up for our monthly News & Notes email newsletter. Sign up online at ReaderService.com or by calling Customer Service at 1-800-873-8635.